SHADOW OF TRUTH: A CHRISTIAN ROMANTIC SUSPENSE

SHADOW LAKE SURVIVAL

SUSAN SLEEMAN

1

Norman Fowler was free to terrorize her again.

Icy-cold fear slid over Megan Cash. She'd imagined this day. How she'd imagined it.

Terrifying, breath-stopping, the man who'd threatened her with a gun during a bank robbery coming back into her life. Now here he was, striding across the gas station lot, heading toward her car.

Had he seen her? Worse yet, followed her to make good on his threat?

Averting her face, she considered flooring the gas pedal and fleeing, but where could she go?

Two cars in front. One behind. Three at the island to the side. All with nozzles feeding gas tanks like umbilical cords. She was trapped unless she wanted to jump from the car and take off running, making herself even more of a target.

C'mon, Megan. Deep breaths. Maybe it's not him.

She'd seen him hundreds of times in the thirteen years since she'd testified against him. The pockmarked face with the long jaw now covered with a thick beard, jutted out in anger, a tattered Tacoma Rainiers baseball cap snug on his head and hiding long dishwater blond hair.

Hundreds of times she'd been wrong. Had to be wrong. He occupied a federal prison cell for robbing the bank where she'd worked. But today was different. He could have completed his prison sentence and could be free.

A hard knocking sounded on the window. Her heart dropped to her stomach.

"You want gas or what, lady?" the attendant's voice shot through the cracked-open window, letting the caustic smell of gasoline waft in.

Right. Gas. She had to do something or even the lack of action could make Fowler look her way.

Make a small purchase. That's what she would do so she didn't draw attention to herself. When the cars in front of her moved, she would race away. She fished through her wallet and withdrew her credit card.

"Twenty dollars. Regular." Keeping her face averted, she slid her card through the gap and shrank back to watch in the mirror as he went to pump her gas.

Thankfully, she was hiding in the car and not standing by the pump when Fowler advanced her way. She'd never imagined Oregon's restrictions on consumers pumping gas might save her life.

"Hey, dude," her attendant called out. "Didn't know you got sprung."

Was he talking to Fowler? If so, maybe this meeting was a coincidence.

She risked a quick peek—spotted the sharp profile of the lunatic who'd threatened her in the bank, chatting with the attendant on the far side of the pumps.

A shudder of revulsion swept through her, but she couldn't take her eyes off Fowler. Not yet. Not until she was certain he was the man she'd stared at while he threatened to draw a gun and shoot her if she didn't put money from her drawer into a bag.

Why he and his partner had chosen their bank and singled her out, she had no idea—none—and he never explained. As his partner slid a bank robbery note across her counter, Fowler's angry eyes declared he wouldn't hesitate to kill her if she didn't comply. Of course, then she hadn't known Fowler was a suspected killer. He was never charged with killing his best friend due to lack of evidence, but law enforcement believed him guilty.

So in her ignorance, she pressed the silent alarm, grabbed a letter opener from where she'd been opening the branch mail, and plunged it into his arm. He jerked back, slipping on the old marble floor, falling, and breaking his ankle.

The police arrived. His partner fled. Fowler could only crawl. Was arrested on the spot.

He blamed her for his injury and threatened to get even once he was free again.

Now here he was, and she couldn't let that happen. Not with her daughter, Ella, depending on her.

"You move back down here now?" the attendant asked.

"Nah, just staying at the Creek Water Motel for a while." Fowler's gruff voice grated on Megan. "Wanna get a drink to celebrate my freedom?"

Fowler's raspy voice was seared into her memory, but this guy's tone was less grating. Maybe age had changed the timbre. Or her mind could be playing tricks on her.

Was this even Fowler? Physical appearance changed a lot in the passing years and the beard didn't help.

Her gas pump clicked off, and the attendant walked to the rear of her car. Fowler followed. She jerked her head away and held her hand to the side of her face.

"I dunno, man," the attendant said as she heard him latching the nozzle into the pump. "I'm not supposed to associate with you."

"Don't be a sissy," Fowler answered, the voice similar to the one he'd used at the bank. "I'll be at our usual spot, PJ's, at eight. Be a man for once and show up."

Fowler laughed, and the memories of him standing before her, the threat of drawing a gun, cut through her. The baseball cap pulled low over his hard eyes. Sadistic grin on his face.

Her hands turned moist and clammy, and she swiped them over her jeans. Too bad God didn't hear her prayers anymore or she would pray. But He didn't listen. Even when the prayers were for Ella.

Ella. Precious Ella. Lying helpless in a hospital bed. Chemotherapy weakening her immune system. Making her susceptible to every bug going around.

Hot tears filled Megan's eyes.

No. Stop. Don't let this man make you cry. Don't let him make you do anything. Not anymore.

She took a cleansing breath, inhaling the gasoline fumes and irritating her airway. She let it out slowly. No way she would cough and draw attention to herself. She'd survived the terror inflicted by Fowler once. She could do it again. This time for Ella.

Megan's daughter had no one else to protect her. No one.

Footsteps approached her window. *Please let it be the gas attendant.*

"Here you go, lady. Merry Christmas." The holiday greeting was as lackluster as the sagging garland on the pumps.

She reached for her card.

He released it, and scratching his bearded chin, he walked away. "I'll be there, man, but only one drink."

"I knew I could talk you into it." Fowler laughed again, but the taunting sound drifted away as if he was heading toward his pickup.

C'mon, hurry up. Drive away.

The cars in front of her slowly pulled forward, but she sat, watching until Fowler roared to the exit in a rusty white pickup truck.

He was leaving. She was safe. She exhaled and panted for another breath.

He turned right on the road leading to the hospital, exhaust trailing behind and tainting the air. *Wait.* Toward the hospital? Did he know about Ella, or was Megan being paranoid?

Maybe he pretended not to see Megan to make her think he didn't care about her anymore. Let her relax. Put her guard down. Become an easier target.

That seemed logical. The city of Medford was too big for such a chance meeting. They were near her home and the hospital. He could've followed her when she'd left Ella at the hospital to go home to get Ella's well-loved Boo-Boo bear.

Or had his truck been at the station when she'd driven in? Was it really Fowler?

Now she wasn't sure. Memories could do funny things.

Maybe she really *had* mistaken his identity. After all, the Department of Justice's Victim Notification Service should have contacted her about his release, and she hadn't heard from them. But she'd given them her home number and hadn't been home to take the call. She needed to call their hotline. Later. After she was certain Ella was okay.

Megan fumbled with the key in the ignition, her hand shaking and slowing her down. She finally revved the car and peeled out of the lot in hot pursuit of the truck. She raced down the streets decorated with Christmas lights coming to life in the dusky skies. She pushed her older car. Raced above the speed limit and the engine groaned with the effort.

Still, it took only minutes before she careened to a stop next to a white pickup parked in the visitor lot.

She climbed from her car and gave the truck a quick once-over. Looked like the same vehicle from the gas station, but she couldn't be positive. Pulse ratcheting up, she jumped out and pressed her hand on the hood.

Warm. Hot, actually. As if the engine had recently been turned off.

Fowler.

Oh, no. No. She bolted through the lot and into the lobby as the sun sank to the horizon. She charged across the open space and around a brightly decorated Christmas tree with colorful packages stacked below, heart pounding wildly.

She glanced at the elevators. All on floors above five. No time to wait for the car. Ella's room was only on the second floor.

Megan took the stairs two at a time, her mind flooding with terrible possibilities. What would she do if she found Fowler in Ella's room? Attack him? Yell at him? Scream?

She didn't know. Didn't matter. Ella needed her.

Megan pulled open the heavy fire door. Rushed into the antiseptic-smelling hallway. She raced ahead and made a hard right turn into the corridor leading to Ella's room.

She slammed into a nurse, and they both tumbled to the hard tile. She rolled and peered down the hall.

Fowler stood outside Ella's room, his back to her, his hand resting against an open door.

Megan's heart lodged in her throat, and she let her voice spiral into an ear-piercing scream.

Fowler spun. His hot, ugly eyes met hers. A knowing smirk slid across his face. The same one he'd worn when he'd threatened her at the bank. He let it linger on Megan for a long moment. Then his sneer disappeared into the hard expression that said he wouldn't hesitate to kill

6

someone—had killed someone—and he turned and walked away.

~

The woman's scream pierced Reid Maddox's ears. He knew this cry well.

Please help this woman in whatever distress she's facing.

Even as the wail drifted into nothingness, the earsplitting shriek remained in his head. As a former FBI agent working on the Child Abduction Rapid Deployment team, he'd heard the keening cry of a mother whose child would never come home again more than he heard the happy laughter of a reunion.

"Oh dear, what do you think happened?" Nurse Mary Waldron asked from behind the nurse's station.

"I don't know, but I have to check it out." Reid glanced at his old family friend. "Can Jessie and Bandit hang with you until I come back?"

"Of course." Mary stepped around the desk and rested a hand on his eight-year-old daughter Jessie's shoulder.

Reid looked at her. "I'll check this out and be right back. Okay?"

Eyes wide and fearful, she tightened her hold on their therapy dog's leash and nodded.

He hated leaving her, but he couldn't ignore a woman's distress cry. Ever. He charged the other way and rounded the corner. A petite woman raced toward him, a nurse hot on her heels.

"Stop him," the woman called out, gesturing to the corridor behind him. "Please, don't let him get away."

Reid turned back. Searched the hallway. Didn't see a man, much less one trying to get away.

"There's no one there." He moved toward the woman.

For a moment, their gazes connected, and he caught the sheer terror claiming her eyes. A spark of recognition flashed in his brain. He knew her. That he was sure of. But from where? Before he could determine her identity, she jerked her eyes away.

She pointed at the corridor behind him. "That way. He's heading for his truck. A white one. In the main lot. Please stop him. I have to—" Her words drifted off as she darted into a patient's room.

Should he follow her or go after this elusive man? From the look of determination on the nurse's face as she caught up to the woman, maybe she was the problem, not the supposed fleeing man.

"I called security," the nurse got out between deep breaths. "She'll be fine."

Should Reid stay anyway? No. He knew better. He might not have worked a case in over three years, and his skills might be rusty, but he knew abject terror when he witnessed it and couldn't ignore this woman's request.

He spun and went down the hallway, his eyes alert and cautious. No telling what the guy had done to bring out such fear in this woman. The supposed man could be armed and dangerous, and Reid wasn't carrying.

He worked his way down the hall and into the stairwell, racing down the steps to the lobby. A quick sweep of the open area produced nothing but visitors, patients, and medical staff wandering through the lobby. He stepped into the gloomy late afternoon, made bright only by the tall Christmas tree at the end of the walkway with thousands of twinkling white lights.

Keeping his back to the entrance, he scanned the lot for a white pickup.

Howling winds picked up from the west, whipping hard rain into his eyes and clouding his vision. He lifted a hand to ward it off and searched the lot shadowed by ominous clouds.

Unease skated down his body. He would feel a lot more secure in stepping out into the open like this if he had his Glock in hand. He wanted to carry. All the time. But since his wife died and he left the FBI to be more available to Jessie, he didn't carry whenever he was with his daughter. She really freaked out at the sight of weapons. She was only now recovering from losing her mother to cancer three years ago, and guns made her think she'd lose him too. He couldn't add fear to a young child who was already dealing with so much. Not simply to soothe his ingrained need to feel safe.

He completed his search of the lot. *Odd.* No trucks. None. Either parked or exiting the lot.

Maybe the woman's fear caused her to confuse the truck's exact location. He jogged around the hospital perimeter and checked all three parking lots. Rain penetrated his clothing and hair, but nothing unusual caught his interest or made him the least bit suspicious.

Back in the main lot, he found a police car parked in the patient-loading area.

Good. The city police were likely here because of the woman. They'd get to the bottom of this, and he could return to Jessie and their therapy visits.

Entering the lobby, he slicked the moisture from his hair and shook it from his jacket. To the sweet sound of children caroling in the distance, he took the stairs two at a time.

In the hallway, he spotted the woman outside a patient's open door. Her hands were curled tight, voice surprisingly loud for such a small person and standing next to a police officer.

"But you can't just leave, Officer York." She looked at

9

him with feverish eyes. "What about my daughter? He could come back."

York lifted his narrow shoulders under his uniform shirt. "I'm sorry, ma'am. But this guy hasn't made contact with you or your daughter or threatened you today. As much as I would like to help, there's not much I can do other than file a report."

"A report?" Her emotion-choked voice cut into Reid. "What good will a report do when he comes after Ella again? How will a report keep him from killing her?"

Officer York looked away, helplessness written all over his face.

Reid recognized that expression. The man wanted to do more for this woman, but budget constraints didn't allow police officers to pursue every problem presented, and they often had to prioritize resources.

She searched the area, and her eyes lighted on Reid. "There. That's the guy who went after him. Maybe he saw him or at least saw his truck."

The officer summoned Reid with a crook of his finger.

"Reid Maddox," he said as he glanced at the woman, still trying to place her, and flashed a look of apology before he told her he hadn't seen the supposed offender.

"Reid," she whispered his name like an involuntary breath.

Oh, man. Megan. Megan Singleton.

He knew her. Knew her well, but he couldn't acknowledge it. He was frozen in place, and he couldn't manage to move his mouth, let alone drop it open as she was doing.

He hadn't seen her since she'd testified at a bank robbery case he'd headed up for the FBI when he was a young agent. As a federal crime, bank robbery fell under the FBI's jurisdiction, and the case had been assigned to him. A big break. His first chance to prove himself in a leadership role.

He first met her at the bank. He'd never forget the moment. She was wide-eyed and shivering with fear, and he could do nothing about it. He had to see beyond the cowering woman to convince her to let go of her fear and testify against Norman Fowler. That was the beginning of months spent together preparing for and sitting through the trial.

Now here she was after all this time. *Wow.* Here in front of him. Peering at him with the same terrified expression. The same urge to hold her until it all went away was nearly stronger than he could resist. He shoved his hands into his pockets and looked away.

York glanced between them. "I take it you two know each other."

"Unfortunately, we do." Megan's shoulders stiffened. "Figures the FBI would send the perfect company man to tell me Norman Fowler was out of prison."

Reid blinked at her. "What? Fowler?"

"C'mon, Reid. Don't play dumb with me. I know why you're here."

At her unusual display of temper, heaviness settled into Reid. He'd done that to her—him—and he wished he could change it. "The Bureau didn't send me. I was just down the hall with my daughter and our therapy dog when I heard you scream."

She arched an eyebrow. "So you're not here to tell me about Fowler?"

He met her gaze. "I'm not an agent anymore. Haven't been one for three years."

Her eyes, a soft blue and rimmed with thick lashes, widened, and he could see her working to process the information.

York took a step closer. "Mind filling me in on what's going on here?"

"I was the special agent in charge of Norman Fowler's bank robbery case. Ms. Singleton—"

"Cash," Megan said. "My name is Cash now."

Right. She'd married and divorced, but surprise at seeing her had made him forget that piece of info. "Sorry, Ms. Cash was the teller at the bank Fowler attempted to rob, and she testified at the trial."

York turned to Megan. "Why are you so angry with Mr. Maddox?"

"That's personal and between us."

York planted his hands on his waist. "Not if it has a bearing on this situation, it's not."

Megan fixed her jaw in a hard line and eyed Reid as if expecting him to explain their past and why she would be upset with him. No way Reid would mention his failed romance with Megan. York didn't need those details.

"What exactly is *the situation*?" Reid asked hoping to redirect York.

"Ms. Cash claims she saw Norman Fowler." York paused and checked his notes.

"So Fowler's out then?" Reid quickly did the math. Fowler had threatened Megan with a hidden gun, but neither him or his partner were armed. In exchange for thirteen years prison stay plus three years of supervisory release out of a twenty year max sentence, Fowler had ratted out his partner, who was the brains behind the robbery.

The prison portion of his sentence had passed, and now the guy was free to exact his revenge. He wasn't free and clear, though. He still had to comply with the supervisory release criteria, which was much like parole criteria, plus he had to report to a federal probation officer on a regular basis.

York shifted on his feet. "First time she claimed to have seen him was a half hour ago at Speedy Fill gas station just down the road. Then again here, outside her daughter's door."

"It's not a claim," Megan said. "I *did* see him."

"Maybe the station has security cameras, and he was caught on video," Reid suggested.

York shook his head. "Small mom-and-pop station, and they never put cameras in. I know as we've suggested it countless times, but they're old school, close to retirement, and don't see the reason to spend the money."

"You could believe me," Megan said. "Fowler was here to make good on his threat to me by hurting Ella." With a shaking hand, she slipped a lock of curly hair behind her ear and glanced into the open door at her daughter.

"About that." York faced Reid. "Can you confirm Fowler issued a threat against Ms. Cash at the trial?"

Reid nodded. "After the trial, when deputies carted him off. He also blamed her for his arrest and threatened her then too. If incarceration didn't change him, I'm sure he'll make good on the threat."

York jotted a note on his pad. "So you consider him a violent man?"

"The Fowler I knew wouldn't hesitate to hurt Megan." Reid glanced at her.

She curled her shoulders in as she'd done often enough in the past when she was uneasy.

Too bad he had to say Fowler was dangerous, but this officer had to see what they were facing here, if indeed Fowler had made an appearance. Not that he doubted Megan. Not at all. If she said she saw Fowler, Reid believed her. "I hope you'll take this situation seriously and provide protection for her."

"I wish we could." York flipped his notepad closed. "But

it's not a crime to go to a gas station or be in a hospital hallway. And no offense, Ms. Cash, but we don't have any proof that this Fowler guy was even here."

"So you've said," Megan mumbled under her breath.

"I'm here with my daughter and our therapy dog, and I heard Ms. Cash's scream when she saw him. It wasn't faked. She was terrified. That I can assure you." Reid scanned the long hallway floor to ceiling. "I don't see any cameras, but the ones in the lobby could have caught him entering the building."

"Not today," York said. "The hospital's updating their system, and it's offline for a few hours."

"He said he was staying at the Creek Water Motel if that helps," Megan said.

York nodded. "I can stop by there and see if a Norman Fowler's registered, but they might require a warrant to provide that information, and I have no probable cause for such a warrant."

Reid knew he spoke the truth. "But you'll let Ms. Cash know what you learn either way?"

"Will do." York pulled out business cards. He handed one to each of them. "We'll make sure our other officers are aware of Fowler's release, and I'll talk to security on the way out to make sure they know what's going on here. They can make a point of checking in on you now and then."

Reid took the card and swallowed his anger at York's action. But York didn't deserve it. He'd behaved much like Reid would've done in the past as an agent when he couldn't really help a traumatized victim.

With the police not taking action, the question was, what was going to happen to Megan and her sick daughter?

2

More than anything right now, Reid wanted to take off. To return to Jessie. Instead, he followed Megan's gaze as she watched York march toward the security guard, her shoulders drooping. Reid finally processed the fact that she'd cut her waist-length hair to her shoulders, leaving it curly. It was still blond as he remembered and seemed as soft as the last day of Fowler's trial, when Reid had crossed the boundaries of professional ethics and moved a stray strand from her face.

Right after the deputies took hold of Fowler to transport him to a federal prison, he turned on Megan, spewing threats in an angry, almost visceral tone. She'd sought comfort from Reid as she'd done every time her fears had taken over in the six months between the robbery and Fowler's trial. They'd spent a lot of time together, and the comfort soon turned into feelings for each other. But she was a witness, and he was a professional. No matter how much both of them had wanted to pursue their feelings, his ethics stopped him from crossing that line until the case wrapped up.

On the final day of the trial, he didn't have to worry

about ethics anymore. So when she complained of a headache, he'd rubbed her shoulders and told her how he felt about her. It had lasted until his supervisor caught sight of them in the conference room and had taken him aside to say if Reid wanted a career at the FBI, a relationship with a witness—even a former witness—was out of the question. An agent who wanted to advance in the Bureau would never do such an unprofessional thing.

Man, Reid had been conflicted. He'd wanted to be an agent since he was a little boy, and he struggled to decide his course of action. In the long run, he'd said goodbye to Megan, hurting her in a way he'd never thought he was capable of doing. He didn't have his priorities right. Hadn't for years. Losing his wife Diane showed him what was most important.

I'm sorry for hurting you. For being such a jerk back then.

He bit his tongue to keep from blurting it out. From seeking forgiveness he didn't deserve. He shook his head too, as if physically warning himself to stop the direction of his thoughts. The last thing she needed right now was for him to mention the day he'd told her his job was more important than her.

As if feeling his eyes on her, she turned and studied him like she would a bug she planned to annihilate under her shoe.

Keep the attention on Fowler. That's what they needed right now.

"I'm surprised you thought I'd be the one to tell you about Fowler's release," Reid said.

"Why? Because you got what you wanted from me to advance your precious career and ran the other way?" She skewered him with a defiant yet challenging stare.

Ah, another personal jab. One he had coming, but one he wouldn't defend himself against and send them down a personal rabbit hole. "That's not what I meant. The Justice Department should notify you of Fowler's release."

A tinge of remorse flashed on her face, and that added to his guilt. "I haven't heard anything from them, so when I saw you, I thought maybe they changed procedures."

"They didn't contact you?"

"No, but they have my home phone number on file, and I spent the night here." She glanced at her daughter's room again. "If I was the only one involved, I wouldn't be as worried, but I have Ella to think about."

He shifted his gaze to the sleeping child, who was definitely younger than his daughter. Maybe five. Megan's messy divorce from a local news anchor had made all the news, and he knew she had a daughter. But this child's gaunt face and bald head left little resemblance to Megan. She seemed very sick. Chemotherapy had taken a toll. A big one.

He had to look beyond the sickness—as he had with his wife, Diane—to find the person before chemo erased her health. Maybe her pert little nose resembled Megan's.

"She looks so peaceful," he said.

"Wait until she wakes up and finds out I didn't get Boo-Boo." Megan shook her head. "She'll be anything but peaceful."

"Boo-Boo?"

"Ella's bear." She aimed a soft smile at her daughter. "She insists on taking him to every appointment. I was in a hurry to get to the emergency room yesterday and forgot him." Her voice died off, and she paused. Drew in a breath. "I stopped to get gas on my way to get him and spotted Fowler. I don't know what I'll do when she wakes up and I don't have the bear. He's gotten her through so many rough days, and she counts on him." Tears pooled in Megan's eyes, washing over the pain and uncertainty.

So much like the trial, when testifying frightened her,

and he'd helped her work through her despair. Maybe he could do the same thing now.

He opened his mouth, but before he could say anything, a sudden resolve tightened her face, and she lifted her shoulders.

"She may want Boo-Boo, but as long as Fowler's free, I'm not leaving her at risk." She'd turned into a fierce protector over the years and didn't need his help coping anymore.

He gave her a sympathetic smile. "I have a daughter too, so I completely understand."

Megan responded with a flat look. One that held a message. She didn't want to hear anything about his personal life. She only talked with him because she was afraid of Fowler.

Exactly what he deserved and he would keep the focus off himself. "Is there someone you can call to pick up the bear?"

"I won't risk sending anyone to my house with Fowler on the loose."

"Dad," Jessie's voice came from behind. "Is everything okay?"

Reid spun. Jessie and Mary were standing behind him. He hadn't heard them approach. He let out a breath and put on a smile for her. "I'll be done in a minute, Bug. How about waiting near Tommy's door for me?"

She glanced at Megan then into the room before searching Reid's face, her expression unsure and worried. She may be only eight, but losing her mother had made her grow up fast, and she was particularly sensitive to other people's body language and demeanor. He needed to make sure she knew he was fine.

He squeezed her arm. "Everything's okay, Jess. I'll be right there."

"Hurry up, okay?"

"Okay, sweetheart." When Jessie strode down the hall, he turned his attention to Megan. "My daughter, Jessie. We visit patients with our dog, Bandit, and I have to go."

"No worries. I remember how good you are at leaving." She pulled back her shoulders in a hard line.

She was mad at him. So mad. But fear had taken over. He hated to leave her all worried and distressed. But he had no choice. Jessie was his responsibility.

"I'm sorry," she said quickly. "That was uncalled for. Your daughter needs you. Of course you have to go. I totally understand."

"Thank you," he said.

"One thing before you go," she said. "Can Fowler even leave Portland under the terms of his release?"

"His judgment order probably has generic terms stating he has to remain within the boundaries of the judicial district named in the order. Oregon only has one federal judicial district and it encompasses the entire state."

"So if he left the state he could go back to prison?"

Reid hoped she wasn't thinking about luring him out of the state. "He could, but more likely he'd only get additional time on his supervised release or receive some other non-prison punishment. But it would put him on his probation officer's radar, and he would likely have to return to Portland if he didn't want to return to prison."

"I hoped this would be enough to keep him away from us."

"After the commotion you caused, I can't imagine he'll show up again. At least not today."

"And tomorrow? Or the next day?" She clutched her arms around her body.

Her dejection nearly had him stepping forward to take her into his arms, but that wouldn't comfort her so he remained in place. "While Jessie interacts with the patients,

I'll make a call to a former associate to see what I can find out about Fowler's release. When we're finished with our rounds, I'll come back and update you. That is, if you want me to."

"So you believe me, then? That I saw Fowler and he's coming after us?"

"Of course, I believe you."

"Thank you." Her lips tipped in an unexpected smile, reminding him of the innocent college student working part-time at the bank who'd bravely testified against a bank robber so long ago. And the woman who'd put every ounce of her trust in him, yet he'd left her high and dry.

He wouldn't do it again.

"Our visits will take a couple of hours." He dug his phone from his pocket. "Let's trade numbers in case you need me before then."

She nodded but her uneasy body language was still palpable. He wanted to stay. To make up for the past, maybe ask for her forgiveness. He glanced down the hallway. Jessie stood patiently waiting, holding Bandit's leash. He couldn't let her down.

Why make me decide between them? Can't I help them both?

But God was silent all of a sudden.

Reid blew out his frustration and tapped in Megan's phone number. She followed suit.

"I'll be on this floor the whole time." He shoved his phone into his pocket. "Call me if anything, and I mean anything, happens that makes you uncomfortable, and I'll come right back. Okay?"

She nodded and went into Ella's room, dismissing him without a word.

He'd hurt her badly, and she had to be terrified if she was willing to accept his help in any way.

He went down the hall to Jessie. She slipped her hand

into his and peered up at him, her blue eyes so like his own, filled with questions. "That lady looked freaked out. Is she gonna be okay?"

"She'll be fine," he answered.

Megan had to be, right?

He glanced at their door and an ominous feeling settled over him.

What if, by walking away, he'd left Megan and Ella in the sights of a crazed man? A man who'd already proved his willingness to hurt Megan—and wouldn't think twice about inflicting more terror.

Reid stood in the doorway of the newest patient's room, keeping a distance from the patient as he always did. Since losing Diane to cancer, no way he wanted to come face-to-face with it again. Not in an adult. Certainly not in a child. But the therapy sessions helped Jessie deal with the loss of her mother and an incident when she was abducted last year, and he would do anything to help her cope.

But now his mind was divided. An hour of therapy time had passed, and he still couldn't let go of his thoughts of Megan. Or Ella, either. They needed help, but he wasn't the guy to provide it, was he? Not with their history.

He could help with prayer, though. He took a moment. Asked for Megan and Ella's safety. Selfishly asking God to help her forgive him too, when he deserved nothing. To heal Ella.

Heal the child in front of him as well. All children going through such illness.

His brave, caring Jessie helping them. She held Bandit on the bed where the young boy fired rapid questions at her about the dog. The child hadn't stopped smiling since they arrived, revealing wide gaps where baby teeth had fallen out.

The picture cut Reid to the core. These children lost teeth, grew out of their shoes, played. Were regular kids in many ways. They just wanted to feel normal and return to their everyday lives. Their weekly visit with Bandit helped them reconnect with life outside the hospital. The visits were especially appreciated this Christmas week when children missed their homes and families even more.

Reid's phone vibrated in his pocket. He dug it out. Jack Duger's name appeared on the screen. Reid stepped into the hall but kept Jessie in his sight. Due to Jessie's age, Reid was listed as the official dog handler, and their agreement with the hospital dictated he be in the room when Bandit was with a patient.

He answered the call from his former partner at the FBI. "Thanks for getting back to me so quickly."

"Are you okay? Your message was kinda frantic."

Frantic? He'd left a very calm and direct message, hadn't he? Maybe the excitement after being out of this business for some time had made him sound like a rookie. Something Jack would have a field day with if Reid stayed on the subject, which he wouldn't do.

"I could use your help." He explained Megan's problem, including the local police department's inability to provide protection. "Can you get a hold of Fowler's supervised release judgment order? He said he was staying at a local motel, but also get a current address for him so we can see if he should be here. Then talk with your office about arranging a protective detail for her?"

A hiss of air was his answer. Typical of Jack.

Reid was more of a make-snap-decisions-and-take-action kind of guy. Jack had to think things through first. Made them a good team and made Jack an invaluable friend. If Reid remembered to be patient, that was, but right now, he wanted Jack to speak.

"You there?" Reid asked.

"You think this is a good idea? Helping her, I mean."

Ah, yes. Reid had no doubt about Jack's reaction. His skeptical tone said it all. Wouldn't deter Reid, though. "I don't see a problem here."

"I don't know, man. You weren't exactly objective about her. Almost cost you your job. What makes you think you can be objective now?"

What difference did it make if Reid was objective? No supervisor kept tabs on Reid now telling him it was wrong to get personally involved with a former witness. He was free to help anyone he wanted. Besides, the only help he planned to offer was passing her off to the FBI for protection. Not get personally involved in any way. Right?

Right. And Reid didn't like Jack questioning him about it. "I'm not an agent anymore and helping her won't hurt anyone."

"You hope."

"What's that supposed to mean?" Reid was getting testy.

"First," Jack paused dramatically, "Megan needs support from someone who doesn't have past baggage clouding his judgment. You do not fit that profile. Second, you said you want to return to the Bureau when Jessie is older. This is a small world and word gets around. Carmichael will get wind of it. Doesn't help if you want back on the CARD team."

Jack and Reid served together on the FBI's elite Child Abduction Rapid Deployment team. Jack had a point about CARD, but Reid wasn't going to ignore Megan's plight over fear of his old supervisor hearing about it. He loved working on the CARD team, but he wouldn't love returning to the team if Fowler harmed Megan because Reid didn't come to her aid. And the old baggage? So many years had passed, and Reid was sure he could keep that under control.

Now all he had to do was convince Jack to help.

"Don't tell me you've forgotten how to work this kind of case." Reid used a teasing tone to keep Jack focused on the first concern.

"Funny, Maddox. Don't think I missed your avoidance of the personal issues here. Even more proof that I'm right, but I'll do you a solid. I'll get the judgment order, and I should be able to get his current address. The protection detail is another story. Without Fowler having committed a crime, I doubt that will fly."

Reid let this comment slide. "Just ask and let me know what you find out as soon as you can."

"And you stay vigilant. It's been a few years since you've had to look over your shoulder. Wouldn't want you to act like a rookie and embarrass both of us." Jack chuckled and disconnected.

Man, he missed working with Jack. Missed the camaraderie. Missed the sense of purpose rescuing abducted children gave him. Managing Shadow Lake Survival, his family's newest business that involved training people in survival skills, didn't bring the same reward. But it did make him available to Jessie.

That had to be enough right now.

He shoved his phone into his pocket. Jessie had left the excited little boy and moved to the other bed nearer the window. Her usual smile was fixed in place, but something about the way this patient clutched her doll instead of showing any interest in Bandit drew Reid into the room.

She was thin with dark circles under her eyes. Spotted bald patches dotted her head. Her anguished eyes spoke to the struggles she faced to remain alive. Like Ella.

She'd been peacefully sleeping when he'd seen Ella, but

what would happen when she woke up? How would she react when she learned her bear wasn't available for hugging tight as this little girl was doing with her doll?

Jessie's white bear came to mind. Well, it wasn't so white anymore. Not after she slept with it every night since Diane died. She even smuggled it in the bottom of her sleeping bag when she went on sleepovers so the other girls didn't know she needed the bear at her age.

His heart constricted for this child. For Jessie. For Ella. For all the children in this hospital. And their parents. He'd watched Diane struggle with cancer, but he couldn't imagine seeing Jessie in this situation. As a parent, he would thank God for anyone who could help his child.

Even someone who'd hurt him in the past.

That settled it. So much for hands-off. He would help Megan in any way she needed—if she let him. And there was only one way he could see that happening. He had to ask for her forgiveness for the way he hurt her. The sooner the better. To do that he needed time alone with her.

Maybe he could talk to her and help her with Ella at the same time. If he found someone to stand guard outside Ella's room, he could take Megan home to get Boo-Boo, and on the way, he could apologize.

Now who should he call to guard Ella? Had to be someone he trusted implicitly. Someone he'd be willing to leave in charge of Jessie if she were in this situation.

Jack fit that bill, but if something went down while he was standing guard, his career could be in jeopardy. Reid might not be worried about risking his own future at the FBI, but he wouldn't do the same thing to Jack. Besides, it would take him too long to get here from Portland.

But he could ask his brother. As Emerson County Sheriff, Russ was the perfect candidate for a protective detail for Ella. More importantly, Russ was someone Reid fully trusted. Little more than a handful of men fit that criteria. His brothers, plus their Shadow Lake Survival team members. But Russ was the only man outside of the FBI who'd had to use a show of force in the line of duty and wouldn't hesitate to use it if Megan or Ella were in danger.

Resolved, Reid stepped into the hallway and dialed his brother. If Russ was available, Reid could keep a child safe and maybe, just maybe, make up a little bit for the way he'd hurt her mother.

3

Megan watched Ella's chest rise and fall in the even breaths of sleep. Had watched her for the past few hours, not sure what to fear most. Losing her sweet little daughter to another tumor or Fowler killing them both. An impossible choice. Maybe both. She had to think about both.

She glanced at the closed door, her imagination coming to life. Seeing the door fly open. The pockmarked face now sporting a thick beard poking around it. A snide smile and crazy eyes directed at her baby.

Megan sucked in oxygen. These thoughts had to stop. *She* had to stop them. Or she would drive herself insane. She exhaled and took in more air.

In. Out. In. Out. That's it. Don't panic.

But they were so vulnerable. Sitting ducks. And she was Ella's lone protector. She wanted Reid here. How she wanted him, despite her anger.

He said he would return in a few hours. She glanced at the clock. He should arrive any moment. At least she hoped so. She'd called the DOJ, and they'd confirmed Fowler's release. He'd been out for two weeks and somehow they'd failed to let her know. The person she spoke to had an *oops, my bad* kind of attitude. No apology. No willingness to check into how the department had failed.

Could he have been following her the whole two weeks? It wasn't a farfetched thought as she hadn't known he was out, and she hadn't been watching for him. Now every noise in the hallway tightened the hard ball of worry in her stomach, and anxiety gnawed at it.

If only Reid could've stayed with them. He'd said he was no longer an agent—a surprise beyond all surprises for the man who lived for his job—but he would still know how to protect them if Fowler burst into the room.

Reid. Did she really want him here or just someone trained on how to keep them safe? She had to face the truth. She wanted Reid. The man she'd loved more than any man in her life. But he was married. His ring finger declared it louder than having a daughter.

She hadn't seen him in years, but seeing him today? Time fell away. It seemed like yesterday that she'd fallen for him, and he'd taken off, breaking her heart. Oh, how could she want him here? Foolishness. Or desperation. Maybe it was because she was at the end of her rope.

Asking for anything from the man who'd broken her heart without so much as a backward glance was ludicrous. Right?

No. This was different. Times were different. This was for Ella.

Ella shifted in the bed and stretched, kicking off her sheet. Eyes rimmed with dark shadows opened. She looked around to gain her bearings and confusion settled into her chocolate-brown eyes so like her father's.

Megan's heart constricted as if a knife twisted in her chest.

"Mommy." Ella's scratchy whisper added to Megan's unease.

"I'm right here, sweetie." Megan poured her daughter a glass of water and hoped the raspy voice was only from sleep and not a sore throat, signaling an impending illness was attacking her suppressed immune system.

Megan brushed her daughter's soft hair from her forehead. "Did you have a good sleep?"

She yawned and reached for the cup. Taking a long sip of the ice water through the straw and looking around, she patted the sheets. "Where's Boo-Boo?"

"I'm sorry, sweetie. Something came up and I couldn't get him." Megan set the cup on the table and braced for the reaction.

As predicted, Ella's chin started to tremble. "But I need him, Mommy."

Megan took Ella's hand. "I know you like to have him with you, but you don't need him here. I'm with you."

"I need him." Ella burst into tears.

Megan sat on the bed and drew her crying daughter into her arms. Why had she fostered Ella's dependence on a stuffed animal? Sure, Boo-Boo had seemed like a good idea after the first surgery for a brain tumor when Ella was three. Now, three years later, it didn't seem so wise.

"Shh." Megan stroked Ella's back.

"Ca-nn you get him, now-ww?" Sobs nearly tore away her words.

How Megan wished she could, but Fowler was free. Stalking them. She wouldn't leave Ella alone, and she wouldn't go to her house alone, either.

Ella's slight body trembled in Megan's arms. *Oh, gosh.* Megan's heart shredded. Not only at her daughter's thin frame but for Ella's sadness that could've been prevented if not for Fowler. That creep. Killer. Robber.

Megan couldn't do anything about Fowler right now. She could distract Ella, but how?

Maybe use one of the many she'd had to employ in situations like this for years. Alone to be both mother and father. Why couldn't Orrin fulfill his marriage vows and be here to help them? In sickness and health. Orrin obviously didn't know the meaning of those words. The first sign of a major problem and he'd run. Just as Reid had bailed on her.

Reid. That's it! Maybe he would bring his cute little dog to see Ella. No, not maybe. Megan would convince him.

She pushed back and locked gazes with Ella. "I have something better for you. There's a man and his daughter bringing a special surprise to patients today. He'll be here in a few minutes." Megan regretted promising something she wasn't sure she could deliver, but when Ella's eyes brightened, it was worth the risk of failure and more disappointment.

For the moment at least.

"When?" Her chest jerked as she tried to stop crying.

"Soon."

"But how long is soon?"

"Not long. We just have to wait patiently."

"I don't think I can." Her mouth started quivering.

Megan couldn't watch her ill child start crying again. "Tell you what. I'll call him to see if I can speed him up. Okay?"

"'K."

Megan gave Ella's hand a squeeze then crossed the room to get her phone from her purse. Putting herself in debt with Reid was probably a bigger mistake than Boo-Boo had been. But Megan would go to any lengths to help ease her daughter's suffering.

Even if it meant partnering with a man she never really wanted to see again.

~

Reid escorted Jessie down the hallway toward the next patient's room, the happy jingle from bells Jessie had strapped on Bandit's collar belied the danger facing Megan. As did the hallways and rooms decorated with wreaths, wrapping paper, and cardboard Christmas cutouts. Christmas was less than a week away, but any holiday mood he'd managed to find had disappeared with Megan's scream and remained buried during the visits to the children with desperate parents trying to cheer them on.

These families with sick children never ceased to amaze Reid. How in the world did they keep their spirits so high? If only he knew he could employ the optimism in his life, but he couldn't do it. Especially not around a holiday. He could fake it. Or at least try his best. For Jessie.

"Dad?" She stopped near a brightly lit tree with presents stacked high underneath the wide branches and peered up at him. So did Bandit, the circles in a black mask around his eyes in a white face that gave him his name appearing lighter in the bright hospital lighting.

Reid didn't like her serious expression, but he smiled anyway. "What, kiddo?"

She scrunched up her eyes, reminding him of Diane, the sight putting an ache in Reid's heart.

"You haven't forgotten about Christmas, have you?" she asked.

"Now, why would you ask me that?"

She let out a long sigh. "We haven't even decorated the tree, and there aren't any presents under it yet."

He rubbed his knuckles over her head and pulled her close. "Have I ever missed a Christmas?"

"No-o-o."

He heard a "but" in her tone. A "but" telling him that he didn't do holidays as well as her mother had. He tried his best but came up short every time. His mom helped, but nothing had been the same since Diane died.

"We'll get the tree done soon. I promise." He hugged her tight, hoping he could find the time in managing a thriving business and everyday life with a young child and dog to do all the extras she craved.

She looked at him, hope and expectation alive in her eyes. "And the presents?"

He didn't want to disappoint her, but the conversation had gotten too heavy with memories of Diane. "Now *that* I'll have to think about." He chuckled.

She eased out from under his arm and shot him a playful punch.

"You're so mean," she said but giggled.

He laughed along.

His phone vibrated. Hopefully Jack was calling back with more information on Fowler than the text Reid received a few minutes ago listing Fowler's current address in Portland.

Reid dug the phone from his pocket and glanced at caller ID. *Megan.*

He'd left her vulnerable. Had something happened?

His pulse kicked up as he answered. "Is everything okay?"

"Fine. I was wondering if you could bring your dog to see Ella."

"That's it? You're all right?" He let out a deep breath, drawing Jessie's attention.

"Yes. Ella's crying for Boo-Boo, and I thought maybe a visit with your dog would cheer her up."

"We're on our way." He ended the call and turned to Jessie. "That was the mom I was talking to earlier. Sounds like her daughter needs a visit from Bandit."

"Can I ask you something, Dad?" Jessie chewed on her lip.

He ruffled her hair to lighten the tense mood that his concern had likely created. "What is it, Bug?"

"You seem worried. Is this girl gonna die like Mom?"

Was she? He had no idea of Ella's condition, but he shook his head anyway and urged Jessie forward.

They'd met many children in their visits. Most of them made it through their treatments, but some of them died. Jessie handled the losses like a trouper and seemed to grow stronger in her purpose each time. Just as her counselor predicted she would when she encouraged them to follow through on Jessie's desire to train Bandit as a therapy dog.

Why couldn't he do the same thing instead of letting a slice of his heart disappear with each death? He only wished he could focus his loss on something positive, as Jessie had. God kept telling him to do so. To get beyond himself and use his pain to help others, but he couldn't manage it no matter how hard he tried. How much he prayed.

They reached Ella's room, and he pushed open the door.

Megan sat on the edge of Ella's bed, her lips pressed into a colorless line. He offered a reassuring smile, and she visibly relaxed as if she believed he could protect them. Surprisingly, the ache in his gut lessened too.

Maybe there was a reason for running into her today. A reason beyond helping her with Fowler. Maybe this was the opportunity Reid needed to right his life. To look beyond his own suffering to help others. If so, was he ready for it?

Jessie pushed past him and went straight to Ella's bed. The pale child squealed. Bandit took it in stride and trotted to the bed, his head tilted as he sat to wait for direction from Jessie.

"Puppy!" Ella shouted. "Can I pet him?"

"Sure." Jessie thrust her chest out. They'd recently

adopted Bandit from his brother Ryan's wife of a year, and to say Jessie was a proud owner was an understatement.

Ella smiled at her mother. "This is the best surprise ever, Mommy."

The sweet voice coming from a body ravaged by chemotherapy tore at Reid's already shredded heart.

She's so sick. I want to help them beyond today, but I don't think I can. It's hard enough seeing kids I don't know in these beds, but Ella is Megan's daughter. Megan's!

He forced his attention to Jessie. She kept the professional approach her training dictated and set Bandit on Ella's lap. Bandit settled down, and Ella stroked his head, a dazzling smile breaking free.

Oh man, this was worse for sure. She looked like a mini-Megan.

Reid shifted his focus to Megan. Expected to see her pain lessened, but a deep anguish lingered in her eyes, darkening them. Stealing his breath. He had to help her. Had to move heaven and earth to take away her anguish. To take away the despair of wondering if someone she loved was going to die as Diane had.

Diane's face as she slipped away to heaven came back to him as clearly as if she were in the room. Peaceful, serene. His heart ripping in two. Jessie sobbing and clutching his hand.

No. No. I can't do this. Can't watch as the child of someone I once cared for suffers. I just can't.

4

Reid turned away. Took a few steps toward the door. He'd never been one to run from his problems, but he'd found himself wanting to bolt lately when the going got overly tough. Like now. With Ella.

And what kind of man does that make you?

He stopped.

He'd run out on Megan before and couldn't abandon her again. Especially when the stakes were higher.

Quit focusing on Ella's illness. Keep your thoughts on Fowler. Yeah, do that. He might be able to do something about Fowler.

The child's illness, he'd have to play by ear. Maybe work through the impact it was having on him. Not alone, but with God's help.

He curled his fingers tight and stepped into the detached mode the FBI had taught him to adopt when bad things happened to good people. He'd had to do that many times and could do it now. Sure, he could.

He swallowed. "Megan."

She faced him, and he tipped his head at the doorway.

She nodded and leaned close to Ella. "While you play

with Bandit, I'm going out in the hallway for a minute. Okay?"

Ella, eyes fixed on Bandit, gave an absent nod. Megan crossed the room, and Reid moved, allowing her to exit into the hallway.

He leaned on the door frame. "I need to stay here where I can see Jessie. The hospital made an exception to let an underage volunteer do the therapy work, so I don't want to risk her losing this opportunity by not keeping her in view."

"I understand."

He glanced at the trio in the room. "I don't think they'll pay us much attention anyway. We could probably shout at each other and Ella wouldn't notice."

Megan's gaze returned to Ella. The start of a smile found her lips, but then she focused on Reid and it disappeared. "Did you learn anything about Fowler?"

All business, the way he kept thinking he wanted it. So why was he disappointed?

"You remember Jack Duger?" Reid asked.

"One of the agents who helped you with Fowler's investigation."

Reid nodded. "I had him check into a few things for me. He learned that Fowler's release record shows him living in Portland."

"So he really has no business being here." She rubbed her neck. "He talked to the gas station attendant like he was an old friend."

Helpful information. "Did you catch the attendant's name?"

"Fowler might've said it, but I don't remember. Is it important?"

Reid shrugged to play it down so she didn't feel bad about not remembering, when knowing this name could help them locate Fowler. "Could be important if this guy does indeed have a record. Fowler's terms of release will prohibit him from consorting with a known felon unless an exception was made."

"The friend said something about that, and he didn't sound like he really wanted to meet with Fowler. So if Fowler's caught with this other guy, is that enough to send him back to prison?" A flicker of hope lit in her eyes.

"Possibly." Reid didn't want to go into details about how a supervised release was specific to each individual and nothing was cut and dried. Exceptions could be made in having contact with other felons. "Jack is checking into Fowler's judgment order, and hopefully he'll call soon with the details."

"Can you also tell him Fowler is meeting this guy at PJ's Sports Bar at eight?"

Too bad that didn't narrow down where they might be meeting to a singular location. Not when PJ's operated several pubs in the city. Unless... "They say which location?"

"No." She tilted her head. "I'm guessing it's the one closest to here. Do you think Jack can go over there? Maybe catch Fowler with this guy and report him for violating his order?"

If only. "Jack's in Portland. He would never make it here on time for their meeting." Reid hated to douse her flame of hope, but he had to be realistic. "Besides, it's a long shot to assume they'll go to the closest pub. They could be meeting in an area of town where they live or have lived in the past."

"Is there any way someone could still check out the bar near here? Just to see if he shows up." She looked at him with the same confidence in his abilities as she'd had when he'd helped her through her testimony.

He couldn't let her down. "I'll have one of the guys from our team head over there. And another one stake out Fowler's motel in case he shows there."

"Team?" she asked.

"My business in Shadow Lake."

"You have a business now." She blinked at him. "How did that happen?"

He didn't want to get into personal details more than needed, but he also didn't want to be rude. "My parents owned and operated a resort there. Valley View. I think I told you about it."

"I remember." She crossed her arms. "You were so proud of it and said you were going to show it to me."

"I'm sorry about that," he said sincerely, but his cheeks burned under the guilt of failing her in so many ways. "They wanted to retire and none of us wanted to run a resort, so they closed the business but held onto the property. That was before my wife passed away."

"I'm so sorry for your loss.

Her gentle tone made his chest hurt, and he couldn't take his eyes off her. He looked deep into the pale blue of her eyes. Eyes he'd once thought would blend well with his sharper blue to create a child with amazing color. He'd ruined all of that. Still, a connection remained, but instead of fresh young love, they shared pain in seeing a loved one suffer.

"Thank you," he finally managed to get out. "That's when I decided to bring Jessie back to Shadow Lake to live, and my parents sold Valley View to me so I could start Shadow Lake Survival with my brothers. The business is thriving, and we had to hire three other guys to keep up with it."

She arched a brow. "What exactly do you do?"

"We train people in survival skills and ways to live off-grid."

She kept her eyes on him. "Sounds like something you'd like to do."

"If I can't be an agent, it's the next best choice."

"But you'd rather be an agent?"

"I would, but Jessie comes first, and right now that means living near family."

She frowned. "And I'm taking you away from her."

He waved a hand. "No worries. I'm sure this will be wrapped up before you know it."

"Thank you for your help." She kneaded her shoulders and rolled her head. "All of this is giving me a fierce headache."

He'd been in this situation with her before. On the last day of Fowler's trial. Ah, yes, that day. He smiled over the memory. Surprising amidst all this pain. Had his life really ever been so filled with the innocence of his younger days? Before he'd seen so many examples in his job of all that was wrong with mankind. Before he'd let down a woman he cared about. Before the loss of Diane.

He couldn't even fathom it, and his good mood evaporated. He looked away before transmitting the change to Megan. His brother, Russ, dressed in his official khaki uniform, rounded the corner and charged their way like an approaching storm.

Good. Russ's usual impatience and no-nonsense personality would keep Reid's thoughts right where they needed to be. On Fowler.

Reid nodded a greeting and waited for his brother to arrive.

"Hey, bro." Russ clapped Reid on the shoulder and gave Megan a quick once-over in a thorough appraisal only law enforcement officers made. "This Megan?"

Reid nodded and faced her. "My brother, Russ. He's the sheriff of Emerson County, about an hour from here where Jessie and I live."

"So you need my help," Russ said.

Megan took a step back and looked between Russ and Reid. "I don't know what you're doing here."

Russ rubbed his neck and stared at Reid. "Thought this was all arranged."

Reid returned the stare. "I didn't think you'd get here this fast, and I haven't had a chance to tell her yet."

"Tell me what?" Megan set her jaw.

"I asked Russ to stand guard outside Ella's door so I can take you to get her bear."

Megan blinked at Russ. "You drove all this way just so I could get Boo-Boo?"

"I know. Crazy, right?" Russ rolled his eyes.

Reid punched his brother in the arm, and a sheepish expression crept onto his face. "I owe Reid a few favors."

"Whatever the reason, thank you." A warm smile lit her face like a ray of sunshine that often glowed over Shadow Lake.

Reid drew in a breath and didn't want to turn away, but he also didn't want to give his nosy brother the wrong impression.

"Fill me in on this Fowler guy so if he shows up I can protect Ella," Russ said.

And just like that, all warmth disappeared from Megan's face and fear for her child's and maybe her own life took over, drawing down her mouth.

Reid grabbed his phone and located a photo from a news story on the bank robbery for his brother. "Texting you Fowler's picture. Can you also check DMV and confirm he owns a white pickup?"

Russ nodded. "I'll do it while you're getting that bear. I can also contact Chief Gleason if you want. Ask him to open an investigation. Don't know if he will, but he might."

"You think he'll help?" Megan asked.

Russ shrugged. "Depends on how happy he is with his officer's actions."

Megan kept her attention on Russ. "Would you have handled things like the officer did when you were on patrol?"

"No," Russ said. "But in those days we didn't have the extreme staff shortages that exist today, and we could take more time at a call. Still, I would've flagged it for my sergeant. At the very least, he would want to know there could be a dangerous criminal in the area. And he could contact the probation officer to make him aware of the potential problem in hopes that they would make a follow-up call to Fowler. But again, they're overworked too and might not act at all with the limited information we have."

"Still, call the chief." Reid's phone rang, and he checked caller ID. Jack. Perfect. If he had good news it might erase Megan's fearful expression.

"Excuse me a minute." He stepped out of earshot. He couldn't see Jessie any longer, but he had to risk it. "Please tell me you have something positive for me."

"Afraid not," Jack answered. "I'm emailing you Fowler's judgment order. I took a quick glance at it, and he's not violating his order by being there. Still, I assume his probation officer could be interested to know he's in your neck of the woods. I could report it for you, but you have no proof he's there, so it'll probably go nowhere. Still, if he shows his face again..."

"Not if." Reid swallowed a bitter taste in his mouth. "When. Any mention in the order about staying away from Megan?"

"No. We should've thought to have it added at the time."

"Rookie mistake." There were a lot of things Reid should've done differently, like not fall for Megan. "And the protection detail? Did you get approval for that?"

"Request refused."

"Why?" Reid's voice rose, drawing Megan's worried gaze and Russ's questioning appraisal. Reid turned his back to them to hide his anger.

"Come on, Reid. I told you it was iffy at best, and you honestly didn't think our office would respond any differently than the local PD, did you?"

"You bet I did." Reid snapped. "The Bureau got her into this mess. I figured now that Fowler's out of prison they'd man up and take care of her." Reid wanted to place responsibility on the FBI, but her dilemma sat squarely on his shoulders. Fowler's threat had Megan changing her mind about testifying, and Reid convinced her to go through with it. After all, testifying was the right thing to do, but Reid had also selfishly wanted to make his first case.

"I'm sorry," Jack said. "I know how much she once meant to you. If I could do anything about our response, I would. If things escalate I can ask again."

Jack spoke the truth. He was a good man, and he didn't like leaving Megan at risk for Fowler's attack any more than Reid did.

Didn't mean he couldn't help in other areas. "Maybe you can redeem yourself by getting the name and address of the attendant Fowler was talking to at the gas station."

Jack didn't answer right away. "I might have better luck with that, but you know the privacy issues are more important these days. It'll likely take a warrant."

"Which no one in your office is going to approve when no crime, especially not a federal one, has been committed." Reid shoved his free hand into his hair.

"You know I'll do everything I can to help and won't let it go at that."

"I know." And Reid would do everything he could too. Starting with asking Russ to see what he could do about getting the locals to request a warrant too. It might be a challenge and even if the locals got the warrant, it didn't mean they would share the information, but at least they would be working on finding Fowler.

"Just like you aren't going to let Megan's need for protection go," Jack said.

Reid didn't deny it as he would be lying. "And?"

"And when you finalize a plan, call me. I'll do what I can to help."

"Thanks." Reid disconnected.

Before he returned to Megan, he wanted to have something positive to report. Like help from his teammates. He would start with Colin Graham, who Reid once worked closely with at the FBI. He and his brother, Devan, along with Micha Nichols, were invaluable members of the Shadow Lake Survival team. Dev was a former Clackamas County Deputy, and Micha served with Russ as a Marine weapons expert before he moved to military investigations.

Reid wouldn't even have to reschedule their classes as Shadow Lake Survival was closed for the holidays. The guys had little real family of their own, and the team had become like family, so they stayed on site to celebrate.

"Yo, boss man," Colin answered. "What can I do you for?"

Reid heard Christmas music playing in the background and hated to interrupt Colin's holiday. But he would. He explained the situation. "I was hoping you'd see if the guy's staying at the motel and keep an eye on him."

"Sure thing," he replied without hesitation. "You want me to take Dev along?"

"I have another job for him," Reid said.

"He didn't mention it."

"Haven't told him yet."

"He's right here if you want to talk to him.

"I would."

"Hang on."

Reid heard Colin explain the situation to Devan before he came on the line.

"Takes a real lowlife to threaten a woman and sick kid." Dev's tone vibrated with anger. "I'm in. What do you want me to do?"

Reid explained his need for someone to go to the bar in case Fowler showed his face there. "I know you're off, and I wouldn't ask if it wasn't important. Colin will watch Fowler's motel. Russ is helping me here with protection, and I'll be calling Micha in too. Ryan is home with the new baby, but I know he'll still spell Colin."

"So I'm last choice, huh?"

"I didn't want to have to call you at all. Not after the grueling training schedule you had last week."

"I'm just messing with you." He laughed. "I'm glad to go so Ryan can spend more time at home with the little fella. I was starting to go a little stir-crazy anyway. Too much time hanging with a brother like Colin can do that to you."

"Hey," Colin yelled in the background. "Goes both ways."

Dev laughed. "Do you have a picture of this guy?"

"I'll text it to you. It's from the bank robbery years ago. Still Megan recognized him so he must look basically the same."

"Roger that. I'll start at the location closest to the hospital. If they don't show there, I'll move on."

"Thanks. Keep me updated." Reid shoved his phone into his pocket and returned to Megan and Russ.

She crossed her arms. Had she picked up on his mood? Probably. He would tell her Colin and Dev were onboard, but he didn't intend to tell her about his conversation with

Jack yet. Didn't want her to stress over not having anyone watching out for her and Ella.

First, Reid needed to create a plan to keep her and Ella safe. To make sure Fowler didn't retaliate by hurting either one of them. A crime a man who allegedly killed his own friend was most definitely capable of committing.

5

All these years later, and now Megan rode with Reid on their way to retrieve Boo-Boo bear. Unbelievable. But here she was. Seated in the buttery softness of the leather seats in his SUV. She stroked Bandit's soft fur and took in the vehicle that was so neat even the rubber floor mats gleamed. That was so very much Reid. Neat. Tidy. Organized. To the extreme.

Would Jessie be that way too? A sweet girl and so dedicated to bringing her therapy dog to sick kids. She'd remained at the hospital with Russ and Ella, but Bandit couldn't stay there without Reid. Megan hadn't expected to hold Bandit for the drive, but the little sweetie curled in a circle on her lap, and his warm body brought her a sense of comfort and peace.

Or maybe it was the man who'd once given her so much strength, sitting tall and strong behind the steering wheel. Sure, he'd brought her equal parts pain, but today she had nothing left to fight him with and simply wanted to feel safe.

She shifted to watch the steady drizzle and familiar sights of the urban streets pass by. Large holiday wreaths with bright red bows hung from doors and garland circled lampposts. They should cheer her, but not with Ella in the hospital and Fowler hot on their heels. She couldn't begin to think about Christmas, much less find the joy of the season. Not that she was succeeding with that even before Fowler appeared—what with Ella's ongoing illness. But Megan would make sure the day was as special as possible for her daughter like she'd insured happened for the past three years.

They turned a corner, revealing the gas station where Fowler had sprung out of nowhere. A lump formed in her throat, cutting off her air. She breathed hard and pointed out the window. "That's where I saw Fowler."

"I've asked Jack to find out the name of the station attendant that Fowler talked to. He'll keep after it until he has it." Reid didn't face her as he spoke. Not even a quick glance. He'd said little since they'd left the hospital, as if distracted and wishing he were anywhere else but with her.

"Sounds like you respect him," she said, hoping to get him talking and lighten the tension between them.

"I'd trust him with my life." He'd said his life, but Megan could read between the lines. Reid would trust Jack to keep her and Ella safe too. And she *was* feeling less threatened at the moment. With Reid by her side. At least for her physical well-being. Her emotional health? Not so much.

She shouldn't look at him. Had tried not to, but he concentrated on negotiating the thick city traffic, and she snuck another quick peek.

His profile was all hard angles, as if chiseled from granite. The perfect profile for an FBI agent, tough and invincible. His dark chocolate-colored hair was short on the sides and back, but longer on top and sleekly held in place. He was still all hard muscle with broad shoulders to carry heavy problems.

He'd always worked out, and she wasn't surprised he

remained fit. What she hadn't expected was to find him volunteering at a children's hospital. And leave the FBI? She'd thought he'd die before doing that, but surprise, surprise, he'd also retired from the Bureau.

Now he was taking her to get Boo-Boo. A sweet gesture from a hard-as-nails man.

But why? Could he have ulterior motives, as when he'd dumped her to move ahead in the FBI?

Did it even matter? She wouldn't tell him to take her back to the hospital anyway. Not when Ella counted on Megan to get her beloved bear. Still, Megan had to know why he was helping her. At least then she could erase the idea of him being one of the good guys now. A crazy idea that was doing a good job at trying to replace her anger toward him.

She swiveled to face him, and Bandit stirred to change positions. "Can I ask you a question?"

He cast her a wary gaze. "I guess."

Okay, so he *would* look at her after all. Good to know. "Why are you doing this?"

"This, meaning what?"

Ah, yes. Just like him. Needing exact words before answering. "Why did you arrange for Russ to stay with Ella so you could drive me home?"

He shrugged, his focus still pinned on the road ahead.

She wouldn't let it drop so easily. "Is it because you feel guilty about our past?"

"Maybe."

This vague answer didn't fit the concise nature of the man she'd fallen for so many years ago. "Maybe—or you don't want to admit the way you treated me was wrong?"

He stopped at a red light and fixed startling blue eyes that had won her heart in one of the darkest times of her life on her. "I'll readily admit the way I treated you was wrong.

What I don't know is why I feel so compelled to help you and Ella, okay?"

The light changed, and his attention returned to his driving. "I'd like to say it's based on putting my faith into action, but I honestly don't think my motives are that pure."

Megan didn't know what to say. She'd thought about this day. The day when they would run into each other again. In every case, she'd walked away and left him hanging as he'd done to her. But now? Even if he weren't helping her get Boo-Boo? The pain in his voice made her want to hear him out.

And if that wasn't enough to sway her toward giving him a break, after he'd said he'd really started embracing his childhood faith, how could she not give him a chance to explain? Even if her walk with God was iffy at the moment, she should treat a brother in Christ with respect and kindness.

But what about the sting of his rejection? Could she get beyond the residual pain for any reason?

At the next stoplight, he glanced at her again. "I didn't want to walk away from you, but I have to admit I wanted to advance in the FBI more."

"Wow." She eyed him. "You couldn't be more blunt than that."

"What good would it do to sugarcoat it? I was young and stupid. I thought my career was the most important thing, so I chose it."

"And now?"

"Now I know better, and I'm sorry for how I treated you," he said in a steady lower-pitched voice. "I hope you can forgive me for being such a jerk."

She wanted to pull her gaze away, maybe to yell at him for hurting her, but she couldn't move.

49

Horns honked behind them, and he jerked his attention to the road.

Good timing. She didn't know what to say anyway. The pain of his betrayal remained lodged in her chest, and a simple apology, no matter how sincere he sounded, couldn't erase the hurt in a flash.

So what should she do? Did she let him off the hook this easily? He didn't deserve it, did he?

They turned the corner, and her house came into view. She usually loved coming home, but even her outdoor manger sitting in her yard which should remind her of Jesus's birth, couldn't calm the acid in her stomach.

Dark shadows clung to the small bungalow she and Ella shared. Fowler could be there. Hiding. Watching them.

She had no business thinking about Reid and what she did or didn't want to do about her feelings for him. A lunatic might be stalking her, and her daughter lay in the hospital.

Possible death in any form trumped a broken heart.

Megan's demeanor transformed like a change in weather, and Reid would rather see her angry at him than this ongoing fear. She'd seemed as if she was ready to talk about their past, maybe offer her forgiveness. Or at least that's what he was getting from her. Until they reached her street, then her whole body tensed as if she expected to find Fowler standing on her doorstep.

Reid really hoped the creep had a change of character in prison and wasn't actually stalking her. But then why had he come to the hospital? Reid had to remember that and not relax his stance a fraction until he was certain the guy wouldn't harm Megan.

He parked in her driveway and made a quick visual

sweep of the property. A generous lot surrounded a contemporary home boasting odd roof angles with icicle lights glowing in neat rows. Even in the drizzling rain and setting sun, the beige house appeared welcoming with the vivid green lawn, neatly trimmed shrubbery, and landscape lighting the walkway to a door featuring a large pinecone-studded wreath.

Tranquil. But he wouldn't let the peaceful setting lull him into a false sense of security.

"You wait here while I make a quick check of the perimeter." He opened the lock on the gun safe bolted to the floor between the seats. He withdrew his handgun and slipped in the clip before shoving the holster into his jacket pocket.

"Is that really necessary?" Her voice was low, her eyes watchful.

"Probably not." He gave her a quick smile to help ease her fears yet not make her relax enough to put herself in danger. "Keep the doors locked. Call me if anything seems odd. Okay?"

She nodded, and he climbed out of the SUV. To keep any neighbors who might be watching from calling the police, he double checked that his gun was concealed in his jacket pocket. It was out of sight yet easy to reach if needed.

He circled the home, checking windows and doors for any breach. He had to give Megan props for having a security system. Though systems weren't foolproof and not a great help against a determined stalker, they did help deter random burglars.

He slipped through a gate to the backyard and made a visual search of the area. Well past prime growing season, he could still see the shape of a large garden that was groomed to perfection. He checked the patio door before returning to the front of the house and sweeping the street.

Satisfied nothing was out of the ordinary, he went to the SUV and opened Megan's door. "We're clear."

She slipped out, holding Bandit's leash.

Seeing her upset left him unsettled, and he wanted to distract her. "You have a beautiful house."

"Thanks." She gave a wobbly smile. "We love it here."

"Seems like a great neighborhood for kids."

"It is." She glanced around, falling silent. She was worried.

He kept his eyes on the area. "Everything will be okay."

"How can you say that?" She gaped at him. "We don't have a clue where Fowler is."

"We'll find him." His words rang hollow even to himself, so he kept quiet and headed up the walk.

At the door, she unlocked the deadbolt and silenced the security system in the entryway.

"Stay here until I clear the place," he said to her and eyed Bandit. "Sit," he commanded.

Thankfully the dog's training made him comply, and he followed directions, peering at Reid with a cocked head.

Reid took out his handgun and entered the family room where a Charlie Brown kind of tree stood in the corner with half a string of lights placed on it and the other half dangling on the floor. Boxes of ornaments and silvery tinsel lay scattered on the floor as if they'd been interrupted in the middle of tree trimming. Maybe that's when Megan had to rush Ella to the hospital.

Reid had done it a few times with Diane when her chemo got the best of her. Terrifying, awful moments when he feared he would lose her.

He shook off the thoughts and caught a whiff of the tree's fresh pine scent. Among the chaos, he glimpsed warm contemporary furnishings mixed with toys and a child's artwork. He went down the hall. Checked the three bedrooms and two baths, then returned to a state-of-the-art kitchen with dirty dishes in the sink. Maybe more evidence that they'd left in a hurry. He opened several closets and then returned to the entry.

"All clear," he said.

Megan let out a rush of air and slipped off her jacket, damp with drizzle. "I didn't really expect you to find anything, but I have to admit I was worried." She hung her jacket on a hook by the door.

He followed suit, using the hook next to hers. "I'm sure I overreacted, but in my former line of work there is no such thing as being too careful."

"I still can't believe you left the FBI."

"It was the only choice. Jessie needed me around more."

She laid her hand on his forearm and gently squeezed. "I said this before, but I'm very sorry for your loss. I can only imagine how hard losing your wife must have been for you."

Her voice cracked. She had to be visualizing losing Ella. He didn't want her to go down that path.

"Now, where is that bear I've heard so much about?" He ended with a smile meant to push away her concerns.

She removed her hand, but her concern didn't disappear. "I'll get him. If we have time, I'd like to pack a bag too. When we headed to the ER yesterday we didn't know Ella would be admitted, and I'd love some fresh clothes."

"We have plenty of time."

"What about your brother? Sounded like he needed to get back."

Reid sincerely laughed and all the tension left his body. "If you knew Russ, you'd realize he always has somewhere to be other than where he is."

She returned his smile.

The urge to touch the side of her face and run a thumb

along her jaw nearly made him forget he had no right to do so.

He shoved his hand in his pocket. "Why don't you pack while I take Bandit for a short walk? After being cooped up all day, he needs to release some energy."

And so do I before I follow through on my impulses.

"Sounds good."

Oblivious to his warring emotions, she turned toward the hallway leading to the bedrooms, and he kept an eye on her until she disappeared around the corner. He retrieved his jacket and exhaled out his thoughts.

The last thing he needed was to get involved with Megan again. Correction. The last thing he needed was to get involved with any woman. Especially a woman whose child's life hung in the balance. He'd barely survived losing Diane. He could never survive losing a child.

He lifted his jacket collar to keep the drizzle from soaking his shirt and blew out the last of his feelings. He reached for the doorknob, and a piercing scream sounded from deep inside the house.

He dropped Bandit's leash and jerked out his gun. Pulse kicking up, he moved cautiously into the home, flattening his back against the wall. His heart thumped wildly. He wanted to race to Megan, but rushing into the unknown could get them both killed.

He counted to three. Glanced around the corner.

Clear.

He moved through the family room. Another corner. Quick look.

Clear.

He went down the short hallway to the first bedroom and swung his gun around the corner.

Empty.

To the next bedroom. Sliding slowly. Same procedure. He hissed out a breath and lowered his weapon.

Megan stood alone in the middle of Ella's room, a child's suitcase in her hand and her face fixed straight ahead as if in a trance. He'd checked this room on his walkthrough and hadn't seen anything odd.

So what made her scream?

"What is it?" he asked.

She didn't speak but pointed at the dresser. He tucked the gun into his holster and followed the direction of her finger.

On Ella's dresser sat a raggedy brown bear with a Band-Aid on one paw. Boo-Boo, he assumed.

"Her bear?" he asked, not understanding.

"Behind it."

He crossed the room and glanced behind it. A full-size baseball cap sat there, a business card too. The cap boasted a silhouette of a mountain and had the words Tacoma Rainiers embroidered on it. This was once the official cap of the minor league team Fowler followed. The team had changed logos. The old logo meant this cap could be the one Fowler wore during the robbery.

The very cap Megan kept referring to when Reid had questioned her, and a memory she'd associated so closely with Fowler that anytime she'd seen the picture of it during the trial, a cold sweat had broken out on her face.

"He's going to kill me," she said, her attention fixed on the dresser.

As if protecting her, Bandit trotted across the room, dragging his leash and sitting with his side touching her leg. He was taking over where Reid had failed.

He shouldn't have missed seeing the cap on his sweep. But he was looking for something dangerous, not a baseball cap hiding behind a bear. Still, Megan's rigid posture and shell-shocked stare were all his fault.

Nothing would comfort her at the moment. At least nothing Reid could say. Without thinking, he drew her into his arms and turned her away from the dresser.

"I won't let him get to you," he promised on a whisper. He held her close and stroked her back.

She settled closer, but then, as if thinking better of it, pushed away from him and crossed over to the cap.

"Don't touch it," he warned. "We need to preserve the evidence."

She leaned closer to the dresser. "The card's from the Willamette Bank."

Reid grabbed a tissue from the nightstand and grabbed the card from the very bank Megan had worked for and the one Fowler had robbed.

She wrapped her arms around her waist. She was afraid and trying to soothe herself. Her fear was justified. Her home had been invaded by the man who'd threatened to kill her.

How he got in was the question Reid needed to answer in order to stop him from doing it again. There'd been no sign of forced entry on Reid's very thorough sweep of the place. Fowler had to have a key or gotten someone to let him in. Things Reid would ask Megan, but not yet. He would give her time to regain her composure.

Then Reid had to do everything within his power to keep Fowler from terrorizing her again. And if he wanted to succeed, he had to step up his game. Not miss little details like a baseball cap. Not miss anything.

Fowler had already proved to be a worthy foe declaring war, and Reid needed to be ready for battle.

6

Reid clicked End on his cell phone. He'd called Russ to warn him to be extra vigilant and phoned Micha Nichols to report here to Megan's house. Now that Fowler had breached her private sanctuary, Reid would take no chances, and no one was better to assess the situation and offer protection advice than a weapons expert like Micha.

At least one thing had gone in their favor. Russ confirmed Fowler owned a white pickup and located the plate number, so it could be used in an alert if Gleason agreed to issue one. Gleason hadn't committed yet. He wanted to talk to his officer before he did anything and would get back to Russ.

Megan sat shell-shocked on her sofa, and Reid didn't think she heard him make his calls. He'd failed her today. Big time. He could've prevented her from seeing the threat. He couldn't—wouldn't—let her down again.

He crossed the room to the sofa.

Her face deathly pale and her hands clasped between her knees, she rocked and let her gaze dart around the room as if she expected Fowler to return any moment. Even with

Bandit curled by her side, she seemed so alone and afraid. What a kick to the gut.

Please give her peace and comfort. Let her know You're here beside her. And don't let me disappoint her again. Ever.

She looked up and blinked as if just noticing he was in the room.

"Did you talk to your brother? Is Ella okay?" Her words rushed out on top of each other.

"Ella's fine. Russ said she's playing a board game with Jessie and having a good time." Reid sat in a club chair across from Megan.

She nibbled on her lower lip. "But you told Russ to be extra careful, right? I mean now that Fowler's been here and all."

"Don't worry about Ella." Reid put as much confidence as he could muster into his words. "Russ won't let Fowler get to her."

Megan shrunk into her chair. "So what happens next?"

"When Micha—one of the Shadow Lake Survival team members—gets here, we'll make a thorough search of your house."

"Why wait for him?"

"I don't want to miss anything. Another pair of eyes will help with that." Plus, Micha had a rare calming effect on people in turmoil, and if the search located anything more, Micha could make things easier for Megan. No need to share that and unnecessarily worry her, though.

She tilted her head. "What about the police? Won't they do the same thing?"

"Yes, but odds are good that Micha and I have more experience and training in evaluating the situation than the locals, so we'll do a search before I call them. Since Fowler got in here without any sign of forced entry, we need to bring our A-game."

She resumed rocking. "He's going to kill me, isn't he?"

"Trust me, I won't let that happen. But we also need to consider that he has other motives. He might not have any intention of really hurting you, and he's just trying to scare you."

"Well, he's doing a good job." She shuddered. "I *am* scared." She clasped her arms around her middle, much like at the bank robbery and her terror for months afterward.

The memories catapulted him to the bank, to the day when officers dragged Fowler away, his hot beady eyes locked on Megan. Spewing obscenities and threats. Megan withdrawing into her chair as if trying to disappear. Much as she was trying to do now.

But she was a different person now. She'd become a fiercely independent woman. He'd seen that at the hospital. She needed to get in touch with that strength again to ease the panic.

Maybe he could help. He took her hand, ice-cold and trembling.

"You and Ella will be fine." He squeezed her fingers. "I know you're worried, but I also know you can handle anything that comes your way for Ella's sake."

She sat up higher, but then a knock sounded on the door, and she jerked her hand away to clutch her body again.

"Relax. That's got to be Micha." Not that Reid wouldn't be careful before opening the door. Hand on the butt of his gun, he peered through the peephole.

Micha stared at the door, his black hair and matching close-cut beard darker in the shadows. He frowned, drawing down his face. Reid had seen this scowl many times with Micha when a survivalist challenged him.

Reid unlocked the door and opened it for Russ's military friend.

Reid moved close to Micha. "Megan's really freaked out. Keep your comments positive when she's in earshot."

Micha responded with a raised eyebrow but didn't speak. They entered the family room. Megan had come to her feet, and Reid made the introductions.

She shook Micha's hand. "Thanks for coming. I appreciate it."

Micha smiled. His good looks attracted women like flies to honey, but on the job, his demeanor changed and put women at ease. Like Megan now. Some tension had left her posture. Reid was glad she'd calmed a bit. He really was, but jealousy stabbed his gut. There once was a time when he'd had a soothing effect on her. Now just being in the same room seemed to agitate her.

"So," Micha said loudly, drawing Reid to the present. "Let's get the show on the road."

"We'll start in Ella's room." Reid wanted to ask Megan to stay put in the family room, but he knew she'd balk at it.

"After you." He held out his hand for her to precede them down the hallway. She hurried ahead.

"Stay," Reid said to Bandit and set off beside Micha.

"No sign of forced entry at all?" Micha asked in a whisper after Megan was out of range.

"None," Reid replied, his tone low. "Fowler either got someone to let him in, had a key, or could pick a lock. Either way, he also had to know the code for the alarm system."

Micha frowned. "Maybe we'll get lucky and find his prints on the keypad."

"I'm guessing he wore gloves," Reid said.

"If he's smart he did."

"He's not the brightest bulb," Reid said as they moved down the hall. "But he literally got away with murder, so he does know how to commit a crime and get away with it."

At Ella's door, Reid let Micha enter first. Reid had

instructed his teammate to bring supplies, and he handed a pair of latex gloves to Reid, then put on his own pair and systematically searched the space. Reid followed suit, sifting through toys, clothes, and craft supplies as he periodically glanced at Megan.

A myriad of emotions wandered over her face, and he could almost see the wheels in her head turning as she tried to make sense of the situation. In the end, she set her jaw. Good. The strong woman from the hospital had returned.

Micha turned from the tall white dresser with alphabet blocks for handles. "Everything's like you described."

Reid joined him and lifted the cap. "Definitely well-worn. Could be the actual cap Fowler wore at the robbery. If so, the police should be able to retrieve his DNA, and they'll take the incident seriously."

"Maybe." Micha pinched his lips together. "With no sign of forced entry, there's nothing to prove Fowler left it here."

Megan's hand flew to her chest. "Do you think someone else might have done it?"

"No," Reid answered honestly.

She frowned. "But if they find his DNA on the cap that should prove he was here, right?"

Reid hated to answer her question, but he had to let her know what was to come. "Actually, the DNA would only prove that he wore it. With no sign of forced entry, the police could assume that when I took Bandit outside, you placed the cap here."

"How would I even get his cap?" She clenched her hands together. "And why on earth would I put it here?"

"People do all kinds of strange things to get attention these days," Reid said. "The police have to explore all angles, and that includes you."

She released her hands to run one over her hair. "But if

the cap has Fowler's DNA on it, won't the threat be more believable to them?"

"Could be," Reid said. "It would also be helpful if we can figure out when Fowler was here. They can then focus their questions when they canvass the neighborhood."

Reid didn't add *if* they canvassed. If they didn't think the threat credible, they would file a report and move on the same way Officer York had at the hospital.

"Reid said your alarm hadn't gone off, so your intruder would need to have accessed it," Micha said. "Your security company should be able to give you a list of status change times while you were at the hospital."

"Their number is on my desk. I'll go call them." She hurried from the room.

Micha locked gazes with Reid. "You're certain she didn't do this herself?"

"I can't believe you even have to ask that." He'd explained when he called Micha how he'd met Megan and how Fowler victimized her. "I know Megan. Know her well. You spend as much time as I did with her, and you get to know them inside and out. Especially when prepping them for testimony at a trial."

Micha shoved his hands into the pockets of his tactical pants. "Yeah, but you haven't seen her in years. People change. She might not be the same woman you knew, right? And she's the only one who's actually seen this guy."

Reid's gut said she hadn't changed from a private person to an attention seeker who would perpetrate a stunt like this. She might have developed a strong determination she hadn't once possessed, but her soft, caring demeanor had remained intact, and deep inside she was the same woman he'd fallen for. But a guy couldn't always count on his gut. Not when the intuition he developed as an agent also said

Micha's apprehension was justified, and Reid needed to think with his brain, not his heart.

"I'll keep your point in mind," he said, even if it was reluctantly.

Micha fixed a narrow-eyed gaze on Reid. "Why do I think you won't?"

Uncomfortable under his teammate's study, Reid forced a smile. "I won't pretend to understand the way you think."

Micha stepped closer, as if he planned to issue a word of warning, but Megan returned and drew their attention.

She stopped inside the door, her lips flattened into a grim line. "They confirmed that my code was used to enter the house at three-seventeen a.m. and reset the alarm at four this morning." She shivered. "He was here. Right here. In my house for forty minutes. Mine! While I was with Ella at the hospital. What could he possibly be doing for that long?"

Reid had no clue, but he *did* know speculating on Fowler's actions wasn't in Megan's best interest. Not in the least. Reid wouldn't reply and would keep his expression neutral.

Or would at least try. Not easy when visions of Fowler pawing through Megan's personal possessions consumed his thoughts. Still, he didn't want to amp up her concern again. Especially when her rigid body language continued to emit waves of fear.

Planning to rest a hand on her arm to let her know he was here for her, he took a step forward.

"Easy, man." Micha snagged Reid's arm and leaned close to whisper, "You're not doing a very good job of hiding your concern. You're too close to this. Let me talk to her."

Reid shrugged off the hand but heeded the warning and nodded for Micha to proceed.

Micha's compassionate expression of earlier was

replaced by a blank one that was totally unreadable. "Can anyone vouch for you being at the hospital during that time?"

She tapped her chin. "I was in Ella's room, but I'm not sure if a nurse came in during that time or not. Still, my car would be in the lot, and security would've caught me leaving and coming back, right?"

"We'll check into that." He smiled again. "Did you give your security code to anyone?"

"My parents have it, but no one else." She crossed her arms. "I never give it out."

"No repairman, house sitter, anything like that?"

"No."

"Does anyone else have a key to your house?"

"My parents."

"And you're sure they wouldn't share the code with anyone else?"

"No one." Megan's expression tightened. "Wait, are you saying my parents are involved in this somehow?" Her nostrils flared.

An urge to shelter her from Micha's questioning had Reid stepping between them.

"I'm sure Micha doesn't think your parents did anything wrong." Reid purposefully kept his tone soft. "Fowler could've somehow conned it and the key out of them. Maybe you should call them and ask."

"They're on a cruise." She rubbed her hands over her arms. "I hate to bother them unless absolutely necessary."

"How long have they been gone?" Micha asked.

"A week."

Micha kept his focus pinned to her. "Do you know if they took your keys with them?"

"Doubtful. There would be no point." She took a slight step away. "They hang them on a hook by their back door.

64

They can never remember the security code, so they put it on a tag on the ring. I never thought it would be a problem because if someone took the keys, they wouldn't know whose house they were for, but..."

"But if Fowler's been planning this for a while, he likely knows who your parents are." Reid turned to Micha. "Can you—"

"Head over to their house and check?" Micha answered, as he often did before Reid posed a full question. "I'll need the address."

"I'll get some paper and write it down for you." Megan charged out of the room as if Fowler himself were chasing her.

"Let's finish our search of the property so you can get on your way while I report this to the locals." Reid held out his hand to direct Micha into the hallway.

He made the move but then paused. "Good thing the parents went on vacation."

Reid didn't like Micha's expression, but he'd had the same thought. If Megan's parents had been home and Fowler wanted the keys, he might've killed them.

Reid stepped onto the back patio to begin the exterior search. "If I need you, might you be able to spell me tonight at the hospital?"

"And then maybe get a few minutes of sleep?" His sarcasm flowed liberally in his words.

"Sorry. I know this is going to be a long day for you too."

"No worries, I'm good to help. Just have to give you a hard time about it." He arched an eyebrow.

Reid rolled his eyes, and Micha grinned. Bandit perked up but Reid signaled for him to stay put, before he stepped into the hallway with Micha.

Holding out a slip of paper, Megan joined them. "I don't get why Fowler went to all the trouble of getting the key and code. It would only take a few seconds to place the hat and card, so why not break in, drop it, then run?"

Reid shared a knowing look with Micha, warning his teammate not to answer. Reid believed that Fowler hoped the police would think this was a hoax and wouldn't take it seriously enough to protect Megan. Then Fowler could have his way with her.

Right now, Reid was certain that included physically hurting—if not killing—both her and Ella.

7

Megan shivered. Her house wasn't cold. Not by any means. Detective Wilson's insinuation that she'd planted the cap and card herself for attention had given her a chill. She'd told him she was at the hospital during that time, and he agreed to check her alibi, but she honestly didn't know if a nurse had come into the room then or not, as Megan had been sleeping on a cot next to Ella's bed.

She glanced at Reid for comfort, and he cast her a knowing look. Yeah, he'd warned her of the detective's potential response.

She took a fortifying breath and looked the detective square in the eyes. "I would have no reason to leave the cap and card in my house. One of the last things I want to remember is that bank robbery."

"I'm sorry, Ms. Cash," Wilson said earnestly. "I have to consider all avenues and since we have no proof Norman Fowler even entered your home, we have to investigate all key holders for the residence. You said the only people with a key are you and your parents, and they're on a cruise so that leaves you."

Megan clenched her hands. "And I also told you I was at

the hospital during the intrusion, and we think their keys had to be stolen."

"Again, you don't know that for sure at the moment, but we will certainly check out their residence to confirm it and your alibi." He spoke like he might believe her, but his eyebrows were drawn close together, and his face tight. "I'll also have forensics process the cap and card for fingerprints. This place too. And if my lieutenant agrees that we have the funds, we'll also test for DNA."

"Funds?" she cried out when she should be trying to remain in control. "How can that play into this when my life could be at stake?"

"Again, we have no proof of a break-in, ma'am, so there isn't any proof of a crime being committed and DNA is expensive to run."

She gritted her teeth and then let out a breath. "However Fowler did this, it has to be him. Check with the gas station attendant. He'll tell you Fowler was at the station down the road."

"Not a crime, unless of course, he has conditions tied to his release that tell him to refrain from making any contact with you. But then again, he didn't make contact."

She wanted to scream. "Sounds like you're on his side. The side of a bank robber."

"Not on his side, Ms. Cash. Not at all. Just telling you that I have to work within the constraints of the law."

"Will you at least go to the gas station? Please?"

He sat forward as if planning to leave. "I'll ask the uniform I sent over to your parent's address to follow up there too."

"And if they say he was there?"

"It doesn't really change anything, but if there's any sign of a forced entry at your parent's home, we'll be looking for Fowler, and this attendant might be the key to locating him."

"And if no sign of forced entry?" Reid stepped in when he'd told her he didn't plan to, as he didn't want to make the officer think he was trying to do his job for him and put him on the defensive.

Wilson met Reid's gaze with confidence. "Then I'm afraid all we can do is have our officers keep an eye out for his truck and stop him to see what he's doing in our area."

"Officer York was going to go by the motel to check on him," Megan said.

"He did and didn't see the white truck registered to a Norman Fowler. The clerk wouldn't give out any information without a warrant, which—"

"You can't get because no crime has been committed," Megan said. "Trust me. I get it."

"What about calling his probation officer?" Reid asked. "I've reviewed his judgment order. As long as he remains in the state he's not violating it, but the PO might have restricted his travel for some reason."

Wilson stood and peered at Megan. "After I know what's going on at your parent's place I can make that call. Tell the PO it's possible Fowler's down here harassing Ms. Cash. Maybe breaking the law. Not sure how seriously they'll take me without any proof, though."

Reid shoved his hands into his pockets. "A good PO will at least call him."

"And with mobile phones, he could lie to his PO about his location, but they could require him to report in, and that could stop this for the time being anyway." He handed Megan a business card. "Now excuse me. I'll make that call to my uniform and get forensics out here."

"Can we leave a house key with you so I can get Ms. Cash back to her sick daughter and you all can secure the property?" Reid asked.

"Of course."

Megan wanted to sag in her seat, but Ella needed her. She stood and picked up a key from the table where the locksmith had left them after he changed the locks and handed it to the detective, who pocketed it.

"Am I free to pack a bag and take the bear I came to get?" Megan asked.

"Don't see why not. I'll be in touch." The detective stepped from the room.

"I'll get things packed so we can get going," she said to Reid, then rushed from the room before she started crying.

But she held it in, got hers and Ella's things, including Boo-Boo, into a bag, and Reid escorted her through the darkness to his SUV. She wished it didn't get dark before five as she would feel much safer. Even Bandit seemed to abandon her as he curled up in the backseat this time.

As Reid drove, she didn't know what to say to him. What to do. So she clutched her hands in her lap. Fidgeting. Fighting her fear. And trying to process today's events and figure out what she could talk about without crying.

She snuck a glance at Reid. Such a tough profile, yet she knew he could also be gentle. But he'd pulled away at her house. Seemed to put up a wall and they'd spoken very little after Micha departed for her parents' house.

Sure he stayed by her side when the police arrived in a whirl of activity, but he'd remained reserved. At least now she knew exactly what that mysterious look she'd caught between him and Micha meant. Fowler wanted the police to think she'd planted the cap for attention, because then they wouldn't offer to help her. He wanted her to know that he was out there and coming for her, but the lack of police protection left her exposed and vulnerable. If she hadn't run into Reid at the hospital, she'd be on her own to keep Ella and herself out of Fowler's grasp.

She shivered and rubbed her arms to warm herself.

Reid glanced at her. "Want me to turn up the heater?"

"Please." But she doubted that would chase out her chill. If anything could thaw the fear and help it melt away, it would be Reid. He might've been quiet at her house, but he still took her side in the investigation, stood by her when the police wouldn't and got a locksmith out to change her locks. He even helped her change her security code when she wasn't thinking straight.

She owed him. Not only for his support but the forgiveness he'd asked for earlier. They'd both been young and naive when they'd first met. Both of them were at fault that things ended so badly. She hadn't even tried to talk to him. Let him explain. And she shouldn't have let her feelings get the best of her. But they'd been in love. Oh, so in love. At least she'd been, and she believed he had been too.

It still hurt to look at him. But she did. Again. Subtly so he didn't catch her studying him, remembering when she'd seen the Rainiers cap, and he'd held her against his solid chest. She'd been soothed by the sure sound of his heart, his powerful arms cocooning her. She'd felt as if she wasn't alone for the first time in a long time. Since Orrin abandoned them.

She wanted to let go. Give in. Let Reid take over and hold her again. No. Not a good idea. Not now. Not ever. She could forgive him, but she couldn't let him back into her heart. Not only him. Not any man. They simply couldn't be trusted not to bail when troubles came up.

And she needed to set some ground rules to make sure Reid didn't try to hold her hand—or her—when the going got tough. Question was, how did she broach the subject without drawing attention to her inner conflict?

She could start by thanking him for what he'd done so far and then play it by ear. "I haven't thanked you for taking me to get Boo-Boo. Without your help today, I don't know what I'd have done."

"You make it sound like I'm going to take off when we get to the hospital." He slowed at a stoplight and flashed a pained look her way. "I know how much I hurt you. Big time, but even as young and foolish as I was then, if Fowler was breathing down your neck like this, I would never have left."

"Wait, no." She swiveled to face him. "You're misunderstanding. I really am thanking you for your help."

"But?" He raised his eyebrow.

"What?"

"There's a 'but' coming. I can hear it in your voice." He stared straight into her eyes.

"Fine. I'm grateful for and appreciate your continued help and support, but I don't want you to be so physical about it the next time I freak out."

"Explain."

"Don't hold my hand. Or me, for that matter. That might've been necessary when you knew me before, but I've grown up, and I don't need a man to hold me anymore and promise everything will be okay." She held her breath and waited for his reaction.

He searched her eyes deeply.

Fine. He didn't like what she'd said. "Now you're mad. That's why I didn't want to say anything."

"I'm not mad."

But he was hurt. She heard it in his voice. Just as well. It would help to keep the wall erected between them. The light changed, and he faced the road to ease the SUV forward.

His phone rang from the holder on his dashboard, and she let out a silent breath of relief at the perfect timing.

He punched his speaker and answered. "Hi, Jess."

"Uncle Russ wants to know when you're coming back. He says he has a lot to do tonight, and he really needs to get going."

Reid smiled but didn't say a word.

"Are you almost here, Dad? I mean, I don't care 'cause I'm having fun, but Uncle Russ is kinda getting crabby."

Reid chuckled.

Megan couldn't help grinning over the change in him. She couldn't help visualizing a warm memory of them laughing together and letting it melt a sliver of the ice around her heart.

"What's so funny?" Jessie asked.

"Nothing. We're on our way and will be there soon."

He ended the call, and Megan swiveled toward him. "Sounds like your brother is getting antsy."

Reid turned and smiled so softly that she wanted to toss away her new resolve and let go. To embrace the way her heart beat faster for him and see if they still had something. She clamped down on her lips and waited for him to continue.

"Russ is always antsy," Reid said.

"And you find that funny?"

"What's funny is how Russ convinces Jessie to call me instead of doing it himself. And she falls for it every time."

"She seems like a great girl."

"She is. The best, actually."

"Seems like you two have a lot of fun together."

He glanced at her again, and his expression sobered. "After losing Diane, I'm grateful for every time we find something that we can laugh about."

The subject was obviously painful for him, but maybe he needed to talk about his loss.

"I can't imagine how hard it was to lose her," she said.

"Yeah." He fell silent for a few moments. "It's been hard.

73

Still is, but the worst part now is seeing Jessie struggle over losing her mother. She's also coping with an incident that happened last year when she was abducted for a few hours. A long story that I don't want to get into."

Wow, oh, wow. Poor little thing. "From what I've seen, it seems like she's adjusting."

"Yeah." He nodded. "Yeah, it's going on three years at this point, and I can say she's finally coming out of it and starting to live again."

"And you? How are you coping?" The minute the words left her mouth and his eyes glazed over, she wanted to take them back. Getting this personal with him was the wrong thing to be doing if she wanted to keep her boundaries intact.

"I still miss her," he answered.

"How long were you together?" she asked, her curiosity winning out over common sense.

"I met her shortly after you and I... ah..." He glanced at her, then away. "After Fowler's trial ended."

So Diane had taken her place in Reid's affections.

"When did you get married?" The question came on a whisper, and Megan knew it was because the answer would hurt, but she couldn't help asking. She fidgeted with her fingers and tensed while waiting for the reply.

"We dated for about a year," he said.

A year. It only took a year to replace his feelings for her. She shouldn't be surprised. She and Reid hadn't actually dated or had an official relationship. But the feelings that had developed between them during the six-month ordeal between the robbery and Fowler's conviction had been very real.

She felt his eyes on her, but she wouldn't face him. And she wouldn't take this conversation any further. She was better off keeping quiet and staring out the window.

"I was surprised to hear you married Orrin," Reid said, his tone letting her know he thought she'd dated on the rebound too.

He was right, of course, but her rebound relationship was different. It didn't last, and she should never have married Orrin. She and Reid had met Orrin when he'd covered Fowler's trial for his job as a television reporter. His stellar coverage of the trial won him a local news anchor slot, and at the end of the trial, he'd asked her out for a celebratory dinner. Reid had just bailed on her and anger propelled her to go. As she and Orrin dated, she'd convinced herself that he was everything Reid wasn't, and as such, he was the right guy for her. But she'd been wrong. So wrong.

"He didn't seem like your type," Reid went on as if she wasn't ignoring him. "Why'd you break up?"

"He couldn't handle Ella's illness," she said quietly.

He gaped at her for a moment. "He left when she got sick?"

"People with seriously sick children often split up," she said, sounding strangely defensive. But why? Nothing could defend Orrin's appalling behavior. "I'm sure you know how hard a serious illness can be on a family."

"Yeah." She heard the pain in his tone and expected him to say more, but he simply nodded at the upcoming driveway to the hospital parking lot. "We're here."

He clearly didn't want to talk about his loss with her, and his unwillingness stung.

You're an idiot, Megan. You can't have things both ways. Move on and let this rest.

He turned into the lot, and though the fog had thickened into a cloudy soup, she spotted her car as they drove in.

"Would it be okay if we stopped to get something from

75

my car? I have a bag in there with magazines and books that I usually take to Ella's appointments. It'll give me something to do tonight if I can't sleep."

"Where did you park?"

"Section C." Memories of the race to catch Fowler earlier in the day brought her unease to the surface again, and as Reid maneuvered through the lot and parked, fear had her searching around. Did the horrible man hide in the shadows waiting to attack? If so, where?

"We need to make it quick." Reid turned off the ignition, grabbed his phone, and opened his gun safe.

Thinking he was leaving his gun in the car and leaving them unprotected, panic threatened to climb out from where she'd buried it. He reached into the safe. With long fingers that had once held her hand, he pulled out another ammo clip, then shoved it into his jacket pocket. He checked the clip already seated in the gun, and then he glanced at the backseat, where Bandit snored softly.

"I'll leave him here for now. You ready?" He smiled but it was forced.

She returned it with a wobbly one of her own and climbed out, Boo-Boo in her arms. The lot was well lit, but fog swirled at their feet and fear crept up over her. She searched the thick haze for Fowler, expecting him to pounce on her. Reid came around the vehicle. One hand was on his holster, the other held out in front.

"Stay close."

She couldn't miss the transformation in him, going from a man feeling the loss of his wife to a former FBI agent, sharp and serious. He didn't have to tell her twice about staying close.

Together they crossed the aisle through the misty rain that seemed to encapsulate them. The slick pavement held unseen puddles, soaking her feet. She knew her car sat only a few feet away, but she couldn't see the entire vehicle.

She inched closer to Reid and hated that she did so. She'd been independent and on her own for years now. Doing fine. But here she was on the day that was second in terror only to the day Fowler held her at gunpoint, letting Reid take care of her again.

So what? This was different. This was life-threatening. She dug into her purse for her key fob and unlocked the door.

Reid opened the door, flooding the interior with light. She leaned in to get her tote bag. Reid grabbed her arm and jerked her out of the car.

"What..." She couldn't finish her statement. Not when ticking from under the hood broke through her brain fog.

"A bomb!" he said. "Run!"

He charged away from the car and dragged her after him. He ran at top speed. She tried to keep up, but her legs were shorter, and she stumbled. He jerked her upright and lifted her into his arms.

They reached a grassy island in the parking lot, and he dove for the ground, turning and cocooning her in his arms to take the brunt of the fall and protect her. He rolled and covered her body with his. Her muscles stiffened, and she waited.

A loud explosion pierced the air. She sent a shrieking scream into the darkness of the night.

Please. Please don't let us die.

8

Reid covered Megan, his muscles tightening in wait for the debris to rain down on them. He took a deep breath—or tried to. His lungs refused to respond. His heart beat a rapid rhythm.

Nothing fell. Silence reigned save Bandit's frantic barking from Reid's SUV.

What was going on? Fragments should've pelted them by now. Sharp. Pummeling.

Time passed. Seconds really. Ticking slowly by like hours.

He lifted his head. Searched for fallout from the bomb. Nothing. Not even the tiniest scrap of metal. Safe to move? Likely.

He rolled off Megan, drew his gun, and came to a crouch. Weapon extended, he pivoted in a circle to perform a threat assessment. No one bearing down on them. No one in sight at all. He focused on Megan's car. White smoke poured from under the hood, but the car remained intact.

A fake bomb or one that failed to detonate? Was it just another attempt to scare Megan?

He kept his focus on the area by her car. "You okay?"

"Yes."

He gave her a quick once-over. She did appear to be okay. Trembling, with Boo-Boo lying on the grass next to her, but okay.

His tension released in a rush. The urge to drag her into his arms and celebrate followed. But he couldn't. Fake bomb or not, he had to keep vigilant. Fowler could've set a trap. Reid couldn't risk them walking across the lot to the entrance or even to his vehicle. And they couldn't stay in the median, out in the open. They had to take cover. Not only in the event it was a trap but in case the bomb wasn't a fake and had failed to properly detonate.

"We need to move behind these vehicles for safety." He pointed at cars parked near the median. "Stay low and move fast."

She didn't question him, but grabbed Boo-Boo—ever the mother, thinking of her child and keeping track of the bear even in such a scary situation—she scooted into position between the cars.

He joined her, keeping watch until he sank down next to her. "The bomb could be a decoy to lure us out into the open. Or it might not have properly detonated. Won't know until we get a bomb squad out here. We'll hunker down until patrol cars arrive and it's safer to move. You have your phone?"

She nodded but her teeth were chattering.

"Call 911 to report the bomb, and I'll update Russ." Keeping his gun in one hand, Reid dug out his phone with the other and made the call.

As the phone rang, Bandit's barking sounded louder from Reid's SUV. Too bad he couldn't calm the little fella, but Bandit would have to stay put and alone until everything got sorted out.

"You on your way?" Russ asked.

"We have an incident." Reid relayed the details as he heard Megan's breathless recounting of the event for the 911 dispatcher.

"I'm guessing it's a warning from Fowler," Reid said into his phone. "By coming to the hospital today, he's shown he's willing to take risks, so be prepared."

"Got it," Russ answered.

Good. He was now on high alert and both girls would be safe in his care.

"We're waiting for the local PD to arrive, and then we'll be up." Reid disconnected.

Megan was staring at him, her body tense, her fingers clutching her phone with a death grip. "The operator said there's a patrol car down the road. You think Fowler's here? Right now? Those beady eyes on us?"

Reid didn't know if her angst was from the fake bomb or the continued threat, but either way he didn't want to scare her more. "He's likely long gone, but we'll still sit tight until the police arrive."

As if the locals heard his comment, sirens sounded in the distance. An engine hummed nearby, and Reid glanced around the cars. A vehicle swung into their aisle. Tires rolled over pavement, coming closer. Reid pivoted. Megan rose up.

"Stay down." He kept his eyes on the vehicle, but in his peripheral vision he saw her comply.

A large black pickup came out of the mist and whipped into a parking space. Could be Micha's truck, but there were millions of black pickups out there and could be anyone. The driver's door opened. A man jumped out and withdrew his gun from a belt holster.

Reid assumed a firing position and waited for the man to face them. He spun.

Micha. Reid let out a breath and lowered his weapon. He

wanted to call out to Micha, but that would identify Micha as their associate. If Fowler was watching, it would make Micha a potential target. No way Reid would do that to a teammate. He waited for Micha to spot them and hoped they wouldn't startle him into firing his weapon.

Micha cautiously moved forward, gun extended. Sirens wound closer. If Fowler was hanging out to enjoy the trauma he caused, with the police on-site, he wouldn't be dumb enough to try anything else, would he?

Micha slipped between cars. His gaze locked with Reid's. Recognition dawned. He hurried forward, his head on a swivel as he moved. "You two okay?"

"Fine. Bomb's likely a fake." Reid explained the situation.

Micha faced Megan. "Sounds like Fowler's trying to mess with your head."

She nodded. "What'd you discover on your visit to my parents' house?"

"Sorry, Megan." Micha squatted next to her. "Someone broke in. Jimmied the back door lock. No major damage, but they stripped the key holder clean."

Reid figured as much, but if Fowler used the other keys to harm someone else, they could have an even bigger problem. He looked at Megan. "Any idea what the other keys they stored there are for?"

"Their car keys and mine." Megan paused and raised her eyes as if thinking. "And they have a beach house in Seaside. That key would be there too."

"Anyone staying at the beach house?" Reid asked. "Renting it, maybe?"

Megan shook her head. "It's only used for family."

"No brothers or sisters staying there?" Micha asked.

"She's an only child," Reid answered for her.

Megan gave him an incredulous stare. Right. She didn't

think he would remember details about her family, but just because he bailed on her didn't mean he didn't remember everything.

He did.

"So no one in immediate danger, then," Micha said, having to talk louder over the approaching siren. "But we'll need to get your parents' house secured."

Reid nodded. "Once we're safely inside, I'll call the guy who changed Megan's locks and have him change everything that needs to be changed." He shifted to a more comfortable position.

A police cruiser careened into the lot. Micha holstered his weapon. Reid stowed his gun too. They were both licensed to carry, but the patrol officers who arrived on scene didn't know that. The officers would draw their own weapons and force them to the ground. The last thing they needed was to be treated as criminals while the police sorted this out.

Reid stood and waved the officers toward him. Siren blaring and lights strobing into the fog, the vehicle screeched to a stop nearby. The headlights cut through the fog and glared at them.

"I'll update the officer." Squinting against the light, Micha wound his way through the cars to the patrol vehicle.

Ignoring Megan's earlier warning not to touch her, Reid held out his hand to help her up. She clutched Boo-Boo to her chest and clasped his hand with chilled fingers. She stood and nearly collapsed, then hopped on one foot.

"What's wrong?" Reid asked.

"My ankle." She limped a few more steps as if testing it but ended by holding her foot in the air. "I think I twisted it."

Reid slipped his arm around her back and put his hand under her elbow for support.

She set her foot down and winced. "It's better."

Why hadn't he done a better job of protecting her? Sure it was only a sore ankle but it could've been so much worse. "We need to get you to a chair."

"I'm fine." She squirmed free from his hold and took a few steps, grimacing with each one.

"You're not fine." He gritted his teeth. "And you don't have to pretend you are so I won't touch you."

She tilted her head. "What?"

"You made it clear in the car that you don't want me touching you." His tone bordered on anger. Surprising. Her earlier comment had hurt more than he thought.

"That's not what this is about. I really can walk. It may hurt, but I'm fine."

Was she really? Her expression was sincere, so he moved away.

"What about Bandit?" Megan asked. "I can hear him barking."

"I'll come back for him once I have you safely inside."

A burly police officer approached them, with Micha following close behind. "Everyone okay here?"

Reid nodded and provided a firsthand account of the incident and the prior ones, as well. "Officer York responded to the hospital incident, and Detective Wilson handled the break-in at Ms. Cash's house."

"And you are?" the officer asked.

"A friend." Reid hoped Megan wouldn't correct him.

The officer gave a sharp nod. "I need you to evacuate the area until the bomb squad gives the all clear."

"We'll escort Ms. Cash inside. Her daughter's in room 238." Reid looked at Micha. "You lead."

Reid motioned for Megan to follow. Keeping his hand poised to retrieve his weapon, Reid trailed the hobbling

Megan and checked the surroundings for anything out of the ordinary.

Without the bomb squad having cleared Megan's car, they gave it a wide berth and arrived at the hospital from the south side. A Peace On Earth sign above the entrance caught his attention. How ironic. Especially with armed security guards standing outside the doors.

Reid was thankful they'd been trained not to approach a vehicle where an explosion had sounded and not put their lives in danger or contaminate the crime scene. He explained the situation to the guards, and they'd been apprised of the earlier incident with Fowler, so even if they'd locked down the exits to this wing of the hospital, they let them pass without a hassle.

Inside, Micha stopped next to the bank of elevators. "I'll coordinate with the locals and meet you upstairs when I'm finished."

Reid clapped his friend's shoulder in thanks.

Micha gave a firm nod as the elevator doors swished open. Reid waited for Megan to limp into the empty car before boarding.

As the doors were sliding closed, Reid locked gazes with Micha. The unease in the tough guy's demeanor left Reid unsettled.

He swallowed it down. He wouldn't let Megan see how much this situation had unnerved him. He put a pleasant tone in his voice. "How's the ankle?"

"It's fine." She let out a shuddering breath. "Thank you, Reid. You've been nothing but helpful, and I've been a real grouch."

"Yeah, you have." He smiled, hoping to lighten the tension. "But you're worried about Ella and your own safety, so I understand." He suspected it was more than her worry for their safety, but now was not the time to get into their past. In fact, until he had a plan for keeping her safe, it was best to make the trip to the room without talking.

He leaned back and listened to the music. *Oh Holy Night* played on the speaker above. Christmas. A few days until his family gathered around the tree. Would this issue be resolved before the big day? He still had shopping to do. As much as he'd joked with Jessie earlier about the presents, he would do everything within his abilities not to disappoint his daughter. He might need to arrange for Russ's wife, Sydney, to help him out while he made sure Megan and Ella lived to see the holidays.

That thought removed all thoughts of a joyful holiday, and he remained alert and ready for danger again.

The elevator dinged, and the doors slid open.

"Stay here until I signal." He fixed his hand on his holster and stepped out to check the area. Confident it was safe, he waved Megan on.

She walked close to his side without him needing to ask, something he appreciated. This allowed him to do his job. At each turn in the hallway, he stepped ahead, and she fully cooperated, limping toward him only when he gave her the signal.

On the final turn, Reid spotted Russ outside Ella's door. He wore his usual scowl, and his hand rested securely on his holster. He waited, eyes watchful and alert, his posture rigid and a wide stance warning anyone who came near to be wary.

But Megan walked right up to him and squeezed his arm. "Thank you for staying so long. I know you wanted to get going sooner."

He actually blushed under her kindness. "Jess kept Ella entertained, so it wasn't too much of a hardship."

"Well, thanks anyway." With a quick glance at Reid,

Megan slipped into the room to the ecstatic voice of Ella crying Boo-Boo's name.

He waited for the door to close and turned to his brother. "Everything still okay here?"

"No issues. Unless you consider a nosy nurse a problem."

Reid laughed and shook his head over his brother's take on life.

"What?" Russ asked.

"I'm just glad to have a brother like you."

"Seriously, we have a lunatic on the loose, and you're gonna get all mushy like a little girl," he said gruffly.

"Point taken," Reid said for his brother's benefit. Russ would do just about anything not to show his feelings. Except when it came to Sydney. Then he was a big old teddy bear.

"So what's the latest?" Russ asked.

"I think the local PD will take things more seriously now. But even after this bomb, I'm not sure they have the resources to provide a protection detail for Megan. I'd like to spend the night here to keep an eye on her and Ella. Would it be okay if Jess and Bandit stayed with you and Sydney tonight?"

"Syd will be ecstatic to spend time with them. Especially since we're now all settled in the cabin. She and Nikki can start a fire and the three of them can make s'mores." Russ made it sound as if his wife was the only one who wanted them, but it was more of his tough-guy front. "Want to run your plan by me before I go?"

"I don't have one yet. Micha's talking to the locals, and we'll hash it out when he gets here."

"Let me know if you need any more help other than trying to get Gleason to try for a warrant for that gas station attendant's name, which I have to say he's balking at, but maybe this incident will change his mind."

"Yeah, maybe," Reid said, not holding out hope that even if he got the warrant that he would share the information.

"But like I said. Let me know what else I can do. Wouldn't mind participating in something more challenging than my usual daily paperwork."

"I don't think Sydney would appreciate you getting involved in this." Russ's wife was a police officer in Shadow Lake and would know Russ would face risks on such an assignment.

"She wouldn't like it, but she would understand." A smitten look flashed across his face as it always did when he talked about her.

"In that case, we could talk about forensics," Reid said. "I don't have a lot of confidence in the local forensics staff, and this has escalated significantly. With a bomb, even a fake one, we should try to get the state techs on site."

"Agreed. Even a decoy bomb could tell us a lot about the person who built it."

"Since you know the chief, could you persuade him to call in State?"

Russ gnawed on his cheek for a moment. "Better yet, I'll ask him to call in the Veritas Center bomb expert. Gleason won't have a budget for that, but since we know the Veritas partners, we should be able to get this done pro bono. I doubt he'll say no to that."

"Sounds good. Make the arrangements."

"Will do." He arched a brow. "You should know, though, if the Veritas contract is with Gleason's agency, they won't be able to share what they find with us. But I should be able to get the chief to disclose the information."

"Thanks, man." He gave his brother's arm a light punch. "Bandit's in my car, but I'll go tell Jess about our arrangements so once the bomb squad gives the all clear you can be on your way."

In Ella's room, Megan was seated in a chair by the window. She came to the edge of her chair, but he raised a hand to keep her from standing. Thankfully, the room was located on the opposite side of the parking lot where the bomb squad was likely swarming Megan's car, and neither Ella nor Jessie were aware of the situation.

He went to Jessie, who sat on the bed with Ella, a snow-man-shaped tic-tac-toe game on a table between them.

Jessie made eye contact, and Reid told her about the change in plans. Her wide smile confirmed staying at her uncle's cabin for the night was a special treat. "Go ahead and keep playing but be ready to go when Uncle Russ is ready."

"I know. I know. He doesn't like to wait for anyone." She wrinkled her freckled nose.

She knew her uncle well.

Reid's phone rang. Seeing Colin's name, he excused himself and stepped into the hallway. Russ locked gazes with Reid, but he held up his phone and answered the call.

"Fowler's registered here, but he's not in." Colin's no-nonsense tone came across loud and clear. "You want me to search his room."

Reid did. How he did, but he didn't want his friend and teammate to get caught breaking the law. At least not yet. "We'll see on that. Maybe later."

"Want me to keep an eye on the room in case he shows up?"

Reid didn't answer right away. He was taking advantage of Colin's time off, but Megan and Ella needed the entire team, so he would ask for as much as they would give. He updated Colin on the bomb situation. "I'd appreciate that if you're willing to give up more of your vacation."

88

"You need me, I'm here." Unquestionable support. That was the hallmark of all of the team members.

Reid was blessed beyond words to have such fine men working for him, and he would never forget Colin's sacrifice. "Thanks, man. Keep me updated, and if this goes on for long, I'll get Ryan to spell you."

"Nah, don't call him in. He's got the new baby and all. I'll be fine."

"I'm sure Ryan will appreciate a few hours away from diaper duty." Reid laughed as he remembered the first exhausting weeks of Jessie's life.

"Yeah, okay. Maybe for a few hours. I'll let you know if I need it."

Reid thanked him again and ended the call to share the conversation with Russ. "Our first official proof Fowler's in town."

"Not really official," Russ said. "Just hearsay of a desk clerk Colin charmed, which isn't going to change anything. We need to see the official records. Need a warrant for that, and I doubt the chief will request one based on what we have so far."

"Not that it will do any good either," Reid said. "So Fowler's in town. We still don't have concrete proof that he's stalking Megan, and the locals won't act on it until we do."

"Forensics from the bomb could provide that," Russ said. "I'll approach Gleason, and we can go from there."

Reid nodded as Micha rounded the corner. "Bomb squad's given the all clear. Detective Wilson is here, and he wants to talk to us."

"Not me," Russ said. "I'll grab Jess and get going home."

"Hang out here, and I'll say good night to her first." Reid reentered the room and held his arms out to Jessie for a hug. "Uncle Russ is ready to go, so I'll see you tomorrow."

She rushed into his arms, then suddenly backed away. "Why do you have your gun?"

Reid knelt down at her eye level and pulled her close to keep Ella from overhearing. "I'm sorry, Jess. I know I promised not to carry one, but a man threatened Megan and Ella. I want to be sure that nothing happens to them, and this is just a precaution."

Her chin wobbled. "Will you be okay?"

"Sure. Everyone will be fine." Feeling like a heel for potentially misleading his daughter, he pulled her into his arms and peered over her shoulder at Megan.

Thankfully, Jessie couldn't see the fear still lodged firmly in Megan's gorgeous eyes, or she wouldn't believe him. The last thing he wanted to do was scare Jessie, but Megan and Ella needed him, and he wasn't going anywhere until he was sure they were safe from Fowler's revenge.

9

_____

After making sure Ella was soundly asleep with Boo-Boo in her arms, Megan joined Reid, who was with Micha and Detective Wilson in the hallway. She tried to pay attention to the conversation. Tried hard. But she couldn't concentrate when her mind kept racing over the explosion.

Each detail played in her head as vividly as if she were still hearing the explosion. The feel of Reid's strong arms lifting her like a doll and holding her close, taking her breath. Them falling and his solid body covering her, protecting her, and risking his life for her. His heart had beat wildly, the thumping against her back—as reassuring as it was terrifying—told her the event scared even a strong man like Reid.

What would've happened if the bomb had been real? She wouldn't be standing here, that was for sure. She could be dead or severely injured.

If the bomb was meant to take her out, even Reid, the tall tower of strength gazing down on her with a flicker of concern in his expression, couldn't have protected her from the deadly force.

Fear clutched her heart, and she shuddered.

Stop thinking about this. Stop now. It's doing no good.

"Like I said." Wilson leaned forward, pausing until she focused on him. "This guy knew what he was doing. Whoever placed it in the car understood how to trigger the device and create the noise and cause little damage."

"Whoever? You mean Fowler?"

"Sorry, ma'am," Wilson said. "But we have no concrete proof Fowler is behind this incident. Good news is that hospital security is back online and the video captured a potential suspect near your car about an hour before the device exploded. If you're willing to leave your daughter for a few minutes, I'd like you to come down to the security office to look at it."

Micha tipped his head at the door. "I'll stay with Ella, and Reid can accompany you."

Megan offered a smile of thanks to Reid's team member, who was proving to be very helpful and considerate. She faced Wilson. "Let's do this, then."

He came to attention. "The security office is in the basement. Follow me."

She started forward, putting as little pressure on her sore ankle as possible, making the going slow.

Reid eased up beside her, his jacket pushed back, hand on his gun. "Stay close and do as I say when I say. Okay?"

She nodded, swallowing down the unease his tone caused and taking some comfort in his nearness.

At the hallway intersection, Wilson turned left, walking at a quick clip, and Reid held his hand out to stop her. He stepped into the corridor and searched the area. After a few moments, he waved her on, and they made the rest of the trip to the security office in the same fashion. By the time they arrived, Wilson stood over a seated security guard who'd loaded the video on his computer.

Wilson pointed at the chair next to the guard. "By the

way, Ms. Cash, we did confirm your alibi for the night of the supposed break-in at your home. A nurse named Nora said she saw you during that time."

Megan wanted to shout *I told you so*, but simply nodded and took a seat. The moment she took the weight off her twisted ankle, sharp pain stabbed her leg. She gripped the armrests of the chair and tried to ignore the throbbing.

Reid moved to her side but focused on the screen. The video started with a partial view of the rear of her vehicle. Soon a man, wearing a Rainiers baseball cap and shouldering a black bag, came into view. He stopped, his eyes raising and he offered a taunting grin through a thick salt-and-pepper beard.

Megan gasped and drew back. Reid moved forward and rested a hand over hers. She thought to withdraw, but why? His touch made seeing this man easier.

"It's not clear enough," she whispered searching the face shadowed by the cap and the overhead light. "I'm not sure it's Fowler."

"Can you pause the feed?" Reid asked the guard, and he stopped it. "Zoom in closer."

Expecting the menacing expression to raise the memories of the bank robbery, she held her breath. The face grew larger. She desperately wanted to identify Fowler. To say this man was the same guy who had terrorized her. The same guy from the gas station. From the hallway, but she couldn't. The picture quality disintegrated as it got larger and the shadowed areas darkened, revealing nothing to help her confirm his identity. She couldn't be sure. Not at all.

"Is that Fowler?" Wilson asked from behind.

"Could be." Memories of the bank robbery returned— Fowler standing over her while he spewed terrifying threats. She breathed deeply and studied the video again.

"I can't be sure." She *was* sure the fear radiating through her own voice scared her.

Reid squeezed her hand. "Let's review the rest of the tape. Maybe we'll catch something else that'll help."

Wilson narrowed his eyes, but the video started again. Fowler moved offscreen.

"Nothing happens for nearly an hour," Wilson said. "Go ahead and fast-forward it to the next timestamp we set."

The security guard advanced the video and started it playing again.

Minutes dragged by with nothing on the screen but a static picture of the rear of her car. With the hood where the bomb had been planted not visible, she didn't know how this recording was going to help. Finally, the suspect appeared in camera range again and disappeared from view.

"He's aware of the camera location, and he's using it to make sure we know he was here." Reid crouched next to her, staring at the screen. She couldn't read his expression, but his voice was hard and angry and served to tighten the knot in her stomach.

"Exactly," Wilson said. "He's playing with you."

"Be that as it may." She spun her chair to face Wilson. "I can't positively ID him as Norman Fowler."

Wilson frowned. "Would be good if you could, but it's not like this video implicates him in the incident."

"What?" she asked. "What do you mean?"

Reid stood. "He was here, but the video doesn't actually show him plant the bomb."

Wilson eyed Reid. "But positive ID added to other evidence we discover could help us make a case against him. And if we had that, I could likely get a protection detail for you."

She wanted to sigh but controlled herself. "I won't lie

and say it's him when I don't know for sure. So what happens now?"

Wilson lifted his chin. "We're still talking to potential witnesses. If their statements give us a lead or additional evidence is recovered, we'll pursue it."

So nothing really. Not yet anyway. "But otherwise you're done, and Ella and I are on our own?"

"Sorry, Ms. Cash." Wilson took a step back. "As soon as I have concrete proof that Fowler is behind the incidents threatening you, I'll apply for a warrant to compel the Creek Water Motel to open their records to us, and then we can check out his room. I have applied for a protective detail, but we've yet to have any credible proof that Fowler is stalking you with the intent of harming you."

Reid drew in a sharp breath but didn't speak.

"But the bomb," she said.

"Wasn't designed to harm you, " Wilson said quickly. "Or to create physical damage, and we have no evidence that you're in grave danger. Nor do we have any physical proof Fowler was connected to it. With staffing shortages, it's possible my request won't be approved."

"Unbelievable." She shook her head. "You hear horror stories in the news about stalkers killing their victims even after the police have been informed, but I never imagined I'd be one of those people."

Nearing nine p.m. outside Ella's room, Reid's phone rang, and he grabbed it before the ringing woke Ella.

"Russ," he answered as Megan changed her attention to him through the crack in the doorway. "I hope you have good news for me."

"I do. Chief Gleason is on board with Veritas, and they

agreed to help. They're sending their bomb expert, Trent Ingram. He'll be here by eight a.m., and Gleason has officers protecting the scene until then."

"That *is* good news." Reid let out a relieved breath.

"Even better, they're also sending additional staff, including their new eDNA expert, Dr. Andi Clarke. She's pioneering a study on pulling DNA from the air, and we might be able to get Fowler's DNA from Megan's car that way."

"Say what?" Reid blinked a few times. "DNA from the air?"

"Yeah, sounds unbelievable, right? A Sci-fi kind of thing, but I guess it's possible to collect human DNA from the air, sequence it, and match it to a specific person."

"Never heard of such a thing."

"eDNA or environmental DNA, falls under a new area of DNA study as far as criminal forensics go. If Fowler was in the vehicle for any amount of time, they believe they can recover his DNA."

"That's great. Should put a smile on Megan's face."

"So will the fact that I got Gleason to authorize Veritas to share their findings with us."

Interesting. Shocking, really. "What did you have to do to make that happen?"

"I'll be providing a few training workshops for his team." Russ's sullen tone said what he thought about having to make such a sacrifice.

"Sorry about that, but thanks."

"Oh, you'll owe me, bro. Big time." Russ chuckled.

"But they're still not willing to put a protective detail on Megan."

"Willing, yes," Russ said. "No staff. Which I can understand. Besides he knows you and our team are taking watch."

"I wish I didn't understand," Reid said. "But I do."

"If we can only get some actual evidence that Fowler is behind the bombing, I know Gleason will reconsider. That DNA from thin air might do the trick."

Reid's phone signaled a call from Devan. "Got a call coming in. Catch you later." He accepted the call.

The background was filled with loud voices and a television. "I'm texting you a PJ's bartender's name."

"You found the location Fowler met his friend?" Reid's hope climbed higher.

"You ask. I deliver." Devan chuckled. "Had to go to all five locations before I learned where they'd met, but I did. They're gone now, but I'll text the location address too."

"I'll try to get Russ over there."

"Glad to wait here for him if you want me to. In case the dude comes back."

Reid appreciated his team member always thinking ahead. "Thanks, man. Hang tight, and I'll text Russ's arrival time."

Reid ended the call and tapped his brother's name.

"I've never felt so wanted." Russ laughed.

Reid told him about the bartender.

"I assume you're going to the bar. You can go alone, or I'll go with you if you want. You know. Put the fear of the law in her."

Reid couldn't believe his luck. He didn't even have to ask Russ to go to the bar. "Sounds good."

"One thing," Russ said. "I'm driving, and that's not up for discussion. No pulling the older brother card."

"Wouldn't think of arguing."

"Hah!" Russ ended the call.

Reid texted Devan to let him know of their impending visit, stowed his phone, and turned to Megan. Her pinched lips revealed frustration, maybe ongoing fear, and he was glad to finally have some good news to share.

He joined her, careful to be quiet and not wake Ella. "Devan found the PJ's location where Fowler met his friend. I'll head over there now with Russ while Micha stands watch outside your door. I'll come back after we talk to the bartender."

Megan gave a sharp nod but didn't seem happy with the news.

Reid had no idea why but left it alone. "Russ also got the Veritas team to agree to handle your car and bomb forensics. They are one of the best forensics teams in the country and have experts in all areas. And they're on the cutting edge with procedures that law enforcement labs have yet to employ."

"That's great." She offered a weak smile. "I'll have to thank Russ when I see him next."

He wanted more than the halfhearted smile so he shared about recovering DNA from the air.

"You weren't kidding that this is good news." She smiled in earnest.

He nodded and now prayed that this DNA in the air wasn't some nonsense and that the Veritas team wouldn't let him down but retrieve the evidence to prove Fowler was behind the bombing.

10

___

Reid observed PJ's parking lot as Russ pulled in. The long building had twinkling, colorful Christmas lights strung around a large picture window. The lights brightened the parking lot but competed with the big sports sign comprised of sports balls and equipment surrounding the bar's name.

"Lot's nearly full for a weeknight." Russ scanned for a parking space.

"Could be people off for the holiday or the Trailblazers have a game tonight."

Win or lose the Portland basketball team always drew a big crowd.

Russ found a space, and they headed for the building in the crisp night air. Russ had driven his pickup and wore tactical pants and a jacket since he wasn't on official business. Who knows, he might've dressed this way anyway as there was no such thing as entering a bar incognito while dressed in uniform. Reid spotted Devan's pickup near the door, but he wasn't inside the vehicle.

Reid pushed open the door. The smell of stale beer and long ago cigarette smoke still living in the walls hit him. He quickly spotted several surveillance cameras, and his hope for obtaining footage of Fowler's meeting with his friend rose.

They headed for the long wood bar crowded with patrons watching the Blazers game on big televisions behind the bar. They located a few seats open, likely because they didn't have a good view of the TVs. He caught sight of Devan at the other end and nodded at him.

He joined them at the open stools and gave an almost imperceptible nod at the female behind the bar. "That's the bartender who recognized Fowler's picture. Her name's Oakley."

The tall, lanky young woman with black hair in a pony-tail took long strides their way. She wore a green and gold Oregon Ducks college basketball jersey over a green long-sleeved T-shirt. The bright team colors stood out in the dark atmosphere. Reid pegged her for an athlete. Maybe she played basketball for the Ducks.

She smiled at them, but she shifted to take Devan in, and her eyes narrowed. "What can I get you guys?"

"Information." Russ held out his credentials, staring at her, his expression serious. "Sheriff Russ Maddox."

"A sheriff. For real?" She blinked.

"For real." He smiled this time. "Devan here says you were working around eight tonight."

Her smile wavered, and she stared at Devan until he backed up, signaling his intent to remain out of the conversation.

"Yeah, I was here," she said to Russ.

"And you remembered seeing this guy? He was meeting a friend." Russ displayed a picture of Fowler on his phone. She might have ID'd Fowler for Devan, but it was something Russ would do in a formal interview.

She studied the picture. "Yeah. Like I told your guy. He was here."

"Lots of men in here tonight," Reid said. "What about the guy made you remember him?"

"He had that ick creep factor going on, you know? And then of course, he had to hit on me. " She faked a deep shudder. "Why is it always the creeps who think they're all that who hit on you?"

Reid didn't want them to go down a rabbit hole. Especially not one like that. "Did you happen to hear him mention his friend's name or overhear any of their conversation?"

She shook her head, her ponytail swishing like a pendulum. "They were here less than an hour, and every time I came close, they clammed up like they didn't want me to hear what they were talking about."

"So nothing at all then?" Reid asked again, desperate for a lead of any kind.

"Nope, nothing."

"Did they get along with each other?" Russ asked.

She shifted her attention to him. "Mostly. There was one point when the one whose picture you showed me shoved the other guy, but then they seemed to get over it."

"Anything else you can tell us about them?" Reid asked.

"One of them smelled like gasoline."

Russ held up his phone hand. "Not this one, though."

She shook her head. "The other one."

Reid nodded at the nearest camera. "I see you have electronic surveillance. Can we see the footage from that time?"

She rested her hands on the bar. "That's above my pay grade. You'll have to talk to a manager."

"Can you get him or her for us?" Russ asked.

"Him and yes." She strode away, her steps quick and sure to a phone behind the bar to make a call. She listened and frowned, then returned. "He's meeting with someone right now. You can wait to talk to him, but he said there was no point. He said you'll need a warrant for the video. Get him one and you can have it. No warrant. No video."

Reid glanced at Russ, trying to ask nonverbally if it was worth demanding to see the manager.

Russ stood and planted his hands on the bar. "This manager have a name and does he work again tomorrow?"

"Guy Fletcher." She moved back a few paces. "We both come in at six."

"You have a day manager?" Reid asked, hoping he could locate someone who could get the warrant as fast as possible.

She nodded. "Patrick—Pat—Vogel."

"Tell them both we'll return with a warrant, and we expect to talk to one of them even *if* they're busy." Gone was Russ's Mr. Nice Guy routine, and the woman flinched.

Russ laid his card on the bar. "Thanks for your help."

He stormed out of the bar. To prove a point that he wasn't happy with the manager? Maybe, or maybe he was acting. Either way, Reid and Devan had to book it to keep up.

Russ flexed his fingers a few times and peered at Devan. "She tell you anything she didn't tell us?"

"No, but I didn't probe after she told me Fowler had been here. Figured you'd want to do that and didn't want to give her time to fabricate a story if she needed one."

Reid felt like a proud dad over his employee's sound thinking.

"You're right about that." Russ frowned. "I should probably have demanded to see the guy, but what good would it have done? Just make him mad and that won't make him cooperate."

"Trust me, I get it." Reid met his brother's gaze. "Been there too many times in my career not to. You think you can get the warrant for the video?"

"I can talk to Gleason but it's not likely he'll comply. Still no probable cause at this point."

Reid expected as much. "Then the key now is to find someone to request a warrant so we can come back and slap it into that manager's hand."

~

Reid parked in the lot of the rundown Creek Water Motel. He'd made call after call from the hospital and had struck out on getting any warrants. He was tired of not having any leads or cooperation from the officials. Tired of sitting around. Doing nothing. Not moving ahead.

So he was taking things into his own hands for once. Moving forward. He had Micha to keep an eye on Megan and Ella, freeing Reid to act.

He cut the engine and turned his attention to the unsavory-looking property. The poorly lit area held shadows in every corner and space. Places where Fowler could retreat and take a stand if he had a mind to. Still, Colin would've likely made Fowler if he'd shown up.

Reid crossed the lot to where Colin leaned against his truck.

He frowned at Reid.

"I know you don't like this," Reid said. "You can stay in your truck if you want."

Colin shook his head. "You know I'm not a natural rule follower, but this? Illegally entering a suspect's room and potentially contaminating evidence. That makes me pause."

They'd both been trained well on following protocol at the FBI, and Reid understood Colin's hesitancy. "I get it. Trust me. I do. But no one is willing to get a warrant, and I need to move forward to keep Megan safe."

"Can't Russ help with that?"

"I wish he could. He asked Chief Gleason and struck out. The chief said if the forensics from the bomb implicate Fowler, he'll be all over requesting a warrant. For now there's no probable cause. Ditto for the warrant for the gas station records. And before you ask, Jack wasn't any help either."

"Okay, then we go in. I just don't like it." Colin pushed off the truck and held a key out to Reid. "Guess with this at least we won't be breaking and entering. Room seven."

Reid sought out the correct room and kept his eyes on it. "And how did you get this?"

"I went to the front desk after you called to say you were coming. Clerk on duty tonight is young and female and might've been susceptible to my many charms. Maybe too susceptible." Colin laughed.

Reid grinned and shook his head. "Thanks for sacrificing yourself for the team."

Colin nodded. "Let's get it done before she changes her mind and comes looking for the key. Or me."

They crossed the lot, and Reid took in the building with chipping paint, cracked windows, and trash in the parking strip where the grass had given way to weeds. "The kind of neighborhood I'd rather visit in daylight."

"Amen to that, bro." Colin pulled back his camo jacket and rested his hand on the butt of his sidearm as he struck out toward room seven.

Reid followed, and they traveled down the fractured sidewalk stained with things Reid didn't want to guess at. Fowler's room sat near the end of the two-story building. The door held small, vibrant blue patches, but most of the paint had faded to gray with bare splotches of metal showing through.

Reid pounded on the door. "Fowler. We need to talk to you."

Reid stepped to the side of the door as had Colin. A suspect who felt cornered might plug the door full of bullets and it wouldn't be good to be standing in the line of fire.

Not today, though. Fowler didn't fire a single shot. Nor did he answer.

Reid unlocked the door, drew his weapon, and shoved the door in. "Show yourself, Fowler!"

He waited, counting down to ten with his fingers, then nodded his intent to breach before entering. He went straight ahead into the large suite that smelled like dirty socks and stale beer. Empty bottles lay on a scarred coffee table next to a small sofa in a sitting area. Stained sheets and ragged blankets were bunched at one end of a bed, and a lumpy pillow propped on the other end.

Reid motioned at the single door that led from the room and then crossed to it. He shoved it open to reveal a small bathroom with a chipped sink and tub.

"Clear," he called out and holstered his weapon before stepping back out to do a more thorough inspection.

"Looks like he slept here at least one night, and the cleaning crew hasn't come in," Colin said. "Had to be before I had eyes on the place."

Reid nodded. "No sign of a suitcase or bag."

"Maybe he moved on but didn't check out."

"Which makes no sense," Reid said. "Why pay for a room you aren't occupying?"

"Maybe the room was meant to distract us while he stayed elsewhere."

"Could be."

"Nothing much here to search."

"I expected to find surveillance pictures of Megan or some indication that he's been watching her."

"Times change and you've been gone from the job too long. Most times now the suspects keep the pictures on their phones so they can access them wherever they are." Colin had only been out of the agent game for about a year, and his disgusted tone said what he thought about the creeps he'd investigated. "As a bonus for them, if they have to bail, they don't leave evidence behind."

Reid hated to hear that. "Maybe I shouldn't be so sad over leaving the Bureau."

"Sad?" Colin eyed him. "You want back in?"

"Somedays, yeah," Reid admitted. "When the survivalists I'm training are out in left field. Or I have to juggle training schedules for all of you guys because the weather's not cooperating. Yeah, I do. But I know I'm where I'm supposed to be for now."

"Well, if you want back in, don't wait too long or you'll age out."

Reid was fully aware of the FBI's age rules for new agents and also the age at which all agents had to retire. Reid was in no danger of exceeding the retirement age of fifty-seven, but the new agent max age of thirty-seven could pose a problem in a few years. But then, would he really be considered a new agent? He didn't know and hadn't asked as there was no point in it. At least not yet.

For now, Reid would return the focus to their job at hand. "Maybe we can find materials that will implicate Fowler in the smoke bomb."

Colin raised an eyebrow at the subject change but handed a pair of disposable gloves to Reid and slipped his hands into another. "I'll check out the kitchenette."

Reid put on the gloves and went to a trash can that he dumped onto the bed to paw through. A few take-out receipts and one for a PJ's Bar location on the other side of town. Reid picked it up. "Cash receipt for PJ's for the time of their visit. Not that it helps us find his friend."

"Agreed." Colin opened a cabinet in the kitchenette.

Reid jerked out a table drawer and dumped it onto the sofa. Basic motel items tumbled out. TV remote, notepad, pen, and a Bible. Nothing to implicate Fowler in any crime. Frustrated, Reid tossed the drawer onto the cushion. It landed bottom side up, revealing a key taped to the underside.

"No sign of bomb-making supplies in here," Colin called out.

"I've got something interesting." Reid ripped the key free and held it up for Colin. "Was taped to the bottom of the drawer. Probably for a padlock. Maybe we're not finding anything because he's keeping things hidden in a storage unit."

Colin joined Reid. "Like those bomb-making supplies."

"Exactly." Reid's heart rate tripped higher as he stared at the key. "Now all we need to do is figure out if we're right and locate the storage facility."

11

_____

Reid held his phone to his ear the next morning, waiting for Russ to answer, and he glanced out the hospital lounge window at the light dusting of snow drifting from above. He only hoped it didn't pick up and make Fowler hunker down wherever he was and not return for that key.

Reid was certain Fowler would return for the key at some point, and he wanted someone in place for when that happened, so he'd left Colin behind. But Reid wasn't going to sit around and wait. Hence his call to Russ.

"Yo, bro," Russ said. "You do know I still have a real job to do, don't you?"

"I wouldn't bother you if it wasn't important."

"Then make it quick."

"We searched Fowler's motel room last night. Was mostly a bust but we found a hidden key. Looks like it's for a padlock. We didn't find anything in the room, so I figure it's for a storage unit he's renting."

"And let me guess. You want me to get Gleason on a warrant for these places to find the location of Fowler's unit."

"Actually, no. We didn't exactly come by the key during a legal search, so we can't tell Gleason about it."

Russ blew a long breath into the phone. Reid really shouldn't be admitting to illegally searching the room to a sheriff who should act on the information. He only hoped right now that the brother card trumped the sheriff's duty.

"Did you take the key?" Russ asked, not sounding pleased.

"No. I left it there so when Gleason gets a warrant for the room, he should find it."

"Unless Fowler comes back to claim it."

"I actually hope he does. Colin is still staking the place out."

"Okay, so what do you want me to do?"

"Call or visit local storage companies. See if you can charm the info out of them."

Russ snorted. "Charm is not my strong suit."

"But you do know how to get information when needed."

"Yeah, that I do." He chuckled.

"So can you do it?"

"I can."

"Thanks, man. You can start with units near the motel." A text sounded on Reid's phone. "Gotta go. Let me know what you find."

Reid ended the call and read the text from Trent Ingram.

Finished preliminary analysis of the bomb. Ready to share details with you.

Be right down, Reid replied. He left Sydney guarding Megan and Ella to rush down the stairs to the parking lot. This was it. The meeting he'd been waiting for this morning. He would get the proof everyone needed for their warrants, and they would finally be on their way to locating Fowler.

He stepped through the snow showers toward Megan's car, surrounded by crime scene tape. A uniformed officer stood guard nearby, his eyes hooded as sleep was beckoning him. At least he didn't have his phone out and seemed aware of his surroundings as he noted Reid advancing on him. Frost covered the grass, and Reid shivered under the cold, but this guy didn't seem fazed by it.

He did stand in Reid's way, though.

A dark-haired guy with a close-cut beard came out from under the hood, his gaze wary in the sun breaking through the snow showers. Had to be Trent. "He's clear. Let him pass."

Reid approached the car. The hood was raised and a woman in protective gear sat inside. She was using a pump to extract air into a tube. Likely Dr. Clarke. Maybe collecting that DNA from the air.

The guy stepped out from under the raised hood. He gave a sharp nod and held his hand up. "Trent Ingram. Gloved up and would rather not change to shake."

"Reid Maddox," Reid said. "I appreciate you coming so quickly and doing the work pro bono."

"No worries." He pointed under the hood. "Brought a few teammates with me. Landon Oliver."

A guy about the same age as Trent stepped out, but where Trent was dark-complected, Landon was blond and fair. Both were fit and looked bright-eyed for having driven hours to get here this morning.

"Landon just started with us last week," Trent said. "His specialties are vehicle forensics and firearms audio forensics."

Say what?

"Firearms audio?" Reid shook his head. "What in the world is that?"

Landon laughed. "I get the same reaction all the time

and am happy to explain. It's no secret our world is filled with electronics. Means recordings are presented as evidence in many criminal investigations. The recordings are from devices like smartphones, private surveillance systems, or body-worn cameras. And when a gunshot is recorded, audio analysis of the recordings can provide spatial and temporal information about the location and orientation of shot sources."

"Interesting," Reid said. "But how does that relate to your vehicle forensics specialty?"

"It doesn't other than both use electronics and my education and experience is in digital forensics. Combine that with a love of firearms gets you the experience in firearms audio forensics and my love of cars with vehicle forensics."

"So basically he gets paid to play with guns and cars all day." Trent laughed.

"Could say the same about you except for the car part. You get to play with things that go boom." Landon chuckled.

Reid rolled his eyes and peered at Landon. "Neither of your specialties are an issue here today, right?"

Trent shook his head. "But your suspect could've connected the switch to the car's electronics. Not something we could tell before we got here and assessed the device. Besides which, Landon is shadowing each of the partners for two weeks to experience what we do."

"And I take it this is your two weeks," Reid said.

"It is indeed."

Landon stepped under the hood again, and movement in the car caught Reid's attention.

"That's Dr. Clarke—Andi—in the car," Trent said. "She's been in there for some time so hopefully she's almost finished with her samples and will be able to update you too." He gestured at the vehicle's engine. "I only hope we can help you figure out who placed this device."

"The who really isn't in question here," Reid said. "Where he is right now is the big question, and we hope something you find will lead us to him."

"From everything you've told me about the investigation, I can see how you would reach that conclusion," Trent said. "You're likely right, but it would be doing this investigation a disservice if we make that assumption. We might be looking at someone else out to scare Ms. Cash."

"True, but the odds point to Fowler."

"They do, but my job isn't to play the odds. My job is to find forensics to give me direction and not make any assumptions."

Reid knew Trent's logical conclusion was right, and Reid shouldn't be assuming Fowler left the bomb, but... "So what have you found? Anything unique?"

He nodded vigorously. "I think so, anyway. Not the devices, though. Not even a bomb."

"Wait what? Not a bomb?" Shocked, Reid stared at the guy. "But I heard the explosion."

"I didn't say there wasn't a noise, but we've got smoke grenades and flash-bangs modified to release through a control panel linked to a pressure switch under the driver's seat. All items are legal and you can purchase them most anywhere in the country."

"Yeah, I know what they are. Used them in tactical training in the FBI." Reid mulled it over, disappointed in himself for misreading the situation. "The noise sounded a lot louder than a flash-bang."

"Try multiple flash-bangs timed to go off at the same time."

"I don't know. Still sounded like more than that." Or Reid wanted it to be more so he didn't feel so dumb for overreacting. Still, if it happened again, he would act the same to protect Megan. Better safe than sorry.

Landon looked up. "Your report said you noted the pressure switch in the car, and you bolted, preparing for a bomb. So that was what you expected to hear. Could make you mishear things."

Yeah, that could've happened. Either way, Reid wouldn't dwell on it. "Okay, say our guy bought these items legally, but it would take more than basic skills to make the switch work, right?"

"Yes, and time. Installing the pressure switch under the seat would take a bit of time to accomplish. Enough time to catch the offender on security video if cameras cover this location."

"I reviewed the feed already," Reid said. "They don't reach as far as the front end of this vehicle. So where do we go from here?"

Trent nodded at the engine. "I'll analyze the components and try to identify the manufacturers and suppliers. When I finish, I'll get the evidence to our fingerprint and DNA experts to process."

"And if we don't get a match?" Reid asked.

"We don't know that Fowler is good for this, and we could be looking at someone who's done the same thing before. So I'll ask other crime labs if they've processed devices with similar characteristics in the handicraft or materials of the bomb maker."

"Handicraft?" Reid asked.

"The way a device is constructed." Trent pointed under the hood.

Reid stepped around the front of the car to see the remnants of flash-bangs in an open wooden box near the motor. Small portions of the flash-bang body, material like thick cardboard, were left, as were the metal fuse casings and detonators, which remained intact. If they hadn't been contained in the box or under the hood, they could've become a projectile in flight and caused serious injuries.

"In this case our suspect took a page out of the Unabomber's book," Trent said. "He placed the items in a meticulously handcrafted wooden box."

"You're talking about Ted Kaczynski." Reid recalled the many bombings of the man his agency dubbed the Unabomber. "Why would our guy do that?"

Trent shrugged. "He might've researched bombs and thought it would distract us if he put the items in a box. Or maybe he wanted to mitigate any damage that could potentially have been done. For Kaczynski, it was theorized that he used a wooden box so he could sand off all DNA and prints on the shipping container, but obviously our suspect didn't ship this device."

"Curious."

"Agreed." Trent's dark eyes narrowed. "The box is a lot of work to go through when he could've bought something commercially. Of course, the suspect could've bought it from someone, and that's a lead you can pursue. It's definitely handmade, so would likely be a local carpenter."

"Or not. Could've gotten it from Etsy or other websites selling handmade items."

"True that. I'll do a more detailed analysis when I get it back to the lab. I'll also run the specifics of the device against ViCAP. See if we get any hits on similar devices. Will be a long shot as our guy didn't hurt anyone, but he might've in the past."

Reid was well familiar with the FBI's Violent Criminal Apprehension Program, a database used to track information on unsolved violent crimes, especially murder. Law enforcement officers entered information into the system to compare their details to other cases in hopes of matching possible connections.

Trent tipped his head at the device. "If you don't have any other questions, I should get to it. You'll receive a copy of my report, which I hope to complete by end of day. When Andi finishes with the air samples, our forensic tech who came along—she's inside getting coffee right now—will process the vehicle for prints and trace evidence."

"No other questions." Thankfully no one was hurt, but Reid was disappointed that these items weren't intended to cause damage, so the feds wouldn't likely get involved. Meant he was stuck with the locals investigating and the limits placed on them by being small potatoes compared to the feds.

The driver's door opened, and a petite blond woman with a square jaw slipped out. She held several tubes and the air pump Reid had seen earlier. She didn't stop to talk to him but went straight to their company van and wrote on the tubes. After storing them, she stripped off her gloves and breathing apparatus and turned to Reid.

"Dr. Andi Clarke." She held out her hand.

"Reid Maddox." He gripped the petite fingers, hoping she might have something positive to report.

"Emory mentioned you. Said you worked a few cases together in the past, and she was sorry to see you leave the FBI."

He nodded as he and Dr. Emory Jenkins, head of the Veritas Center's DNA department, had indeed worked together. "All good things, I hope."

Andi nodded, a slip of hair escaping the rubber band holding it back. She shoved it behind her ear, and Reid noted that she didn't wear a wedding ring. Didn't mean anything. She might not wear it in the field.

"So were you able to collect DNA?" he asked.

"I'm sure I collected something in my filters." She lifted her shoulders. "As to whether any of it belongs to your suspect, I won't know until we process it and run the results against the database."

"No offense, but DNA from the air sounds pretty much like science fiction. How exactly can you find it?"

She smiled, when he suspected she got tired of hearing his questions. "You're not the first person in law enforcement to say that to me. eDNA can come in various forms of genetic material shed by living organisms. Humans shed pieces of hair, skin, or free-floating, naked DNA. I simply use a pump with a filter to draw air from the space and filter out that genetic material."

"Not something that I've heard of before. But then I've been out of law enforcement for a few years now."

"Forensics is evolving rapidly. Far faster than the courts can keep up with." She scratched her neck. "There really isn't any set precedence for this field yet, so they may or may not accept my findings from today."

"If they don't, the local police will hopefully acknowledge Fowler was indeed here and finally offer protection for Ms. Cash and her daughter."

She gave a sharp nod. "Then we'll finish working this scene and hightail it to the lab so we can get you results as fast as possible. "

"I suspect getting your findings is one area that hasn't gotten faster." He frowned as he remembered the days of waiting for results when a child was missing and in need of his help.

"You're right there. DNA still takes twenty-four hours at a minimum. Unless you're doing the rapid tests, but those are only good for Buccal swabs."

"Right. I forgot about that." The FBI had taken lead on limiting the use of rapid DNA tests. When the sample came from a person's swabbed cheek, there were no chances of comingled DNA. But samples recovered elsewhere could contain DNA from someone else, and it needed to be isolated, which meant intervention by a human. "You'll let me know the minute you have any results?"

"Will do, but don't start your countdown yet. We'll likely be here most of the day, then drive home and then the processing."

He nodded. "Thanks again for coming and thank your associate too when she returns." He went into the lobby and spotted Russ, dressed in uniform this morning, coming down a hall toward him. Russ was here to aid in a security detail for Ella so she could attend a Santa party in the lounge on her floor, but Reid had no idea where Russ was coming from.

Reid joined his brother near a blowup of a large snowman playing Christmas music. "What're you up to?"

"Just leaving the security office."

"They have something for us?"

"Nah. I wanted to review all the footage to make sure they weren't missing something or covering something up."

"And?"

"Nothing."

"I just talked to Ingram and Dr. Clarke." Reid filled his brother in.

Russ's phone rang, and he got it out to answer. "Sheriff Maddox."

He listened and then grabbed Reid's shirt sleeve to tug him into an alcove, where he put his phone on speaker. "Surprised to hear from you in the morning, Oakley."

Oakley? The bartender? Reid's interest piqued.

"I'm surprised to be calling you." A nervous laugh sounded over the speaker. "I came in this morning to get my paycheck. Our day manager, Pat, said a vehicle was left in the lot overnight, and he had it towed. He wondered if I knew anything about it."

"And do you?" Russ asked.

"Well, kinda." She fell silent for a moment. "When those two guys were leaving last night, the one whose picture you showed me said his truck had broken down. I didn't mention it cause I forgot until now, but…"

"But you think this is the vehicle that was towed?" Russ asked.

"Don't know, but Pat said it was a pickup."

"Where was it towed?"

"All our vehicles go to First Class Towing."

"Anything else you forgot to tell us last night?" Russ asked, not sounding pleased at her failure to share this bit of news on a timely basis.

"I don't think so."

"Make sure everyone at the bar knows to call me if this guy comes looking for his truck." Russ disconnected.

"We can't trust them to follow through on that," Reid said. "We need our own eyes on the place. I'll get Dev over there."

"Tell him not to be conspicuous. We don't want to spook Fowler if he does show."

Reid got out his phone but caught sight of the time on his watch. "We have plenty of time to check the towing company before Ella's party."

"I'll drive." Russ headed for the door.

Reid could text Dev in the car, so he followed Russ, taking in the early morning visitors and staff in the lobby as he strode through. He half hoped to see Fowler's ugly mug among the groups so he could cuff the creep and haul him in.

After all, arresting the man was the only way Reid could ensure Ella's and Megan's safety today.

The towing company was located a few miles down the road from the hospital, and even with Russ's tendency to speed, it was enough time for Reid to call Devan out to the bar.

"He a go?" Russ asked after Reid hung up.

"Yep."

"You have to agree having our team on our side right now is a huge win." Russ clicked on a blinker and slowed near the towing company's driveway.

"Ditto for Veritas," Reid said. "Trent brought a new guy with him. One of his specialties is, get this, firearm audio forensics."

Russ shot him a wide-eyed look. "Say what?"

"My reaction too." Reid explained as best he could the information Landon had shared. "He came along because they didn't know if the bomb switch was patched through the electronics of Megan's car, plus he's shadowing Trent for a few weeks."

Russ shook his head. "I can't begin to stay current with forensics these days. Specialties I've never heard of are popping up everywhere. No way we'll ever stay current in a rural county."

"As usual, sounds like the Veritas Center is on the cutting edge."

"Too bad they cost so much." Russ swung into the towing company driveway and parked in a spot that said it was for towing company customers only and violators would be towed.

Russ snorted. "See them try to tow me."

He climbed out and Reid followed suit. The morning sun beat down on them, warming Reid's back as they made their way across the paved lot to a booth connected to a high fence with barbed wire that surrounded the property. The burly man in the booth had hair as greasy as his coveralls, and he was chowing down on a breakfast burrito. Signs were plastered everywhere, giving people unfortunate enough to have their vehicles towed the rates and procedures for reclaiming them.

Reid hung in the background as Russ displayed his credentials through bulletproof glass. "You towed a pickup from PJ's Sports Bar this morning."

The attendant set down his burrito and took a long swig on a straw in a takeout glass. "I did."

"We'd like to see it," Russ said.

The guy arched a bushy eyebrow but didn't move or speak.

Russ drew in a breath. "We have reason to believe it was used in a serious crime, and the owner could come looking for it."

"Warrant man. Need a warrant." He picked up his burrito again.

Russ's jaw muscles jumped. "I assume if a dangerous criminal shows up on your doorstep, you'll want police protection. Or not. You cooperate and we cooperate. That's how it's done, and it's your choice."

"Fine. Follow me." The beefy man took a last bite of his burrito. Cheese oozing down his chin, he pushed off his stool and lumbered out the door.

Russ gave a heavy sigh as he and Reid followed the guy, winding their way past vehicles of all sizes and colors to a white pickup. The plate number matched Fowler's registration.

A jolt of adrenaline at the potential lead hit Reid, but he kept his mouth shut and let his brother take lead as this guy seemed to think that despite Russ being the sheriff in another county, he had jurisdiction here. Could be because Russ never mentioned the county he oversaw, but whatever the reason, Reid was thankful the guy had cooperated.

"You been inside this vehicle?" Russ demanded.

The guy lifted his hands. "Haven't touched the thing other than to haul it in and park it."

Russ planted his feet as if he expected a fight. "We'll be taking charge of the truck now. You can return to your office, and we'll let you know what's going on when our plans are finalized."

"Fine by me. As long as I get my money." He spun and took his time moving across the lot.

Reid dug out his phone. "I'll call Trent. See if we can get Landon over here to process the truck."

"Agreed."

Reid made the call and explained his need to Trent.

"Text me the address, and I'll send Landon your way," Trent said.

Reid ended the call and fired off a text with the towing company's address. "We need to get the chief to approve an expansion of Veritas's duties to include this vehicle."

"Not a problem. I can convince him of that."

"You call him. I'll go to the gate and wait for Landon to make sure the owner lets him in."

Russ got out his phone, and Reid took a quick walk around the vehicle. Why, he didn't know. Maybe he hoped to see something that would instantly tell him where to find Fowler. All he discovered was a dirty truck with food wrappers and empty drinks littering the cab. The mess reminded him of Ryan's pickup. Reid sure would like to have Ryan helping out more, but didn't want to pull him away from the first month of his son's life more than was absolutely necessary.

Reid headed for the front of the property and arrived when Landon was pulling in. In the office, Reid arranged to have Landon let through. He hadn't noticed the smell of body odor on the first visit, likely because the burrito was covering it up, but now the odor permeated the space.

"I'm gonna get my money, right?" The owner lifted an eyebrow and held his hand over the switch that would open the door for Landon.

"I'll be sure the people in charge are aware of your outstanding fee," Reid said, but it was the least of his concerns right now.

The owner seemed satisfied and tapped the switch.

The door swung open, and Landon entered the building. He'd shed his Tyvek suit and wore tactical pants and a polo shirt with the Veritas logo on his chest. He carried a field kit and wore a serious expression as he approached Reid.

The minute they were alone, he asked, "What do we have?

"A Ford F150. Maybe ten years old or more. Not sure. Vehicles aren't my thing."

"The year is going to be a big deal." Excitement rode on Landon's words. "We need to hope for a touchscreen and some sort of infotainment system to glean the most data from the vehicle."

Reid hadn't even thought to check for that. "I looked inside but wasn't looking for a screen, so didn't notice one way or the other."

"No worries. That's why you have me."

Reid couldn't fault the guy for lack of eagerness and excitement in his work. Reid had been equally motivated when he was a young agent—too motivated—and could be the reason they were in this situation.

They reached Russ, who was stowing his phone.

Landon split off and peered in the window. "It has one of

the earlier models of a touchscreen that Ford put out. Puts it around 2012, maybe 2013 model."

He continued around the truck, his expression going from a smile to a frown and back again as he circled the vehicle a few times.

Russ leaned close to Reid. "A warrant for the truck's in the works so we can tow it if needed. And the chief has a judge at his beck and call, so should have it within the hour."

"Speedy, especially for a holiday week."

"Hey, you know me." Russ chuckled. "Friends in low places."

Reid rolled his eyes. His brother had lightened up so much the moment he'd gotten engaged to Sydney and grew since their marriage. So what if he made some bad jokes? It was a nice change.

Landon marched their way, and Reid introduced him to his brother.

Russ shook hands. "The new Veritas squint."

"Squint, ha-ha." Landon laughed. "Yeah, I watched Bones too. If only all of it were real."

"The law enforcement part too." Russ rolled his eyes.

"So what's the word on the truck?" Reid asked to draw them back to their mission.

Landon's expression perked up. "It has an infotainment system, and I should be able to get plenty of data from that."

"Data like what?" Russ asked.

Landon tilted his head. "Depends on whether he plugged a smartphone into the system or paired it via Bluetooth. If he did, the system can store navigation history, text messages, and emails. Even internet browsing history and social media feeds. Probably best of all, it can give us Bluetooth and cell tower connections."

"That's all, huh?" Russ joked.

Landon didn't laugh along this time. "Not quite. Vehicles also have electronic control units—ECUs. They're called the brain of the engine as they help with how a vehicle works. Basically it's a computer, switching system, and power management system all wrapped up in a neat little case."

"That do what specifically?" Reid asked.

Landon took a breath. "Most vehicles have more than seventy-five ECUs in them and each one handles a certain task. One might control the fuel injection and the timing of the spark to ignite it. Another air pressure. One could turn on and off lights. You get the picture."

"Impressive," Reid said. "So it shows us how the vehicle was used, and that could tell us where Fowler's been, maybe telling us where he is now."

"Or with internet search history, what he's planning next," Russ said.

"You got it." Landon smiled.

"How long before you can get that data?" Reid asked.

Landon's smile fell. "I'll need to dismantle the truck. Our forensics staff will want to do that too. So the best thing is to have this vehicle delivered to our garage at Veritas. There, we can tear it apart in a clean environment, and we can stand behind our results."

"Not sure I like the transport time to Portland," Reid said. "But if it's the right thing to do, then that's what we'll do."

Landon peered at Russ. "I assume you have a warrant for impounding the vehicle."

"Not yet, but hope to have it within the hour."

Landon glanced around the lot. "Seems like this place only has rollback tow trucks. I'll need you to make arrangements to have the truck hauled on a flatbed."

"I can do that," Russ said.

"Good. Good." Landon clapped his hands. "I'll head

back to the hospital to talk to Trent. I hope he'll agree to let me ride with the tow truck driver so I can get to work on the vehicle right away."

"Hey thanks, man," Reid said, wondering how they would ever find Fowler if they didn't have this fine team on their side. Thankfully, God had provided, and Reid should trust in that provision.

So why did he still fear he wouldn't find Fowler before the creep brought further terror to Megan and Ella?

12

_____

Megan applied her makeup in the hospital bathroom. The night had dragged by. A sleepless night, leaving its mark on her. Emotionally and physically. She dabbed cover-up under her eyes. But why bother? The strongest make-up in the world couldn't hide the evidence of her lack of sleep.

She'd tossed and turned on the cot next to Ella's bed. Her mind flashing over the terrifying events, then settling on how good it was to see Reid again. To have him with her, helping to keep them safe. Her traitorous feelings making her mad and sleep eluding her more.

Even her hot shower here in Ella's bathroom couldn't keep her mind from Reid stationed outside the room all night. She'd wanted to go out and talk with him, yet feared doing that very thing. Thankfully, he'd taken a break to go talk to the forensic team this morning, and Russ's wife was on guard duty now. But he could've finished with the team and be outside Ella's door now.

"Enough, Megan," she said to her reflection in the mirror. "Let it go. You're wasting your time and effort thinking about him. Hopefully, Ella will be discharged today, and you'll be out of his life before you know it."

Maybe. At least, she hoped.

Ella had improved enough after dinner to be fever-free, and her white blood cell counts had reached an acceptable level. If they stayed stable today, the doctor would release her, and Megan could take Ella as far away from Fowler as possible. Fortunately, a generous divorce settlement from Orrin gave her the freedom not to work. She hadn't wanted to accept his money, but she took it because Ella needed a full-time mother during her illness. With no job holding Megan back, they could go anywhere.

But where would be safe?

The beach house? It had always been a place of refuge when life got too difficult. Like after the bank robbery, Reid's disappearing act, and especially when Orrin bailed on them. She'd found solace there. No matter the time of year.

Even now, in December, she loved hearing stormy waves crash on the beach. Loved hearing howling winds whip pelting rain against the floor-to-ceiling windows while snuggled in front of a blazing fire, a cup of hot cocoa in her hands. Too bad. That was the last place they could go now. Fowler stole the keys and he now knew about the place.

She shuddered at the thought of him invading her place of sanctuary. She would have to find another place to go.

She packed her toiletries and took one last look in the mirror to put on a cheerful face for Ella before she headed into the room. Ella looked up from watching a video of classic Christmas specials, and Megan smiled.

Ella's eyes were alive and hopeful in her ashy face. "Is it time for the party now?"

Megan checked her watch. "Ten more minutes."

"Aw, I wanted to go now." She tugged Boo-Boo closer.

"Be patient, sweetie. Santa is on his way." Megan loved seeing Ella in good spirits, but with Fowler on the loose, she wasn't certain how she felt about taking Ella to a party.

Reid had enlisted help from his fellow teammates to allow her to attend and ensure her safety. Plus, the hospital administrator approved a screening of all attendees before they would be allowed to enter the lounge. Her doctor gave Ella the okay too, as long as she masked.

Megan peered at her sweet little girl. Visions of Fowler standing outside this door yesterday. His malicious and repulsive expression sending a shiver down her body. Despite not being able to confirm him in the grainy video, she was still certain she'd seen him yesterday.

The video ended, and Ella glanced at the door. "Is Jessie here yet?"

"I'm not sure." Megan dug deep for a smile.

"Can you go see?" Ella grinned, revealing a gap from the tooth she'd lost last week.

"Sure." Megan had avoided Reid all morning, but she would see him at the party in a few minutes anyway, so she headed for the door.

In the hallway, Jessie and Bandit, along with a female officer who Megan assumed was Russ's wife, stood by her door instead. Sydney was tall and slim, legs a mile long, with her blond hair pulled into a bun, almost regal-looking despite her drab brown uniform.

She finished chatting with Jessie and turned to Megan. "Hey there. I'm Sydney. Russ's wife."

"And my aunt," Jessie said proudly.

Sydney squeezed Jessie's shoulder. "Most important, Jessie's aunt."

Megan offered her hand. "Megan Cash."

"She's Daddy's friend," Jessie announced in a very serious tone.

"Well then, she's our friend too." Sydney's firm grip squeezed Megan's hand. "Right, Jess?"

"Right." Jessie smiled. "Is Ella awake?"

Megan nodded. "She's been waiting for you to get here."

"Can I go see her?"

"Absolutely."

Jessie peered at Sydney. "Can you watch Bandit? I can't take him in a patient's room without Dad."

"You got it." Sydney accepted the leash and smiled fondly at Jessie.

Jessie went into Ella's room and her daughter squealed with joy.

"Jessie's quite a girl, isn't she?" Sydney said when the door closed.

Megan nodded. "Very mature for her age."

Sydney frowned. "Too bad losing her mother is the reason she had to grow up fast. How are you holding up?"

"Are you talking about Ella's illness or Fowler?"

"Both, I guess, but mainly Fowler. That's something I can help you with."

"It's a minute-by-minute thing. One minute I think we'll be okay, the next—" Her voice broke and drifted off.

"I completely understand." Sydney laid a warm hand on Megan's shoulder. "I was recently in a similar situation. A creep thought I was in possession of something he wanted. He threatened me and everyone I love."

"Seems like that all turned out okay."

"Thanks to Russ." Tenderness softening her gaze, she peered over Megan's head. "There's no one better to have on your side than one of the Maddox brothers."

Megan followed Sydney's gaze down the hallway. Reid, Russ, and Micha strode their way. The three men walked side-by-side, and it seemed as if they moved in slow motion, like the way movies portrayed heroes coming to the rescue. Russ, a man she'd pegged as a real tough guy, returned Sydney's smile with a warm, intimate one of his own. Oh, how Megan wished a man would react to her the same way again. Would join her in life and share her burdens and joys.

She shifted her attention to Reid, surprised at how much he resembled his brother, yet he was his own man. This morning he wore blue jeans and a white button-down shirt under a dark brown blazer. She could see the outline of his gun in the fabric, and as much as she hated weapons, seeing him and the others armed gave her comfort.

She let her gaze return to his face and loved seeing his determination, likely placed there on her behalf. His eyes met hers, and a shiver of awareness rippled through her. When he smiled softly, almost shyly, her heart completely thawed toward him. Poof. Just like that. She forgot all the hurt, the past pain, the present pain, and enjoyed the warm feeling.

Sydney cleared her throat, and Megan broke the pull Reid had on her.

Why couldn't she control her emotions? Especially in front of others. Not good. Not good at all. How could she respond this way to a man who'd bailed on her and hurt her beyond words?

True, she wanted to feel cared for, and this man had once proved he could do that. But she also wanted a man who would stay by her side through all of life's troubles, to share her burdens and help raise Ella.

He wasn't the man she could count on to do that any more than Orrin had been. They'd both demonstrated their willingness to leave her behind when something they wanted more presented itself.

When Megan chanced another peek at Reid, he'd traded his warm expression for a deadly serious one, exactly like the tough FBI agent exterior he'd once portrayed. He stopped in front of Megan, as did Micha, but Russ went to join Sydney. He laid a protective hand on the small of her back. She smiled up at him, and the loss of a life partner hit Megan harder.

Leave it alone. Move on. Full stop.

"So." Reid clapped his hands. His alert, almost hard posture sent all thoughts of a missing partner to the recesses of her mind.

"Let's review the plans one more time," he said. "I'll escort Megan and Ella, along with Jessie and Bandit, to the party. Russ, you'll take the south corridor, Micha the north. Sydney, you'll seal this one off after we leave. Hospital security is on full alert and actively watching for Fowler. If you need backup for any reason, don't hesitate to call." He paused and looked each person full in the face before locking gazes with Megan, communicating his concern for their safety. "I don't have to tell you that Fowler has proven his resourcefulness. So be aware and question anything out of the ordinary. Even the smallest of things."

Breathe, Megan. Just breathe.

"Any questions?" he asked.

Murmurs of no went through the group.

Reid glanced at his watch. "Then let's do this."

Micha and Russ headed down the hallway, and Sydney remained at the door. All three remained at attention and kept their focus vigilant.

"You ready?" Reid opened Ella's door but paused to flash a brilliant smile.

Megan's stomach flip-flopped. Oh man, with him looking at her that way, how could she talk? She swallowed hard. It changed nothing. She didn't want to have these feelings. Had promised herself not to let him get to her again, but somehow he broke through her barrier.

"Everything will be fine. I promise." He cupped her elbow and squeezed gently, the warmth traveling up her arm.

She peered into his eyes. Remembered the way she fit under his arm when he'd wrapped it around her shoulders and squeezed at the end of Fowler's trial.

"Megan?" He narrowed his eyes. "Is everything okay?"

No. Stop looking at me that way.

"Just tired," she said and crossed the room, shaking off the memories as she walked.

"Looks like the ankle's better," he said.

"It barely hurts today."

"You two ready to go to the party?" Reid approached the girls, sounding nothing like the hard-as-nails FBI agent from the hallway. *Right.* He could change fast. She'd seen it. One minute he wanted to pursue a relationship with her, the next minute his career took precedence.

"Um, Jessie's daddy?" Ella peered at Reid.

Reid smiled. "Why don't you call me Reid? It's easier than Jessie's daddy."

Ella looked at Megan. "Is that okay, Mommy?"

"How about Mr. Reid?"

"'K." She turned to Reid. "Since Jessie is my new friend, are you Mommy's new friend too?"

Reid's expression softened as he took Ella's hand and helped her to the edge of the bed. "I'd like to be your mommy's friend if she'll let me."

"I know she will." Ella's seriousness surprised Megan. "She always tells me to be nice to the other kids my age, and you look like you're her age, so she'll be nice to you." Ella looked at Megan. "Won't you, Mommy?"

Megan smiled and nodded. "Let's get going."

"This is gonna be so much fun." Jessie jumped down and charged to the open door, where she grabbed Bandit's leash from Sydney.

Megan settled Ella's mask in place then maneuvered her

IV pole into position to leave. She took Ella's hand and walked to the door held open by Reid.

Worry eating at her, Megan escorted Ella into the hallway and started the short walk to the lounge. Even with Reid by her side and the other security personnel stationed around them, she couldn't relax and prayed they'd put plenty of measures in place to keep Ella safe.

Reid kept his eyes on the party that was starting to wind down. The small lounge was filled with children and parents, nurses, and one large Santa Claus that children had surrounded for the whole event. He tried to ignore Megan standing so close to him. Tried hard, but he kept catching her scent when she moved, and it was all he could do not to turn and ask her about the clean-smelling fragrance he couldn't place.

But he wouldn't ask. Couldn't ask. It was too personal. So what if they'd had a few moments in Ella's room when he almost thought Megan was still interested in him? He still wouldn't go there. He was likely wrong. Probably his ego hoping she was still attracted to him.

He glanced at her and, this time, let his gaze linger. She was a stunning woman. This morning, she'd dressed in dark blue jeans and a deep navy blue top that brought out her soft blue eyes. Eyes that wouldn't let go of her anxiety. He wanted to smooth away the worry line on her forehead. To wave a magic wand and erase all of her problems.

Get a grip, Maddox.

He curled his fingers. She still had a very sick child, and he couldn't go anywhere near that kind of issue.

She sighed, much like he wanted to but didn't. He may

not be able to talk about what was happening between them, but he could reassure her about Fowler.

"Relax. We've taken every precaution, and Ella will be fine."

She warily eyed him. "I wish I *could* relax. Fowler might not show up, but Ella isn't out of the woods in the health department."

"How long has she been sick?" He focused on the room, watching Ella, who stood next to Jessie and Bandit, waiting for Ella's turn on Santa's lap.

"Since she was three."

"And she's how old now?"

"Just turned six," Megan said softly.

The pain in her voice drew his attention. Her focus remained on her daughter. Though clearly upset, the same strength she'd displayed yesterday was in her posture. She could handle whatever happened in the future. She may need him to protect her physically while Fowler was on the prowl, but she could handle herself emotionally.

"They discovered the first tumor just after her third birthday," she continued. He wanted to shut her down before she got too personal, but he'd been in her shoes with Diane and knew it helped to talk about it, so he nodded.

"Surgery and chemo took care of it. She was really sick for a while, but then she was in remission for a few years. Now this." She rubbed a hand over her eyes. "It was the hardest day of my life when the doctor told me the tumor had returned."

Memories of Diane's last few months rose, nearly choking off his air. He wanted to shut down this conversation, but when he talked with Megan, she seemed to fill that huge void Diane had left behind. Despite her fears of Fowler and Ella's health, she hadn't changed from a warm, caring woman, and he wanted to move closer to that. But he couldn't even bring himself to ask about Ella's prognosis.

He searched for something to say, something positive to lift Megan's spirits. In his therapy visits, he'd heard the nurses talking about the various doctors, and they all respected Dr. Browne.

"The good news is that you have the best pediatric oncologist in the area," he said.

"We were so blessed to get in with her this time around."

He nodded but didn't really agree that there was any blessing in having to see your child go through such an ordeal one time, let alone two. "Any idea when Ella will be released?"

"Dr. Browne said if her white blood cell count is high enough this afternoon, she can go home then."

"You're speaking figuratively about home, right?"

She pivoted to face him. "You mean because of Fowler?"

"Yeah. So what are your plans?" He glanced at her and then put his full attention back on Ella.

"Normally, I'd say we'd head to my parents' beach house, but Fowler knows about that too, so I don't know what we'll do. But I'll figure it out. I always do."

Ella crossed the room, her face jubilant, and yet lines of tiredness etched her eyes, and it hurt to look at her. Jessie walked alongside, pushing Ella's IV pole and holding Bandit's leash. This wasn't the kind of conversation to have around either of them. He and Megan had plenty of time to discuss this later.

"I wish the party could last forever." Ella slipped her hand into Megan's.

Megan stroked Ella's cheek with her other hand. "You look tired. We should get to your room so you can rest." She turned to go, but Reid held out his hand, stopping her.

He didn't want to be on the move when so many other

children and parents were milling around. "Let's wait until this room empties before leaving." He urged Ella and Megan to move out of the path of traffic, and Jessie followed.

"So you had a good time?" Megan knelt down in front of Ella.

"It was so fun. Did you see Bandit and Santa?" Ella's face lit up, and Reid could finally see the resemblance between her and Megan.

"I think Bandit likes Santa, don't you?" Megan asked.

"That's silly, Mommy, everybody likes Santa."

"I guess that means you do too." Megan tickled Ella, and she squealed with laughter.

Jessie smiled, seeming happier than he'd seen her in a long time.

Though enjoying the festive mood, Reid stayed vigilant and checked in with Russ and Micha on their comms unit. All was good.

A nurse pushed the last child out in a wheelchair and Santa trailed behind, tying a balloon onto the chair as it moved.

"Bye, Santa Claus," Ella said and waved at the big man.

He winked at Ella, patted Jessie's arm, and then saluted at Megan and Reid before sauntering down the hallway.

"I think Santa Claus likes me better than the other kids." She glanced at Jessie. "Sorry, Jess, but..." She reached into her robe pocket and pulled out a business card. "He put this in my pocket. I watched, and he didn't give one to anybody else." She held it out to Megan. "See?"

She held a business card with the Willamette Bank's logo on it.

Megan jerked the card from Ella's hand.

"Don't tear it, Mommy," Ella protested.

Megan didn't respond but studied the card and flipped it

over to reveal a handwritten message. Reid read over her shoulder.

If you want to keep your child alive, you will meet my demands.

"He was here," Megan whispered.

"Go after Santa!" Reid yelled to Micha.

Micha didn't question but turned and bolted down the hallway. Reid alerted Sydney and Russ to be extra vigilant, and he pinned his focus on the hallway Micha's departure had left unprotected.

"What's wrong, Mommy?" Ella's voice quavered. "Why does Mr. Reid want to stop Santa Claus? Did he do something wrong?"

"I just need to ask him a question." Reid wrapped an arm around Jessie, then glanced at Ella. Her chin trembled so he moved closer and touched her nose with his index finger. "You, little miss, look like you need to take a rest."

She peered at him, her eyes innocent and sweet. The urge to pull her as close as Jessie was and keep her safe—not only from Fowler but also from the cancer—was almost too much to ignore.

Please, I need Your help. I can't get close to Ella. You know I'm not strong enough to handle it.

More importantly, he prayed that the cancer—and the man who sought revenge and seemed to outsmart them at every turn—didn't get to this precious little girl and her mother.

13

___

Staring at her sleeping daughter, Megan sighed, releasing her distress as she searched for a positive attitude. But what was there to be positive about? Fowler had slipped through their defenses, and this time he'd actually interacted with Ella. Person to person. Up close. Touching her. Holding her on his lap.

A fist of fear pressed against Megan's chest. She couldn't let Fowler get near Ella again. He would try again. There would be another attempt to approach them. She knew that as clearly as she knew she had to breathe.

Reid and the others kept saying they would protect her. But despite their best efforts, Fowler walked right up to Ella today. Right up to her! What's to say he couldn't get to Ella again, even with these fine law enforcement officers' training and skills?

She could never let Fowler anywhere near her daughter again. She had to be more proactive. If anything like attending a party was mentioned, she would shut it down fast. No matter what.

Not that she thought she was smarter than Reid or the others. None of them could've anticipated that he would've overpowered the guy who was to play Santa. That was why Ella would simply have to stay in her room until they departed.

She gently laid Ella's hand on the bed, tucked her covers around her and Boo-Boo, and kissed her soft forehead. Tears threatened, but Megan swallowed them down and headed for the door. Outside the room, Russ stood alert, arms crossed and feet solidly planted, blocking the door.

Keeping his attention on the hallway, he stepped aside. "Everything okay in there?"

"Fine. The party wore Ella out. She's asleep."

"Must be hard for a little kid to be so sick."

"It is." She let her nails bite into her hands so she didn't start crying in front of him. "I'm heading down to the lounge to talk to Reid. Ella will likely sleep for a few hours, but can you let me know if she wakes up?"

"Will do, but first let me call Reid so he can escort you."

"Is that really necessary? It's just down the hall."

"If I want to stay alive, it is. Reid's in such a terrible mood from letting Fowler get to Ella, he'd take my head off if I let you go anywhere alone." He lifted his phone from a belt holder.

Not waiting for her agreement, he dialed Reid. She understood Reid's guilt, but they'd done their best, and none of the wonderful people who were helping to protect her and Ella should feel guilty about anything. Easier said than done.

"He's on his way." Russ resumed his surveillance of the hallway. His expression hardened his face into granite, raising her concern again.

Where would she be without these men and Sydney helping her? All four of them had put their lives on hold to make sure she and Ella stayed safe. And if Fowler had gotten to Ella, they'd have stood strong and prevented him from hurting her. She owed them all a huge debt.

She faced Russ. "I don't know how I'll ever repay you for helping us out."

He cleared his throat but didn't make eye contact. "No need. Glad to help."

"Well, thank you. And tell Sydney thanks too."

"Sydney's the first one to help if someone needs it." When he said her name, his posture relaxed a touch and the love for his wife colored his tone, leaving Megan with that deep longing again for a partner in life.

She doubted Orrin's voice ever held such affection for her—even in the beginning of their marriage. He'd always been too busy focusing on his career and working hard to move to a larger broadcast market. And Reid? If he'd once cared this deeply for her, he'd kept it bottled up to keep others from seeing he had a thing for one of his witnesses. And then when he was free to tell her he cared for her, he too, chose his job over her.

But there was a difference. A big difference.

Orrin had promised to stay with her until death parted them, and Reid had never promised anything. He'd only hinted at a future relationship after the trial ended. And to be fair to the guy, she may have put more stock in those hints than he intended. She needed to talk with him and put their past behind them once and for all.

Eager to do so, she focused on the T in the hallway, waiting for him to round the corner. When he did, she gave him a quick once-over. He'd taken off his jacket, and the white fabric of his shirt was crisp and clean against his tanned skin and tapered at the waist, fitting him as if custom-tailored. His shirt cuffs were rolled to his elbows as if he'd been delving into something. His face held the guilt she expected to find, yet a strength showed through at the same time.

Wanting him to know she didn't blame him for Fowler getting so close, she smiled, making sure it was warm and welcoming. She didn't really have to try, because she was honestly happy to see him. As his long strides brought him closer, that safe, cared-for feeling wrapped her in warmth.

He returned her smile with a sideways grin, and her pulse sped up. If she hadn't just decided to let go of their past, her anger would have melted into a warm puddle. She glanced away. Caught Russ studying them. He didn't miss her interaction with Reid. Of course not. He was a perceptive law enforcement officer.

"I'll be going now." She didn't wait for Reid to reach them but took off in his direction.

"How's Ella?" Reid asked when she approached.

"Sleeping." Not wanting Russ to catch her ogling his brother again, she kept walking, remaining silent until they moved out of Russ's view. "Did Jessie go home?"

"Yeah. Sydney took her."

"She seemed upset." Megan glanced at Reid and slowed her steps. "If you want to go home to be with her, I totally understand."

"I'm not leaving you until this is resolved. Jess is fine without me. She may not like the situation I've placed myself in, but she understands you need help." He stopped and gazed down at her until she wanted to squirm out from under his attention. "Unless you're trying to tell me you don't want me here."

"That's not what I'm saying at all."

He raised an eyebrow. "So this doesn't have to do with our past?"

She shook her head. "Ella always wants me around when she's upset, and I figured Jessie might need you."

"Jess's fine. She's with Sydney and we have other family who'll take care of her too. You and Ella are all alone right now." He was right, and it hit her like a punch to the gut.

She turned away. She never thought of herself as being alone. Her parents were always there for her, but they were on vacation, leaving her alone at the moment. Very alone. Vulnerable in so many ways. Ella's illness. Fowler's stalking. Reid's kindness and strength threatening to melt all of that away.

"Megan?" Reid rested his hand on her shoulder.

An invisible pull encouraged her to step closer. To let him wrap an arm around her and hold her until the turmoil and danger went away.

No. Stop. Right now they needed to keep things all business. "So what did you find out about Santa Claus?"

A nurse and patient approached them, and he held out his hand for her to get moving. "Let's finish this discussion in the lounge."

She headed down the hall until she reached the lounge, where she came to an abrupt stop inside the door. Only a few hours ago, this room, brightly decorated with balloons and butterflies on the wall, had been filled with smiling children and caring nurses. Now, the table once lined with refreshments held a laptop, file box, and reports strewn across the top, as if Reid had abandoned them in a hurry. A portable whiteboard with notes about Fowler jotted in vibrant blue stood next to the table. A foldaway cot hugged the corner, and bedding lay on the sofa.

"The hospital let us set up a command post here." Reid's voice came from right behind her and startled her.

"Us?" She looked at him. They were so close that she could see the slices of gold woven through the blue of his eyes.

"Micha is helping me," he whispered. "He went to get something to eat."

His gentle tone made her chest ache, reminding her of the time he'd been there for her, patiently sitting by her side, helping her work through Fowler's attack. Now it set her mind heading in the wrong direction, and she couldn't succumb to it.

She crossed the room to a chair, where she sat and tucked her feet under her body. "So you were going to tell me about Santa."

"Toby Turner, the man hired by the hospital to play Santa, was discovered gagged and tied up in his van." Reid joined her and leaned against the wall, legs crossed at the ankles as if chasing down a creep like Fowler was child's play. He'd mentioned working with a child abduction team, so maybe her situation seemed minor compared to rescuing a child in the hands of a predator. But to her, it was big, terrifying, and confusing.

"Will he be all right?" she asked.

"Someone hit him and he lost consciousness, but he's expected to make a full recovery."

"And did he see who hit him?"

"Unfortunately, no." Reid ran his hands through his hair. "The police have processed his vehicle and lifted finger-prints. Hopefully, they recovered Fowler's prints."

"I hope Toby wasn't hurt. He's the best Santa. We've been here for a few Christmas parties, and he's been the Santa at each one."

"So you know him?"

"Know him? Not really. Just his work, I guess you might say." She tilted her head. "You don't think he could be involved with Fowler, do you? I mean, I can't see it. He's such a sweet old man that he wouldn't associate with a creep like Fowler."

"He doesn't have a record, which really goes without saying as the hospital wouldn't hire an ex-felon to play Santa."

"Oh, right. Good point."

"Early indications say he has no connection to Fowler, but while you were getting Ella to sleep, I called my FBI buddy, Jack, to ask him to run a deeper background. He has a few analysts helping, so we should know something soon."

She pursed her lips. "There's something I don't get. How could Fowler have organized this? He couldn't have known Ella would be in the hospital or at that party. So how could he plan to be here? Especially after being out of prison for such a short time."

"He's most likely been following you since his release and saw you bring Ella to the ER. The nurses posted the party on the whiteboard by the elevator and included Santa's visit in the posting. Fowler most likely noticed the board when he was here yesterday and hoped Ella would attend. If she didn't, it would be no big deal to him, but if she did—"

"He would pounce on an innocent child." She hated the bitterness in her tone, but she still really couldn't fathom that they'd allowed this man to come so close to her daughter. "I can't let go of the thought of him touching Ella."

"Believe me. I understand how you feel." He crossed the room and sat on the coffee table in front of her. He leaned his elbows on his knees and made eye contact. Tension radiated from him, and she held her breath as she waited to hear what he had to say.

"I've worked hundreds of child abduction cases, but last year when Jessie was abducted by that killer, I wasn't prepared for the emotions that hit me."

She fought hard to keep from letting him see her horror

over the situation and further compound his suffering. "I'm so sorry. Would you like to tell me what happened?"

"She witnessed a crime, and the suspect wanted to eliminate her so she couldn't ID him." He flexed his fingers and stared at them. "I wanted to kill him." His voice held a razor-sharp edge she'd never heard before.

She sat back, reflecting on his tone and the sheer determination in his eyes. He knew what it was like to have a child threatened and understood Megan's every emotion. Understood it well.

She was certain he would help protect her child. No matter how Fowler tried to hurt them, Reid would help. Not because he cared for her, not because they had a past, but because he'd lived through the same excruciating pain and came out the other side.

If only she could be sure this situation would end as well for her and Ella.

Reid couldn't handle Megan's piercing gaze, and he looked away. After a night without sleep and Ella's near miss, telling Megan about Jessie's abduction drained his last bit of energy, and he needed to regroup. He couldn't do that under Megan's scrutiny. He waffled between continuing this discussion with a very personal bond connecting them and forcing the conversation to the business at hand.

"Do you want to talk about it?" She laid a hand on his knee.

A flare of awareness raced over his body. Sucking in a breath, he rubbed a hand across his face as if it would erase his response to her touch. For the first time since Diane died, a woman had thawed a small spot of his heart, and he wanted to risk it all again. Everything. Put himself out there and connect with Megan to see where their interest in each other could go.

He lowered his hand and caught her expression. He couldn't decipher her watchful gaze, and it splashed him with a cold dose of reality.

The woman sitting across from him wasn't the Megan he'd once known. The woman who'd gazed at him with adoration and affection. This Megan was wary and on edge. A Megan who hadn't forgiven him.

Sure, she needed him right now. And he would be there for her this time, to do what he could to compensate for how he'd hurt her before, but that was all he would do.

"What time does Dr. Browne usually round?" he asked.

Megan eyed him for a moment then glanced at her watch. "She should be stopping in anytime now."

"Have you thought any more about where you'll go if Ella's discharged?"

"Someplace far away from Fowler." She pushed up her sleeves and thrust her chest out.

Ah, here she was. The determined Megan he knew. A good thing for sure, but he'd seen her determination blind-side her. In this case, it could make her do something dangerous. Maybe unwittingly put herself in Fowler's path.

Reid couldn't let her make any rash decisions. "I asked Micha to find a safe place for you, and he's working on it now."

"If he doesn't find one, you could help us disappear, right?" She pressed her lips together.

She wasn't swayed at all, and Reid didn't like it. Not one bit. "Define disappear."

"I don't know. I'm feeling my way through this. But I'm thinking you could find a house where Ella and I can stay long-term. Somewhere Fowler can't find us."

He returned to his seat, facing her. "I could try to arrange something, but is that really what you want?"

"Why not?"

"Say you go away for a while, and Fowler can't trace you. He's not going anywhere. The minute you return, he'll resume his pursuit."

"Then we won't come back."

"And then what?"

Her eyes narrowed to slits. "I don't care, as long as I keep Fowler away from Ella."

"But what about your family and friends? Ella's doctor? Your life is here?"

She cleared her throat. "We'll make a new life."

He knew she was making a mistake. "A life where you'll be looking over your shoulder all the time. You can't let Fowler control you like that. You have to stand up to him."

"I did that once, remember? I stood up to him, like you said. And now he's out of jail and not only coming after me but Ella too." Pressing her lips into a tight, colorless line, she folded her arms, and memories of that conversation so long ago came back to him.

"I know this is scary, but you can't let a man like Fowler win."

"I can't do this again, Reid." She jumped up, strode to the window, and kept her back to him.

He should stay seated and wait for her to speak, but he hated that she was hurting, and he moved as close to her as he thought she would allow. He placed his hands on her shoulders. "I know this is similar to what happened years ago. But you're not the same person as back then. You're stronger, and you have a child to think of. You have to do what's best for Ella in the long run."

She swiveled, her shoulders curled over her chest.

"What's best for her is getting away from here before Fowler hurts her."

"Maybe in the short term. But running from her home, from her grandparents, that's not good for her in the end. Let me help you, Megan. I can protect both of you."

"Can you?" She stared into his eyes. "I don't mean to doubt your expertise, but it seems like Fowler has the upper hand here, and no matter how good you are, he'll get to us."

"Give me another chance. I won't let you down, I promise."

"You'll stay with us every minute until Fowler is caught?"

"Yes." He pulled her into his arms.

She didn't resist but laid her head on his chest. He rested his chin on the softness of her hair and stroked her back. She snuggled closer, and the same protective urge he had for Jessie had him tightening his arms.

What was he doing? How could he get involved with Megan again?

How could he not?

She needed him more than ever, and he couldn't walk away simply because he was afraid of his obvious feelings for her and her little girl.

"I'm not going anywhere. I promise I won't let Fowler get to you," he whispered the promise that was nearly impossible to keep.

One he would die trying to fulfill.

14

Reid's cell rang. Megan jumped and pushed away from him. What had she been thinking by letting him hold her? She scooted a safe distance away. He'd held her, warm, strong, and yet tender, and she hadn't wanted him to let her go.

What would she have done if his phone hadn't rung? Hoped for more? For a future with him?

How had she let herself so easily fall into this man's arms again? Sure, she was afraid of Fowler, but Reid had proved he wasn't a man she could count on. Was it possible he changed? Could he now be depended on when the going got tough? Not one to run? It sounded like he stayed with his wife through her illness, and a man prone to bolting wouldn't have. She knew that firsthand.

She studied him as he took the call. He'd clamped his hand on the back of his neck and bent forward, staring at the floor, phone to his ear. She admired his rugged profile, his wide and solid jawline.

Her heart rate picked up again. Just from looking at him. Unbelievable.

What're you going to do here, Megan? Use your common

sense and run. From your stalker and your protector, if you know what's good for you.

"We'll be right there," he said into his phone and shoved it into his pocket. "That was Russ. Dr. Browne is with Ella, and she wants to talk to you. I'll walk you to the room."

He moved toward her, eyes intent on her face. She wanted to leave him behind and flee from her wayward feelings, but why? He would chase after her, and she wanted to be safe too. She stayed out of the way as he checked the hallway. He signaled, and she stepped out of the room.

Near the end of the hall, a man rounded the corner. They both jumped. Reid whipped out his gun before lowering it just as fast.

She identified the man as Micha. He held up his hands.

"I come in peace." He laughed, doing nothing to ease the tension.

"What's the word?" Reid asked him, not laughing. Not even smiling.

Micha's smile fell. "Still searching for a safe place for them to go, but haven't located the right location yet."

Reid jammed his weapon back into the holster and flared his nostrils. "They can't go to their house."

Micha didn't back down under Reid's anger but pulled back his shoulders. "I'll keep searching. Worst case, we go to plan B."

"Which is?" Reid continued to stare at his teammate.

Micha shrugged. "I don't know yet, but we'll figure it out. We always do."

Seemed to Megan that the men had forgotten she was standing here. "I need to go. The doctor's waiting."

She started off again and didn't wait for Reid to follow. He would. And he did, coming up beside her near the corridor leading to Ella's room.

"Slow down. Let me make sure it's safe." He slipped his hand around her elbow, and a shiver traveled over her arm.

At the corridor, she stopped, and he moved into it. The impulse to rush away from him and her unwanted feelings was almost too much to bear. And yet, oceans of vulnerability swamped her, urging her to slip under his arm and let him hold her as he'd done in the lounge—let him take care of her and Ella.

Reid waved her forward. "Don't worry. We'll find a safe place for you and Ella."

Had he mistaken her current angst for worry over Fowler? How had that not taken precedence in her thoughts? There was a madman after them, for goodness' sake, and her daughter was in the hospital. Time spent focusing on Reid and her reaction to him was wasted time when she should be thinking of what she would do if Dr. Browne said she would discharge Ella.

At Ella's door, Russ greeted them with a quick nod. "Before you go in, I wanted to let you know I got ahold of Chief Gleason. Forensics hasn't processed those prints from Santa's van yet. I tried to light a fire under him, but he said they're short-staffed for the holiday and working on a murder investigation. He prioritized the work but said they'll finish when they finish."

Reid gritted his teeth. "Thanks for calling him."

"Yeah, I didn't like his answer either, so I pulled two of my deputies to canvass the area. See if they can find someone who saw something. Maybe give us a lead until those prints come in."

"Didn't the locals already do that?" Megan asked.

Russ's expression soured. "They did, but I get the feeling they weren't as thorough as I would want."

Megan suspected not all law enforcement officers had

the same work ethic as Russ, and she really appreciated his dedication.

"Thank you, Russ. I know you are going above and beyond." Megan smiled at him.

Russ seemed as if he was going to say something, but Dr. Browne stepped out of Ella's room. Megan didn't like the tight expression on her face, and she braced herself for the news.

The doctor glanced at Reid, then Russ before training her gaze on Megan. "Maybe we should talk somewhere more private."

"It's okay," Megan said, apprehension making her want Reid by her side. "You can talk in front of them."

Dr. Browne shoved her hands into the pockets of her white coat. "Ella is improving steadily, and she's eager to get out of here for the holidays. I believe discharging her would be in her best interest."

"I hear a 'but' coming." Megan learned that doctors could be evasive when bad news lurked around the corner, and at times she had to force the issue.

"No but." Dr. Browne gave a tight smile. "I'd like to talk about conditions for her discharge. To be on the safe side, I'd like Ella to have labs drawn and see her in my office every morning for the next week or so."

Every morning? Impossible. "I don't know if we can do that. We need to leave town to get away from the man I told you about." Megan glanced at Reid, but couldn't discern his thoughts.

"I completely understand, but I wouldn't recommend travel for Ella right now and would be hesitant to discharge her under such circumstances." She drew her hands from her pockets and crossed her arms.

Megan had been offered a way out of this terrifying ordeal, only for it to be snatched away a moment later. It seemed as though around every turn, life conspired against her. Had God truly turned His back on them? He could change what was happening, but was He hearing her pleas?

She didn't think so and the thought sent nausea swimming in her gut. "I don't know what to do. We can't stay in the city."

Jaw set, Reid stepped forward. "Megan and Ella can stay with my family. We live about forty minutes from here, and I could drive them to the appointment each day. Would that work, Dr. Browne?"

The doctor tilted her head, blinking rapidly. "Yeah, sure. I don't see why not."

Megan spun to face Reid. She and Ella couldn't stay with him. That was crazy talk. Just plain crazy. She didn't need to be in his company twenty-four hours a day.

She opened her mouth to protest, but before she could speak, he pushed up his sleeves and moved into Megan's personal space. She knew that posture. Had seen it many times during Fowler's trial. He wasn't going to back down—no matter what—and arguing would be useless.

Why argue when he was right? The solution he offered fixed their problem. His home was close by. Jessie and Bandit would be there to keep Ella company, and Reid would be on hand to protect them should Fowler somehow learn their location.

"Thank you for the offer. We're glad to accept." Okay, maybe not glad but it would be bad-mannered to act churlish when he was offering sanctuary at his home.

Yes, it was a good plan for all involved. If—and it was a big if—she found a way to ignore her growing feelings for this man who towered over her with a far-too-appealing look of satisfaction on his face.

❧

An hour later, Reid marched up the walkway to the real Santa's, AKA Toby Turner, home in a well-kept subdivision with single story homes built in the sixties. He'd hoped to be driving Megan and Ella to his place by now, but they were waiting on final blood test results for Ella. Reid had alerted security that he would be leaving for an hour or so, and Micha was taking over their protection.

He passed a giant blow-up Santa and rows of large candy canes lining the walkway and reached the house outlined in multi-colored lights to knock on the door holding a pleasant-smelling pine wreath.

The plump man pulled open the door, jingling came from little colored bells dangling as ornaments from a Christmas tree on his gaudy red and green sweater. He had long silvery hair but no beard and wore khaki pants. Still, Reid could easily imagine him in a red suit with a fake beard entertaining children.

Reid introduced himself and shared his reason for being there. "I was hoping you would be willing to talk for a moment."

"Not sure what I can do to help, but sure." He smiled, and his apple cheeks rose.

Reid followed him and the jingle into a sparsely furnished home to a living area connected to a retro-sixties kitchen with aqua appliances. He pointed at a blue velvet sofa. "Get you a cup of eggnog?"

"Thanks for the offer, but no." Reid sat.

Toby plopped onto a straight-backed wood chair, his bells settling into silence as he rested his hands on his large belly. "Now what can I do for you?"

Reid shifted to get comfortable on the hard cushion. "Tell me what happened at the hospital when you were tied up."

"Will never forget that. Not for as long as I live." He

grimaced. "I was changing into my suit at the rear of my van. Been doing this gig at the hospital for ten years now, and I use the same secluded spot every year so no one can see me. Wouldn't want the kids to see Santa without his beard." He grinned, but it faded fast. "Anyway, I was bending down to put my boots on. When I stood up, something slammed into the back of my head. I remember reaching for whatever it was, grabbing onto something, then falling to the ground. The next thing I know, I'm waking up in the van, tied up, and duct tape on my mouth. The door closed."

His lips pursed as if eating something sour, belying the rosy cheeks. "Who would want to tie up Santa?"

"Did the police mention a possible suspect?" Reid asked, not willing to share Fowler's name if the locals hadn't done so.

"Yeah, a guy named Norman Fowler." He frowned. "Showed me his picture too, but I don't have a clue who he is."

Not the answer Reid was hoping for. "Did you have a chance to look through your vehicle after the police freed you to see if anything is missing or odd?"

He started shaking his head but winced and stopped. "The doctors carted me off to the ER right away to check out my head injury. When I was released, the police gave me a ride home."

Exactly like Reid suspected had happened. "The police took an inventory of the items they located in your van. Would you mind reviewing it to see if you notice anything missing?"

"Sure."

Reid called the list up on his phone and held it out to Toby. He took the device and scrolled down the screen, his tongue peeking out the side of his mouth. "Odd. There's a blue stocking cap on here. I don't have a stocking cap in my van, much less a blue one. Everything else is right." He handed Reid's phone to him.

Maybe the cap was the lead they needed. Reid stifled his eagerness from Toby. "Could someone you know have left the cap in the van?"

"No," he said. "I only use the van for work, and I'm the only one who goes in there."

"You mean your Santa job," Reid clarified.

"Yeah, that, but I also deliver flowers."

A flower delivering Santa. Something Reid might laugh at in a different situation. Instead he pondered the cap. Could it belong to Fowler? If so, why had he left it in the van?

"If someone wore a stocking cap, could it fit under your Santa hat?" Reid asked.

"Um, well." He tapped his chin. "Never tried it, but I think it would show."

Okay, then. If it belonged to Fowler, he would've had to take it off to play Santa. But why would he leave a potentially incriminating item in the vehicle? Did he want them to know he attacked Santa?

Questions Reid intended to pose to his team, but for now it was time to conclude this interview. "Is there anything else you think I should know about the incident?"

"Um, no. I don't think so." Toby forced a breath out between clenched teeth. "But I'll ask for your help with the same thing I asked the cops I talked to. It would be great if you could let the hospital know I had nothing to do with this. I sure don't want to lose my Santa gig with them. It doesn't pay much, but seeing these sick kids smile is the highlight of my year."

Reid wouldn't promise anything until the background reports Jack was running on this guy came back clean. "I'll see what I can do."

"I'll walk you to the door." Santa led the way, a waddle in his step.

Reid shook hands with the man and hurried down the walkway to his vehicle. He didn't want to waste any time on letting this potential lead go cold, so he grabbed his iPad from the backseat. He set up a group video conference call for everyone working with him on the investigation and texted them a link.

He leaned back, his eyes on the screen as his team and Jack logged on. Ryan too, whose dark circles under his eyes were what Reid expected from a new dad.

"Oh, man, Ryan," Dev said. "You look worse than Rip Van Winkle before his big nap." Dev's eyes lit with the humor that was often found there.

Ryan scrubbed a hand over his face. "People warn you about what parenthood will be like, but man, they don't do it justice. Both ways. The bad and the good."

"How is the little man?" Reid asked.

"Doing all the things a baby should do." Ryan stifled a yawn. "Of course, he's advanced at all of it." He laughed.

"Mia said Austin already has you wrapped around his little finger," Russ said. "You just proved it."

Ryan didn't try to argue but gave a satisfied smile. "You know how it is, right?"

"I do." Russ's fond smile was likely for his son Zach. "And good news is, you forget the sleepless nights."

"I mean you're so tired, how can you remember them?" Ryan laughed. "So what's been happening?"

Reid brought them all up to speed, including his meeting with Toby. "The guy seemed on the up-and-up."

Jack's gaze sharpened, and he sat forward. "He's clear. Background checks out. The locals also took his prints and a DNA swab for elimination purposes. They recovered only his prints in his van. DNA is processing."

"Thanks, Jack," Reid said, resisting spouting off what he really wanted to say. He'd hoped that van would provide a lead, but he wouldn't bring the guys down with a negative comment. He would be sure to get with the hospital administrator at some point to tell him Toby was in the clear.

Reid turned to his brother's picture on the screen. "Russ, I need you to get with the police on the inventory recovered from Santa's van. They put a blue stocking cap on the list. Toby says it's not his and no one else has access to his van. He also remembers grabbing something after he was hit. Could've pulled this cap off Fowler's head, and we might get a hair for DNA."

"Why would Fowler leave it behind?" Micha asked, his dark brows drawing together, reminding Reid of how he was often the most serious one on the team.

And the one Reid had more in common with. "I don't know. Seems sloppy, but one thing's for sure. He couldn't wear it while impersonating Santa."

Russ arched an eyebrow. "He could've planned to retrieve it when the party was over, and we prevented that from happening."

"Could be," Reid said. "No matter what, they need to consider it evidence and process it for DNA. Also the cap could be unique in some way, and we can trace it to where it was purchased."

"Sounds possible," Russ said. "FYI, the locals also processed the business card that Santa put in Jessie's pocket. They located one print and ran it against AFIS, but didn't return a match to Fowler. To anyone in the system. Not surprising as the Santa impersonator wore gloves."

Not at all what Reid expected. The Automated Fingerprint Identification System was a database managed by the FBI and held prints of most people who'd been incarcerated so Fowler's prints would be in the database.

"Prints could belong to the person who gave the card to Fowler," Jack said.

"Could be, but whoever it is, we don't have their ID." Russ frowned. "I also got Gleason to add Fowler's ball cap and the business card from Megan's house in the package going to Veritas for DNA processing. Prints didn't return a match to anyone on the system either, and I figured Veritas would get DNA results faster, and they would be more thorough too."

"Good thinking, bro," Reid said, though he had to admit disappointment that the cap didn't have Fowler's prints on it. Reid could understand the card, but if Fowler wore this cap on a regular basis, his prints should be on it.

"I get that not locating the guy's prints is a letdown, and we still have no concrete proof that Fowler is in the area," Russ said as if reading Reid's mind. "But I do have one other thing. One of the deputies I had canvassing the hospital area located a potential witness who has the incident on video."

"Way to bury the lead," Micha said.

Russ rolled his eyes. "The father caught the abductor hit Toby over the head outside his van when he was filming his wife putting their new baby into the car. The incident occurs in the background but it's far away and not clear. Also doesn't show the face of Santa's assailant, but I'll forward it to everyone. I've also informed the locals so they can follow up with him."

It might not be the lead Reid expected, but it was something. "You think I should interview him?"

Russ shook his head. "I talked to him on the phone, and he didn't see the attack. He was too focused on his wife, but she noticed it when he showed the video to her. Since he didn't see it, I honestly don't think it's worth your time, but you can be the judge of that after you review the video."

"Now that we know about the cap," Jack said. "We can watch for it in the video."

"Good thinking," Russ said, issuing one of the few hard-earned compliments he ever gave out. "Looked like he was wearing a cap, not sure of the color though."

"Get it to me ASAP," Reid said.

"Doing it right now." Russ looked down.

Reid told them about the key at Fowler's motel. "We think it's for a storage unit, and Russ is trying to run that down."

"Without any success so far," Russ said without looking up.

Reid had texted everyone earlier about the plan for Megan's transport but reviewed it now. "Any questions or anyone else have something to report?"

"No movement at the motel," Colin said, sounding bored.

"You ready for that break?" Ryan asked.

"I can hang in here if someone brings me some food." As if on cue, Colin's stomach grumbled. "See what I mean?"

"Not like that's anything new," Ryan said. "We need to call you Rolly from One Hundred and One Dalmatians."

"I'm hungry, Mother." Ryan's voice went high like a little kid's voice. "Really I am. I'm so hungry I could eat an elephant."

The team laughed at Ryan's impression of Rolly. Reid too. Laughing felt good and reminded him of times when he'd been able to joke with Megan to get her to lighten up. Likely Ryan's intent here. He was the team joker and often used humor to change the mood. Had always done so, even as a kid. Especially when Reid and Russ got into it, which was often in their teen years.

Reid's phone dinged with the text from Russ containing the video. "Micha, can you drop some food off for Colin?"

"I don't know, man, I've only got a regular-sized pickup, and I'm not sure it'll hold enough food for him." Micha laughed.

"Ha-ha." Colin grinned. "I'll text you my order."

"You got it."

"I should let you all know that I got tired of waiting for a warrant and spoke to the gas station manager," Jack said. "Figured I might be able to play on his sympathies. But he wouldn't give up the name of the gas station guy without a warrant, which I haven't yet been able to get. The Santa attack might help with my supervisor, and I'll go back to him. But so far, all of these incidents fall under local jurisdiction, and I don't know how successful I'll be."

"Man, I never thought I'd want the feds to interfere." Russ laughed.

"Russ, why don't you go flash a badge or one of us could hang at the station and question the other workers?" Micha asked.

Reid had thought of that, but... "I don't want to alert the friend that we're looking for him and send him underground. He was already skittish about going back to prison, and if he finds out law enforcement wants a word with him, we might never find him."

"Ah, right," Micha said. "Good point."

"Leave the friend with me," Russ said. "The locals now have an investigation open and seem eager. I'll ask the chief again to apply for that warrant for the gas station."

"Could we get the local PD to put out a BOLO for this guy now that we know what description to use?" Colin asked. "We could get lucky and someone will spot him and we won't need the friend."

A Be On The Lookout alert circulated on the local police radios might be their best opportunity to find Fowler.

"Already done," Russ said. "Chief Gleason took care of that and will notify me of any sightings."

"Thanks," Reid said. "Any other updates?"

"We could put out a plea to the media for anyone who was in the area of the hospital at the time of the attack," Dev suggested.

Russ gazed into the camera. "I'll get on the horn to Gleason the minute we're done and ask him about that. I'll also ask him to revisit the break-in at Megan's house and prioritize the forensics and get the stocking cap out of inventory and into evidence to be processed."

"Then let's get off this call so you can do that." Reid ended the meeting, thankful he had such a competent team. He'd never imagined when he hired the guys to handle training on survival skills that he would need their help in protecting someone, much less his daughter last year and Megan and Ella now.

He opened the video from Russ. Just as Russ had described, a woman loaded her newborn's car seat into the back of her car. In the distance over the vehicle's hood was a guy sneaking up on Santa behind his van, as Toby had described.

The camera caught the guy from behind, but Reid could clearly see he was wearing the blue stocking cap in question. Reid fired off a text to Russ.

Santa's attacker is wearing blue stocking cap in video. Make sure the locals prioritize it. Better yet, convince them to overnight it to Veritas.

On it.

Reid could get used to this ready compliance from his brother, but if it was because he felt bad due to Megan being in danger, then Reid would gladly have the argumentative brother he knew and loved.

Reid gave the text a thumbs-up emoji and cranked his

engine, then pointed his SUV for the hospital. Hopefully, his brother would text after his conversation with the chief. Reid wanted to know if this stocking cap was on its way to Veritas, where he hoped their experts would prove that Fowler was willing to attack an innocent man to exact his revenge on Megan.

15

Megan peered out the rear car window, the rural scenery flying past. Reid was driving her and Ella to his childhood home. Unbelievable. Visiting the place where he'd been raised seemed so intimate, and she didn't want to grow any closer to him.

She glanced at her sweet daughter sleeping in her booster seat next to her. Her chattering during the drive through the city had helped distract Megan, but as the wheels hummed along the pavement, Ella had drifted off to sleep. If only someone else had ridden in the car with them to diffuse the tension. But Micha had gone ahead to clear the route, and Russ followed at a distance in his official police vehicle, making sure no one tailed them.

She shifted into a comfortable position and sighed. This was entirely too long of a drive, and her mind kept betraying her. They had to almost be there.

"How much farther?" she asked.

Reid laughed. "You sound like Jessie on our road trips."

"Sorry. I rarely leave the city, so this seems like a long drive."

"Have you ever been out this way?" He lifted his gorgeous blue eyes to peer at her in his mirror.

She gazed out the window. "My family used to come out here on weekends when I was a kid."

"So you like the outdoors then?"

She stared out the window. "I suppose. Not that I've done a lot of outdoor things since Ella got sick."

"Jess and I like to hike, and we have a lot of great areas around here for that."

She kept her eyes on the scenery. The sun sank lower in the sky, sliding behind towering pines thickly lining the side of the road. Rushing river water tumbled downstream, and she could remember the sound as she'd trekked along it with her mom and dad as a child. Laughing, playing, they'd come home worn out and happy every time.

She smiled at the memory. "I'd forgotten how much fun we used to have out here when I was a kid."

"I love this place." His excited tone confirmed that. "Now that I've come home, I don't think I could live anywhere else. Even if it wasn't such a beautiful part of the country, I can't imagine ever being away from family again."

His life sounded idyllic. On the surface, of course. He'd suffered a great loss, but he seemed to have moved on. Something she could learn from him. Could she find more happiness while Ella remained ill? To make those moments she'd faked joy for Ella to actually be real?

What would it be like to live a normal life again? Maybe heading to a resort here for a fun weekend of hiking instead of rushing away from a stalker or sitting in a hospital as Ella fought for her life.

"Of course, our church family is here," he continued. "They would be hard to leave too."

She studied his face in the mirror. "All those times we talked during Fowler's trial when I told you my faith was the only thing that kept me going, and you said you were raised going to church but didn't ever attend then."

He frowned up in the mirror. "I didn't really live my faith then."

"But you do now. When did that change?"

"When Diane came into my life." He smiled as if the memory of his wife was a good one. "At first, I went to church with her to make her happy. But then I started listening, really listening, and God opened my eyes. When I think about it, I think He was preparing me to survive her loss."

"He could've let her live," Megan mumbled under her breath.

"What?" His gaze briefly met hers.

"Nothing." She turned to the window again.

Her mom called this part of Oregon "God's country." Megan could feel God's power and majesty here as she had as a child. Too bad that it was only here. Not in her everyday life or even when she went to church.

"Do you still go to church?" Reid asked.

"Yes, with my parents," she answered, happy he didn't ask if she still believed in God, because she didn't know how she would answer that question. If push came to shove, she would say she did, but these days she simply attended worship services for her parents and for Ella to experience it. She hadn't found the courage to tell her parents that she thought God had abandoned her.

"When did you say they'd be back from vacation?"

"The first of the year."

"I'm sure you'll be glad when they get home."

"Yeah," she answered, hoping he'd take a clue to her change to short answers and stop trying to continue the conversation she never should have started.

As she stared at the road, a longing to phone her mom and hear her reassurance that everything would be okay hit hard. But she couldn't ruin her parents' anniversary trip, and honestly, after everything that'd happened in her life the past few years, she wouldn't believe her mom anyway. Not after seeing that video of Fowler's vicious attack on Santa, bashing in his head with a tire iron.

She looked at Reid. "If only we could prove Fowler attacked Santa. It could lead to his arrest, and Ella and I would be okay for as long as he was in prison again."

"That might well happen. Russ said right before we left that he got the locals to overnight the stocking cap found in Santa's van to Veritas. If anyone can find DNA on it, they will." He drummed his fingers against the wheel. "And who knows, they might be able to enhance the video. While you were getting Ella ready, I sent it to their tech expert, Nick Thorn. He didn't hold out a lot of hope for that. Still, he's willing to try."

"I'm going to owe so many people after this is all resolved." *If* she lived to thank them, something only God could know.

"We're here." Reid pointed out the window to the left, but she couldn't see anything that slightly resembled a driveway.

He slowed and turned into an opening in the trees barely wide enough for a vehicle the size of his SUV. Rough gravel covered the driveway that wound down a hill to a heavy-duty metal gate where Micha leaned against his pickup parked off to the side. He gave a thumbs up, and Reid lowered his window to punch a code into a keypad posted on the fence. A latch released on the gate and it swung open.

What in the world was going on? "You didn't mention you lived in a fortress."

"A recent development thanks to the business. We had some issues with attendees of the survival camp getting radical and stealing weapons. When a couple of them found their way all the way over here, we secured the compound. That includes this place where Jessie and I live with our cook, Poppy."

"Sounds dangerous."

"You're not in any danger from the business. We put procedures in place and are more cautious about the people we allow into the camp." He took them down the drive into a clearing surrounded by majestic pines soaring toward the sky.

A big log lodge with a wide wraparound porch sat in the middle of the space. The sun hid firmly behind the trees. The darkness should've rekindled Megan's worry over Fowler, but warm beams of light filtered from windows, and white lights twinkled on garland wrapped around the porch railing, giving her a feeling of coming home. Two thick pines covered in multicolored Christmas lights sat at the end of the walkway. The whole scene seemed like a Christmas movie set in Hollywood. The only thing that could add to the ambiance would be a dusting of snow, which the weather forecast hinted at in the coming days.

Reid parked his SUV in front of a three-car garage. Russ came to a stop right behind them.

"Stay here." Reid fired off a warning look and then climbed from the car.

Russ got out and met Reid near Megan's door. They spoke in low tones, but she could still hear everything they said. Russ confirmed that Fowler hadn't followed them, and the mere mention of the creep's name sent her warm feelings fleeing.

Reid directed Russ to sweep the lodge, and his brother headed up the stairs to the porch without question. Reid stood sentry outside her door until Russ stepped out and gave a brisk nod. He remained on the porch, and Reid opened her car door.

"We're good to go." He focused on Ella. "I'll carry her in."

"I can get her." Megan's words drifted into the air, as Reid had already run around the car.

He opened the door, and Ella stirred and rubbed her eyes.

"Are we here?" Excitement bubbled up in her sleepy voice.

"That we are, little one." Reid unhooked her seat belt. "How about I carry you since you're not all the way awake?"

Ella lifted her arms and gazed at him with the same adoration she'd once offered to her father.

The last thing Megan needed was for Ella to form an attachment to another man who'd proved he wouldn't be around for the long haul.

Hoping to take Ella from him, Megan climbed out of the car.

"You go first," Reid said.

"I'll take Ella." She held out her arms.

"No, Mommy," Ella whined. "I can see so much more from up here."

Megan didn't want to make a scene, so she set off, clenching her jaw as she went. She entered the family room, Reid's footsteps right behind her. Ella squealed with delight, and Megan turned to catch the joy on her daughter's face.

She wiggled out of Reid's arms. "Bandit!" she called out.

The excited little dog jumped from an over-stuffed leather sofa in front of a floor-to-ceiling stone fireplace. He trotted to Ella, stopping to sniff a ten-foot or higher spruce tree in the corner waiting for Christmas decorations.

Jessie stood from a matching chair, a book in her hand and an expectant gaze fixed on the door.

"Where's Syd?" Russ asked.

"Upstairs," Jessie said and peeked around him toward Reid as Russ charged up the rustic steps.

"Hey, Bug." Reid flashed his daughter a joyous grin.

She raced across the room and threw her arms around him. "I missed you last night."

"I missed you too." He ruffled her hair then bent to kiss the top of her head.

Why couldn't Orrin have been a father like Reid seemed to be? These two were so connected that it made Megan's heart ache for Ella. As much as this home seemed wonderful and welcoming, they were outsiders here.

Before tears started to fall over everything Ella had lost in her life, Megan turned away to study the room and inhale a savory aroma coming from the open kitchen behind her. Windows filled the entire front wall, and stairs led to a balcony overlooking the room. A massive island surrounded by wrought-iron bar stools separated the kitchen from the large two-story family room.

She could almost see Reid's family as he grew up sitting by a roaring fire, sipping cocoa, and playing games as she'd done with her family. Of course, she was an only child. With three boys, this place probably saw a lot of rough play.

She turned to the kitchen giving off the same homey vibe as the family room. A slow cooker sat on the granite countertop, likely the source of the mouthwatering scent kicking up an appetite that had been missing since she'd spotted Fowler yesterday.

Fowler. Everything was nice and pleasant for once. Why'd she have to think about him?

Voices drifted from upstairs. Russ and Sydney, arm in arm, came across the balcony and headed down the stairs. Of course Russ had immediately gone in search of his wife. That's what a man in love did.

Jessie slipped away from Reid and crossed over to Ella and Bandit. "Wanna play Barbies before dinner?"

"Can Bandit come with us?" Ella asked.

"Sure," Jessie said. "C'mon."

Ella looked up. "Is it okay, Mom?"

"Of course. Take it easy, okay?"

"'K." Ella followed Jessie into a hallway on the far side of the room.

Sydney and Russ reached the first floor and strolled arm-in-arm across the wide plank floor. Up close, the unease in their expressions contradicted their relaxed posture. In love or not, they were fully aware of the danger. These law enforcement professionals wouldn't let their guard down. No matter where they were. No matter if Megan felt safe or not.

They were there for her.

Russ released Sydney and stepped closer to Megan. "I got a call from Chief Gleason on my way here. He put out a public plea for anyone who was in the area during the hospital attack."

"That's good news," Megan said.

Russ nodded. "If you'll provide a key, he'll also have his forensic team go to your house to do a more thorough job. You can give it to me, and I'll make sure he gets it."

She took out the spare she hid in a secret pocket in her purse in case she misplaced her key ring. "Thank you, Russ. For this and for getting that stocking cap sent to Veritas."

"Glad to help." He pocketed the key.

Sydney patted his shoulder. "That's my guy. Helpful. Except when it comes time to doing dishes. Then he makes himself scarce."

Sydney laughed, and Russ joined in. Megan got the feeling he didn't laugh easily, she liked seeing him relax.

Reid pointed at the door. "We should bring in the bags before it's completely dark out."

Russ didn't question but fell into step with his brother on the way to the door.

Megan tracked their exit. Confident. Strong, capable men. Caring and warm. Willing to share their family home. Christmas week, and they were probably busier than usual, yet they put their lives on hold for her and Ella.

"How about a cup of tea?" Sydney headed for the open kitchen.

"That would be great." Megan followed her and took a seat at the counter. "Are you responsible for this wonderful aroma?"

"Poppy—Reid's cook—and Jessie made stew for you guys. Poppy left to stay with her sister for a few days due to Fowler's threats."

Another person affected by this man. "I hate that we displaced her."

Sydney glanced toward the door and then leaned closer. "Between you and me, she was reluctant to go. She feels a huge responsibility to Reid and Jessie since Diane died. But I assured her that you and I could make sure Reid and Jessie were fed. Of course, she's much more than a cook. Like a family member really. She's been working for the family since the Maddox boys were kids."

"Sounds like quite the woman. Too bad I didn't meet her."

"You could if you stayed around." Sydney winked and slid a tea basket across the island. "Choose whatever you want." She went to the stove and poured steaming water from the kettle into two mugs.

Megan pulled out a green tea packet. "You seem right at home here."

"Hard to believe it's been such a short time since Russ

and I reconnected." She turned with the mugs. "In fact, our first kiss was down the hall. I'll share that story someday."

Not likely. Megan liked Sydney and liked the thought of knowing her in the future. But once Fowler was out of the picture, Megan doubted she would be friends with Reid's sister-in-law.

"You look worried." Sydney put her tea bag in the mug. "Russ is sure Fowler didn't follow you here. You're safe."

Megan could point out their earlier worried expressions but decided to keep it to herself. "I don't know how I can ever repay you." Megan took a sip of her tea.

"No need for that." Sydney got a glint in her eye. "Of course, you could consider dating Reid. That would be the best payment ever."

Megan choked on her tea and coughed to clear her throat.

"Why so surprised? Russ said there's something going on between you and Reid."

"Well, Russ is wrong. There was something. Once. A long time ago. But there will never be anything between us again." The vehemence of her tone shocked her.

Instead of responding to Megan, Sydney peered over Megan's shoulder. Megan followed Sydney's gaze.

Reid and Russ stood in the doorway. Thunder darkened Reid's face. Okay, so he'd heard what she'd said.

Good. She hated to be so stern with him. Wished she could take it back. Apologize. But if he was mad at her, she would no longer need to find a way to fight off the feelings for him that seemed to swamp her good intentions.

16

After dinner, Reid held his cell in hand, a text from his buddy, Jack, waiting for a return call. Reid had been antsy to call since the text had come in during their meal of savory stew and buttery homemade rolls. He'd ignored it to have a pleasant meal with the others. He hoped Jack had texted to say he'd gotten his supervisor to approve a safe house for Megan and Ella or obtained a warrant for the employee names from the gas station or for the bar's video. None of which Reid expected because nothing had changed in the probable cause arena, but he had to hope for something.

He headed outside for privacy from Jessie, Megan, and Ella still sitting at the dining table. They'd had a wonderful time at dinner, and Reid didn't want it to end. Especially not the conversation and family atmosphere that'd been missing in his life since Diane's death.

Not that this thing with Megan was going anywhere. She'd made that perfectly—vehemently—clear in her statement to Sydney. It had taken him a few hours to come to grips with the rejection, but if pressed, he would've said the same thing. With Diane's loss still weighing him down, he wasn't free to pursue Megan. Once they apprehended Fowler, he and Megan would go their separate ways.

End of story.

A blustery cold wind whipped in Reid's face and moisture dampened the night air. His breath whispered through the air in white puffs as he tapped Jack's phone number. Reid wouldn't be surprised if the predicted snow *did* fall this week. A fantastic thing with Christmas coming up.

He pulled his jacket tighter and made the call. "You wanted to talk."

"You're not going to like this," Jack said.

Of course it wasn't going to be the good news Reid had hoped for. "What's up?"

"Fowler's gone missing."

Reid sucked in a breath of the crisp air. "What do you mean missing?"

"He was supposed to check in with his probation officer today, but he never showed up."

"Did they send someone out to follow up with him?"

"No. He's starting with a phone call, text, and email. If that fails, they'll call his employer. Then they'll stop by his place. The last resort is to check with known associates. If they still don't find him, they'll issue a warrant for his arrest."

"You're right. I don't like it at all." Reid paused and stared into the dark sky. "He's not at his motel and hasn't shown the whole time Colin's been on duty. I don't like not knowing where he is."

"Sorry for the bad news, but I thought you should know he's not likely in Portland."

"I appreciate it. Not that I think he's at the lodge. I'm certain he didn't follow us."

"Doesn't mean he can't find you, though."

"How?"

"He could remember you from the trial and if he was watching the hospital, saw Megan leave with you. A quick internet search and he could discover that you manage Shadow Lake Survival."

"Even if he did figure that out, we're staying at the lodge. It has no tie to the business." The business was housed on land where his father had run the resort, but his dad had legally separated the resort from the lodge. Fowler wouldn't be able to find any official records to connect the two and lead him to them.

"But the locals know, right?" Jack asked. "He could come to town and chat one of them up. Maybe at a gas station."

Someone like Gladys Miller. The local gas station owner was a real busybody. She'd be glad to share any piece of information she could if the person asking flattered her enough.

"It's possible," Reid admitted reluctantly. He didn't want to think he hadn't done his due diligence and let Fowler find him so easily. Still, he couldn't take any chances and needed help.

Reid thanked Jack and disconnected. He tapped Russ's icon. "You and Sydney wouldn't want to form a protection detail tonight, would you?"

"Fowler figure out where you are?" Russ sounded sleepy.

"I don't think so, but he failed to check in with his probation officer today. Means he's likely still in our area, and it's got me a little spooked. Figured it wouldn't hurt to take a few precautions."

Russ snorted. "Says the guy who gets to spend the coldest night of the year inside."

"C'mon, bro. You'll have Sydney next to you to keep you warm."

"Let me check with her."

Reid heard him asking if she wanted to join him and her quick reply that she'd be happy to do it.

"We'll be over in a few minutes." Russ disconnected.

Reid stowed his phone and walked the porch, gazing into the area surrounding the house. His hand automatically drifted to his gun but found it missing. Jessie's comment about him carrying again had him returning it to his gun safe. He would retrieve it the moment she went to bed.

Confident no one lurked outside, he went in and hung up his jacket.

Ella sat on the sofa. Her eyes were droopy and a big book rested on her lap. Jessie and Megan were in the kitchen chatting like old friends and doing the dishes. *Wow. Just wow.* His daughter was acting like Megan was her new best friend. What a change. Jessie hadn't been able to enjoy life this freely since her mother died.

Megan gazed at him, her eyes narrowed. "Everything okay?"

Jessie's head shot up, and she rubbed her hands on her pant legs.

"Everything's fine." He smiled and headed toward the kitchen. "You want help with the dishes?"

"Sure," Megan answered.

"No, don't let him help." Jessie planted her feet. "He stacks the dishwasher wrong, and the dishes don't get clean."

Megan's smile vanished, and her face took on a mock seriousness. "In that case, I think you better go entertain Ella."

Jessie gave a thumbs-up. "That's a good job for him. He's good with kids."

She was so serious and grown up for her age that it

177

made Reid's heart ache as he headed for the sofa. He sat next to Ella. "What are you reading?"

"It's about Christmas." She lifted the book to display the cover of one of Jessie's favorite Christmas stories. "Will you read it to me?"

"Sure."

She handed the book to him and scooted close. He slipped his arm around her shoulders and started the story of Jesus's birth. As he read, Ella's eyes grew heavier with each page. Before he reached the end, she slid down on the sofa and laid her head on his knee. He stopped reading and studied her. The cute little face was so relaxed in sleep, but the ravages of her illness clung to her like a dark cloud.

He closed the book and set it on the table. Jessie had often fallen asleep to this story, and he'd sat softly stroking her hair until Diane would pick her up, and together, they'd put her to bed. The memories gnawed at him. He'd missed this family atmosphere these past few years.

He glanced at the kitchen where Megan watched him. She had a tender smile for him, her face filled with a longing that must match the feelings permeating him.

"See," Jessie said. "I told you he's good with kids."

Megan crossed the room, seeming to shake off whatever emotions she'd transmitted. "I'll put her to bed."

"Let me carry her for you." Reid got up before Megan protested.

"Bandit's too quiet in there, and I'm going to check on him." Jessie headed down the hall toward the den.

Reid climbed the stairs, and Megan followed him. He could feel her eyes burning into his back. Maybe she didn't want him helping her with Ella. Maybe it reminded her of Ella's absent father, a subject that piqued Reid's curiosity.

He stepped into his former bedroom, the one Megan

and Ella were sharing, and flipped on the light switch with his elbow. "You never said if Orrin spends time with Ella."

Megan went to her suitcase and dug in it, as if ignoring him. "No, I didn't."

"You don't want to talk about him," Reid said, though it was obvious the subject was off-limits.

"No." She pulled out a pair of pink footie pajamas.

"Is this about Orrin or about our past?"

She turned and locked gazes with him, her eyes sincere. "I'm not mad about what happened between us anymore. I've forgiven you and totally let it go now."

He stopped mid-step. "When did that change?"

"I don't know. I guess earlier today, I realized that we didn't ever really discuss a future together." She paused and shook out the pajamas. "You never promised me anything. So how could I be mad at you?"

He made strong eye contact. "You shouldn't let me off so easy. You know as well as I do that we had something together, and when I left, I hurt you."

She shrugged. "It's in the past. Let's forget it and not talk about it anymore. Okay?"

"How can I forget about it? Every time I look in your eyes, I see how much I hurt you."

"I'm fine, Reid. Really, I am." She swiveled and pressed out wrinkles in the pajamas.

He moved closer, bending low and forcing her to face him. "I heard the way you told Sydney there could never be anything between us again. You sounded angry—maybe hurt—but definitely not fine."

"You're reading too much into it. I'm not upset anymore. When I first saw you at the hospital, I was still mad, but you've changed that by being here when we needed you. I've forgiven you for everything that happened and want to move past it." Her words rang sincere.

179

The heavy weight he'd been carrying all these years lifted from his shoulders, but he could tell she was still holding something from him. "Despite what you say, I didn't mistake your tone with Sydney."

She shrugged. "Maybe I came across as mad, but I didn't want Sydney or Russ to get their hopes up when the only reason you and I are together right now is because of Fowler." She held out the pajamas. "Now if you don't mind, I need to get Ella to bed."

End of conversation, just like that, and he would honor her wishes. He laid Ella on the bed as gently as possible, but her eyes blinked open. She focused on him and smiled. The tiny eyes surrounded with dark circles in a gaunt face met his. *Oh, man.* A stab of pain ripped into his chest.

She lifted her little hands and placed them on his face. "I just wanted to see if I was dreaming."

Megan came closer with the pajamas. "Time to get ready for bed, sweetie."

Reid moved away.

"Wait." Ella grabbed his hand. "Will you be here when I wake up?"

"Yes."

"Good." A soft smile lit her face.

A connection that he didn't want to feel drew him to plant a soft kiss on her forehead. No. He didn't want to feel that. Not at all. He focused on not transmitting his horror at his feelings and backed toward the door.

"I like him, Mommy," Ella said before he left the room. "He read to me tonight. Did you see that, Mommy?"

Ella's excitement danced in the air like a promise or wish.

"I did." Megan's words came out in a flat tone. So flat her opinion on the comment was clear. Crystal.

"Daddy was always too busy to read to me. Even at the hospital."

Reid stopped outside the door and rested his head against the wall. What kind of man was always too busy to read to his child? Especially a child who was as sick as Ella. If Reid ever ran into this guy, he didn't think he could keep a civil tongue. But it was none of his business, so he softly pulled the door closed. Closed down his heart too. For everyone but Jessie and his family.

He jogged down the stairs. Some might say ran, but he had to get away from the precious little girl. Away from any emotions forming for a sick child.

Russ and Sydney glanced at him from the sofa.

Reid hurried over to them. "Thanks for coming."

"Anything we need to know before our night of frost-bite?" Russ asked.

"Turn the heater on in the car?" Reid joked to keep them from seeing his anger over the abandonment by Ella's father. Or maybe the way he still cared about Megan and was coming to care for Ella too.

"I'm serious," Russ snapped.

"Relax." Sydney laid her hand on Russ's arm.

Reid could see the touch instantly calm him. She'd been so good for Russ. Changed his life in so many positive ways. Reid was jealous of what his little brother had with Sydney.

He heard Megan coming down the stairs behind him and turned. She descended toward him. This was the woman who'd just sat across the table from him. Who warmed the room with her smile. Who bonded with his daughter and made her feel important. Desire for the same family dynamic he'd had before ached in his gut.

Would Megan be as good for him as Sydney had been for Russ? Or would he only be setting himself up for disappointment and hurt?

Not something he should even ponder. Not only couldn't he survive the unknown of a loved one with cancer, but it wouldn't be right to put Jessie through such pain again. And no matter his renewed interest in Megan, he wouldn't risk connecting with her and then bailing again. That wouldn't be right. Not at all. Especially after her husband had done that. And with a sick child. Reid would be the lowest of low if he treated her that way.

"I didn't know you were coming over." She directed her gaze at Sydney, who didn't respond but cast a questioning look at Reid.

"Jack called to say Fowler's gone AWOL." Reid tried to keep his tone free from any anxiety.

"And you think he found us?" She flashed her worried gaze to the windows.

"No," Reid said. "But I don't want to take any chances, so Russ and Syd will stand guard outside tonight."

"Is this really necessary? I hate to think of the two of you outside in the cold."

"Not necessary, but Reid is right," Russ said. "Better safe than sorry." Russ tugged Sydney to her feet. "See you all in the morning."

"Anything happens, call my cell." Reid followed them to the door. "You have your key in case you need to get in, right?"

"Got it."

Reid locked the door behind them and checked the clock.

"I need to get Jess off to bed," he said to Megan, who'd wandered over to the fireplace. "I'll be right back." He went to the den. His daughter, nose buried in a book as usual, was curled in a large chair.

"Bedtime, Jess," he said.

"Aw." She held up a finger. "Just a few more minutes?" She tried this every night.

"Sorry. You need to stick to your schedule so you're not tired out for Christmas."

"Okay." She placed her bookmark and stood. Reid wrapped his arm around her shoulders, and they strolled down the hallway.

"Want me to tuck you in?" he asked when they reached the stairs.

She rolled her eyes. "I'm not a little kid like Ella, Dad."

He almost laughed as Ella was only two years younger. "Too big for a kiss and hug too?"

She groaned and wrapped her arms around him, then looked up for a kiss. He expected her to head straight upstairs, but she went over to Megan.

"It's fun having you and Ella here," Jessie said.

Megan's fingers touched her parted lips. "Thank you."

"Will you be here tomorrow night too?"

"I'm not sure."

"Hope so." Jessie suddenly seemed shy.

"Me too." Megan reached out and tucked a stray strand of hair behind Jessie's ear. His daughter flashed a satisfied smile. She enjoyed the touch. She really missed a woman in the house. So did he.

Jessie gave Megan an awkward hug then charged up the stairs with Bandit trailing behind.

"Night, Dad," she called on the way, a happiness in her tone that Reid hadn't heard much the past few years.

Reid glanced at Megan. She still seemed surprised, but he saw a hint of the same desire for a family lingered in her expression. Or maybe she was simply longing for a healthy child who could race up the steps as Jessie had. Either way, this was not heading in the right direction, and he needed space to think.

"Make yourself at home," he said. "I'll be right back." He took off for the den to retrieve his gun. Okay, maybe to get away from his thoughts too.

But as he unlocked the gun safe, his mind raced with possibilities. He seated an ammo clip and put the holster on his belt. He almost wished Fowler would come there tonight so they could put an end to his stalking before he and Jessie both became too fond of Megan and Ella.

But he really didn't think Fowler knew where they were, and Megan could be staying here for several days before they apprehended Fowler. Not good for Jessie. Reid's best bet was to have her stay with his parents in town for the duration so she didn't become attached. Jessie loved her grandparents and it would be no hardship for her, but she would likely be mad at Reid as she wanted to stay with Megan and Ella. So what? He would always do what was best for Jessie, even if she got mad at him for it.

Resolved to call his mom tomorrow if needed, Reid closed the gun safe and hurried to the family room.

Megan gazed at a large family portrait hanging above the fireplace. He waited for her to acknowledge him, but she must not have seen him enter the room. He should clear his throat. Let her know he was there. Instead he enjoyed seeing the firelight skip over her face.

How odd it was to have Megan staring at Diane. That particular photo had been taken the Christmas before Diane got sick and was the last family picture of her looking vibrant and healthy.

An ache crept into his heart again. He shook it off and dug deep for the strength to clear his throat.

She turned to him, her expression puzzled. "How did you handle it?"

"Handle what?"

"Losing your wife."

He caught an edge in her voice that hadn't been there since they'd arrived at the lodge. Something flickered in her eyes at a depth that he'd never seen before. Fear. Not fear for her life—fear for Ella.

"You don't really want to talk about this." He approached her. "Ella is going to be fine."

Her whole body stiffened. Was she worried? Fearful?

He stopped closer to her than was good for either of them. "What brought this on?"

"I don't know. Maybe it's spending time with Jessie and seeing how healthy she is. Or maybe it's Fowler." She shook her head. "It just seems like Ella and I can't get a break when all we want is a normal life." She clutched her hands.

He understood. More than she could know. He'd lived with desperation, and he hated to see her suffer.

Ignoring warning bells clanging in his head, he took her hand and twined his fingers through hers. "You really want to know how I handled losing Diane?" He peered into her distraught eyes.

She gave an almost imperceptible nod.

"I had to keep things together for Jessie the same way I've seen you do with Ella. But inside, I was a wreck. I thought it was so unfair. That God was punishing me for something. It took months before God could get through and let me see He didn't hate me or have it out for me."

"Talk about role reversals. I remember telling you about my faith and you humoring me. Now you're the one who's truly living your faith again."

His turn for surprise. "Are you saying you don't?"

She shrugged. "I don't know. I guess I still believe, but everything's falling apart around me, and God's letting it. I can't see Him in my life anymore."

"He's still there. You just have to look for Him."

She tugged her hand away. "I want to believe that, but I can't."

"If we talk about it, maybe I can help."

She stared at the floor and massaged her neck. "I don't know if you can."

He crooked a finger under her chin to tip her head up. "I'd like to try. If you'll let me."

Trust flickered in her expression for a moment before she looked away. "What do you want to say?"

Her brief second of renewed trust in him put a lump in his throat, and he swallowed hard before going on. "When's the last time you remember feeling like God cared about you?"

"I don't know." She shook her head. "I guess I started to question His presence after Ella got sick and Orrin left."

"Tell me about it."

"There's not much to say. It was hard—really hard. I didn't know if Ella was going to make it after her first surgery, and I had no one I could count on to be there for us."

"What about your parents?"

"Well, yeah, they were there, but it's not the same as having the father of your child with you." Tears formed in her eyes. "Imagine if Jessie got sick and you had to carry the burden all alone."

"Having Jessie abducted gave me a glimpse of your struggle, and I know the fear of losing a child has to be almost unbearable for you." He rested a hand on her shoulder.

She shook her head. "Look at me—going on and on about my fears when you actually had to get through the pain of losing your wife." She stepped away from him as if his loss diminished her fear.

He followed her. "Don't shut down like that. Sure I lost

186

my wife, but your fear is still very real, and I'd like to help you see how God can bring you through it."

"I don't think anything you can say will help." Her voice was tiny and weak, as if she'd given up. "And I'm too tired to talk." Her shoulders drooped.

He needed to let this go for another day, but he wouldn't end on a down note. He had to leave her with hope. "Just promise me you'll try to remember what your life was like when God was a part of it. When you could leave all of your problems with Him. Can you do that?"

She held his gaze for a long moment, then gave a brief nod and turned to stare into the fire.

Tonight's conversation was a good start, but he wouldn't give up. With Fowler in the wind and Ella's illness, Megan needed to believe God was beside her. Reid could help her work through her struggles and find her way to God again.

Even if it meant losing his heart in the process.

17

Reid sat on a stiff sofa in the waiting area outside Dr. Browne's office located in the hospital. Ella had blood drawn when they'd first arrived that morning, and a rush order was given to the hospital lab for processing. The moment the results were in, Megan and Ella had gone into the exam room to meet with the doctor. Thirty minutes ago. Long, ticking slowly past, anxious minutes. Reid didn't know how Megan was staying as strong as she was without her faith. He was uneasy and sweaty and would be a wreck in her position.

His phone rang. He lurched.

Calm down, man.

Jack's name popped on caller ID, and Reid quickly answered.

"You're not going to believe this." Jack's voice rose with each word.

Reid could think of only one thing that might be surprising. "You arrested Fowler?"

"No, but he called his probation officer an hour ago. Surprise. Surprise. Said he missed the appointment because he was home sick, and he would check in tomorrow."

"You trace the call?"

"Number's for a burner phone, but we don't have probable cause to have the signal triangulated."

"Of course he would be smart enough to use an untraceable phone." Reid gritted his teeth. He hated that people could buy prepaid phones without providing contact information, and they were virtually untraceable, often with the intent of committing a crime. "I know he's not at the motel. Colin confirmed that not more than ten minutes ago. So we still don't know where he is."

"He could be with his gas station friend."

"You get that warrant yet?"

"I tried again, but nothing's changed, and Kade's still a no-go."

Reid expected that answer, but he was getting desperate. Jack's supervisor, Oliver Kade, who served as Assistant Special Agent in charge of the FBI's Portland Field office, wasn't an easy guy to deal with. Reid had worked under Kade for only six months before leaving the FBI, but had learned from day one that he was a tough guy who made his agents jump through hoops. Seemed like he was doing the same thing with Jack right now.

"Fowler going AWOL could help with that," Reid said.

"How? We don't have an official investigation open yet. Kade still won't go for it." Jack let out a long breath. "Everything else going okay on your end?"

Was it? Reid didn't know. Megan had kept him at arm's length all morning. Maybe she was afraid he would pressure her on her faith. Or maybe she didn't want to deal with him.

"Reid?" Jack pressed.

"As well as can be expected," Reid answered truthfully, as he didn't expect much.

"Something I can help with?"

Reid wasn't about to share the struggle his feelings for

Megan were causing. "Nada. Just keep me updated on Fowler's whereabouts and any new developments with the local PD."

Reid disconnected and let out a long breath. He stood and paced the small area.

Then Megan and Ella stepped out of the doctor's exam room, and Megan flashed him a big smile. Ah, good. The appointment had gone well. They would be returning to the lodge instead of Ella being admitted again.

He met them on the far side of the waiting area.

Ella smiled at Reid and slipped her hand into his. "I don't have to stay."

Megan reached out as if to pull Ella free, but instead she let her hand fall to her side.

Reid didn't like Megan's response, but he wouldn't let Ella see that. He flashed her an enthusiastic smile. "Then we'll be heading to the lodge."

"Yay." Ella swung Reid's hand. "I get to play with Bandit and Jessie."

"Sorry, Ella," Reid said. "But Jessie's staying with her grandparents. She'll likely want to take Bandit with her too."

Ella's chin wobbled. Guilt from causing the child's sadness washed over Reid, but he wouldn't second-guess his decision about what was good for his daughter.

"We can have fun on our own." Megan put on a smile for her daughter. "We should get going."

"Let me confirm Micha's waiting at the exit." Reid dialed his teammate and lifted his phone to his ear.

There'd been no sign of Fowler so far, but Reid wasn't taking any chances and had Micha accompany them to the hospital. With Fowler's brazen behavior, Reid wouldn't be surprised if he was nearby, watching and waiting.

"Everything okay on your end?" he asked when Micha answered.

"Dull as can be."

"Stay alert. We're on our way." Reid ended the call and opened the hallway door. "Let's go."

He tried to release Ella's hand, but she clung to him, so he waited for Megan to exit then followed. He and Ella walked down the hallway hand in hand. Megan stayed close to Ella's other side as if she feared what or who they might encounter. He didn't let the warm little hand clutching his distract him from surveying the area as they walked.

At the parking garage entrance, Reid nodded at Micha and then made eye contact with Megan. "You two wait here while I bring my SUV around." And check things out, he didn't add to keep them from worrying.

Megan didn't have to be told anything to worry about. She knew the risks and a quick shiver told him as much. She shook it off and took Ella's hand.

He narrowed his eyes to warn Micha. "Stay vigilant."

Micha planted his feet wide, and his hand drifted to the butt of his weapon.

Reid went into the garage, moving at a slow pace through the dimly lit area, checking between and under cars. The only person present, his footsteps echoed off the thick concrete walls.

His internal alarm sounded loudly for some reason. He stopped to search every inch of the garage. Visually nothing appeared out of the ordinary. But with Megan's and Ella's lives on the line, he would take no shortcuts.

None.

He set off again and took his time approaching his SUV to make a thorough search. He scanned and rescanned the shadows clinging to the walls and near the stairwell. Over each car. Truck. SUV.

He reached his SUV and gave the exterior a thorough check, including dropping to the ground and examining the underside with a flashlight. Convinced Fowler hadn't planted a bomb underneath, Reid jumped to his feet and opened the door to release the hood for a similar inspection.

As he leaned in, he came up short, and hissed out a breath.

A large white calendar sat on the passenger seat. A thick red circle ringed tomorrow's date, and someone had scrawled large block letters above it.

Your day of reckoning has come. $500,000 will keep you and your child alive. Be ready to meet me with the money.

Of course. Why hadn't Reid thought of that earlier? Tomorrow was the anniversary of the bank robbery. Made sense that Fowler would choose the anniversary to exact his revenge. And with the calendar in Reid's car, Fowler proved that he knew Megan and Reid were still connected.

Reid dug out his phone and quickly updated Jack on the recent development. "We have a direct threat on top of everything else. If this isn't cause for your office to get off the fence and get on board, I don't know what is."

"I agree. Blackmail is a federal crime, and we now have jurisdiction to get involved." Jack's assurance meant the world to Reid right now. "You think the lodge has been compromised?"

Did he? "I doubt it. Russ and Sydney were certain no one was on site last night, and I'm positive he didn't follow us here this morning. He must've been watching the hospital and caught our arrival."

"So he knows you're transporting Megan."

"I'll need to go to plan B. Let me know the minute you have Kade's verdict, and we can make that plan together." Reid stowed his phone.

For now, he had to move Megan to a more secure location and tell her about the calendar. But how did he do that without scaring her more? He would have to play it by ear.

He headed toward the building, eyeing anything and anyone that moved.

On the bright side, the blackmail could actually be good news. If the Bureau got involved, Fowler might freak out and back off.

Reid entered the lobby, and as he ran a hand through his hair to right strands the wind had blown astray, he caught sight of Megan's wary gaze. His heart ached with concern for her—and maybe more than concern.

If the FBI did get involved, they would expect him to leave her in their care. Could he do that? Step away? Resume his life?

No. No way. No matter how many agents worked this case, he wouldn't back off for one second. She was starting to mean too much to him, and he always took care of the people he cared about.

No matter the cost.

~

Chaos. Inside and out. Squad car lights twirling. Uniformed police officers. FBI agents. All scurried around the parking deck as Megan peered out the window of the lounge. Their response was greater than for the fake bomb.

Ella sat unaware in the closed-off lounge, eating a peanut butter sandwich Reid had gotten from the cafeteria and watching a Christmas program on Megan's phone to distract her.

They should all be sitting down to lunch at the lodge right now, but Fowler had taken care of that plan. Not that she could eat a bite with the nausea unsettling her stomach.

She sensed someone's presence at the door and turned. Reid was staring at her. How long he'd been standing there, she didn't know.

"Hey." He crossed the room.

Ella lifted her face to him, eyes bright with excitement. "Are we ready to go home now, Mr. Reid?"

"Not quite yet," Reid answered and drew Megan out of Ella's hearing range.

He shoved his hands in his pockets. "I won't be taking you to the lodge. Jack will."

"Why? What's going on?"

He pulled out a hand and held it up. "Nothing to be concerned about. We've just decided it would be better for Jack to drive you and for me to act as a decoy in case Fowler's watching."

"But you all said you didn't think he would be here with all the law enforcement presence."

"We don't, but there's always a possibility he is, and we don't want him to find out where you're staying."

She didn't like this plan. "But he'll see that I'm not with you."

"Jack arranged for a female agent to stand in for you. Her name is Lauren Nickels, and she looks enough like you that from a distance it should confuse Fowler."

"And what about you? Will you still be coming to the lodge?" Man, she sounded desperate. Totally and completely desperate. As if she could no longer take care of herself. She didn't want to depend on Reid, but she clearly had come to need him.

"Of course I'll be there," he said without hesitating. "Lauren and I'll take a circuitous route. Once we're certain he's not tailing us, we'll head to the lodge."

Megan let out a thankful sigh. What if she'd never run into Reid at the hospital? She would be dealing with Fowler all on her own. The man, as angry as a rabid dog, would've placed his latest demand in her car, and she would've found the note and been left to deal with it on her own.

A shiver started at her head and wormed its way down her body.

"Hey, it's okay." Reid cupped the side of her face. "Fowler asking for money is a good thing. It tells us what he's really after." He stroked a thumb along her jawline, and another shiver raced over her skin.

He moved closer, and the mere proximity sent a new sensation through her body. She moved away before she did or said something foolish.

He arched an eyebrow. He'd clearly noticed her evasive move. So what? It was good for him to know she was fighting her feelings for him.

"With the Bureau involved now, this will all end soon," he said.

She reached for her phone. "I better get my accountant started on securing the cash."

"No. Don't." He flashed up a hand again. "I get that you want to pay Fowler off, but giving him money isn't the answer. He'll only come back for more."

How could Reid balk at this? "That's better than what he'd do to Ella if I don't give him anything. I'm not willing to take a chance with her life."

"We won't let anything happen to her."

She stared straight into his eyes. "You keep saying that, but Fowler keeps getting too close. I can't risk another encounter."

"Pay Fowler or not, a man like him won't stop until we put him behind bars. Give us the chance to do that."

"I just don't know what to do anymore." She clamped a hand on her neck and rubbed stiff muscles.

He continued to eye her and even intensified his gaze. "Trust me in this. I know what I'm doing."

She peered at him, and the warmth and sincerity of his expression made her want to do anything he asked of her, but maybe she was thinking with her heart, not her brain. "I don't know."

He rested his hands on her shoulders. "It's the right thing to do. I promise."

"Okay," she said, but she wasn't sure she was doing the right thing at all.

She would trust him. For now. But if the slightest thing happened where she feared harm would come to Ella, Megan would hand over the cash. Money she could replace. She could never replace her daughter.

"Jack's here." Reid tipped his head at the door. "The police are still processing my vehicle so I've arranged for a rental car, and I'll head out with Lauren."

"Are you sure we can't go with you?" The words came out before she could stop them.

Get a grip, Megan. Quit acting so desperate.

He didn't seem bothered by her neediness. "Jack will make sure you're safe." He gave her a sweet smile. "I'll get Ella."

He went to the sofa and held out his hand. "Ready to go?"

She jumped up and slipped her hand in his.

"My friend, Jack, is going to give you a ride," Reid said.

Her eyes narrowed, and Megan knew her daughter didn't want Jack driving them any more than she did, but she'd already sounded like a woman who couldn't survive without Reid's protection, so she bit her tongue and trudged along next to him down to a secured service area Fowler wouldn't have access to.

Reid scooped Ella into his arms for a hug, then set her down and knelt in front of her. "See you soon. Listen to your mom and Jack, okay?"

"Okay."

He nodded at Megan, and she took Ella to the car to

settle her in her booster seat. Megan climbed in next to her daughter.

Jack remained parked.

"Aren't we leaving?" she asked.

"Right after Reid gets to the front of the building and makes a very public appearance so Fowler thinks he's still here with you. He'll let me know on the comms unit." Jack tapped his earbud.

"Who's Fowler?" Ella asked.

"Just a guy." Megan got out Ella's favorite Christmas book and started reading it to her to distract her.

Jack soon drove off. An odd sense of abandonment settled in Megan's stomach and tears pricked her eyes but she kept reading until the book ended. Ella chattered away, talking about Christmas, but Megan couldn't concentrate on what her daughter was saying. She'd let Reid into their lives, and she'd come to depend on him. Hopefully, it was only because of Fowler. But once the man was no longer a threat, could she let go of these feelings for Reid and go back to her life?

18

_____

Megan settled into the soft leather seat and tried to relax on the long drive as Ella drifted off to sleep, but it wasn't until they pulled into Valley View's driveway that she let out a long breath, and her trembling hands calmed.

Jack wound down the driveway lined with evergreen trees perfuming the air and settling into the vehicle.

A jolting bump woke Ella. "Yay, we're here!"

"We are indeed." Russ's patrol car was parked outside the lodge, and Megan's calm evaporated.

"Why's Russ here?" she asked Jack.

He glanced in the rearview mirror. "He just came by to make sure the house was secure."

"What's secure mean, Mommy?" Ella asked.

Megan turned to Ella. "Nothing for you to worry about, sweetie."

Jack killed the engine and slid out.

Russ joined him. "Everything's clear."

Jack shook Russ's hand. "Appreciate your taking the time to check it out for us since the rest of my team is tied up at the hospital."

"I'll hang out until Reid gets home, but then I need to

take off." Russ tipped his hat at Megan, then strode to his car and leaned against the hood. At first glance, he appeared relaxed but his sharp gaze constantly moved.

Megan unbuckled Ella. She hopped down, and Megan couldn't stop thoughts of how Reid always offered to carry Ella inside. Jack opened her door, but he wouldn't offer something as personal as carrying her daughter.

"It's getting colder." Jack held out his hand for them to precede him up the stairs. "They say it might even snow."

"Snow!" Ella danced.

"Not today, Ella," Megan said so her daughter didn't linger outside to wait for it.

They entered the lodge, and the place had an empty feeling. No meal cooking in the kitchen. No fire in the fireplace like yesterday. No warm welcome from Sydney, Jessie, and Bandit. And especially, no Reid standing tall and filling the room with his rugged presence.

Despite being equally tall and broad-shouldered, Jack didn't seem to be as imposing as Reid. He probably was as commanding, but she'd put Reid on a pedestal from his help all those years ago.

Ella tugged on Megan's hand. "Can I take my jacket off now?"

"Sure." Megan helped her shed her coat, then hung it along with her jacket on a hook at the door.

Ella yawned, and Megan turned to Jack. "I'd like to take Ella upstairs for more of a nap than she got in the car."

"Go ahead," Jack answered.

Megan escorted Ella to the bedroom they'd shared last night and settled her into the bed.

"Do you think Mr. Reid likes us?" Ella asked.

"Why do you ask?"

Ella reached for Boo-Boo sitting on the pillow. "I wondered why he didn't want to come here with us today."

"It's not that he didn't want to. He had some business to take care of."

"But he's coming later?"

"Absolutely."

"Good. I like him." Ella clutched Boo-Boo and snuggled into the blanket. "I wish Jessie and Bandit could come too."

Megan didn't comment but rubbed Ella's back to help her fall asleep. Ella was getting close to Reid, and Megan didn't like that. Not one bit. But she had to admit to falling under his spell too. Something she both hated and relished.

Talk about being wishy-washy.

Ella shifted in the bed. It was as if her daughter knew Megan shouldn't be thinking of Reid like this and moved to warn her that he would break her heart.

But did she really believe he would hurt her again? He wasn't the same man she'd once known. The loss of his wife had changed him. His active faith had changed him. And being a father had changed him.

But had he changed enough?

She let herself get lost in thoughts of a future with him and Jessie. Seeing the complete family she wanted. She didn't know how long she sat there but a car pulling up outside broke her trance. Was it Reid? She hoped so. Despite her misgivings.

She went to the balcony and looked down on the family room.

Jack opened the door. The female agent entered, and Reid followed. He stopped at the threshold and immediately sought her out.

She breathed a small sigh of relief.

He kept his eyes trained on her and smiled sweetly.

She was sure her eyes telegraphed how glad she was that he'd arrived. So what? She *was* glad. More than she cared to admit. But she still couldn't pull free.

"Megan," Jack called up the stairs and drew her attention. "I'd like you to meet Special Agent Lauren Nickels."

Megan came down the stairs toward the stern-looking blonde. Short like Megan, she appeared strong and determined in the way she carried herself across the room. At a distance, Lauren would have served well as a decoy, but the closer they got, the more the resemblance disappeared.

"Nice to meet you, Ms. Cash." Lauren stuck out her hand with a quick jab and gave Megan a no-nonsense shake, quickly dropping Megan's hand and spinning toward Jack. "We secure here?"

Jack nodded. "There's no indication that Fowler knows about this place, but we'll remain on full alert and keep a security detail."

Reid turned the deadbolt and jiggled the handle before coming into the room.

"How about bringing me up to speed." This wasn't a question. Agent or not anymore, his tone made it clear that he didn't expect an argument.

She remembered this tone from Fowler's trial. Reid's strength took center stage then and was obvious now. She liked that about him. Liked feeling as if he could solve any problem at hand.

"Let's all take a seat." Jack tipped his head at the kitchen island and slipped onto a stool.

Reid and Lauren moved across the space to join him, and Megan trailed them. Jack hadn't specifically said he wanted Megan to participate in their conversation, but she wouldn't miss it unless they told her otherwise.

As she drew nearer to the kitchen, her stomach rumbled. She glanced up at the wall clock. Three o'clock. No wonder she was hungry. She may not have the law enforcement skills the trio seated at the island possessed and couldn't help with logistics, but she could at least feed them.

"I'm going to make something to eat," she said. "Anyone else hungry?"

She got an affirmative answer from all three, so she went to the refrigerator and scoped out the contents.

"I can help." Reid's voice came a foot or so from behind her.

She jumped.

"Sorry." He smiled. "I didn't mean to scare you."

She turned. They were so close she could feel the warmth from his body. The urge to lay her head on his chest moved her closer. She hoped he would respond by wrapping his arms around her.

Instead, he sucked in a breath and held it while twining his fingers in hers as he'd done last night. Their gazes held, and he was reflecting the same attraction that she had to be transmitting. An excitement that hadn't zipped through her since she'd fallen in love with him years ago raced through her.

"You plan on joining us, Maddox?" Jack asked.

Jack's voice brought Megan back to reality.

What was she doing? Was she crazy? She was flirting with Reid. Not only flirting with him but doing so in front of a pair of FBI agents.

She jerked her hand free. "Sit. I'll get the sandwich stuff."

He searched her eyes for a moment longer, then stepped away. She spun and stuck her heated face in the cool of the refrigerator as she gathered sandwich fixings she'd seen last night along with condiments and set them on the island.

Reid had put plates and knives on the counter and was now carrying bread and chips from the pantry. She grabbed sodas, and before she could prepare sandwiches, everyone started making their own.

Reid slathered mustard on a thick slice of homemade wheat bread. "So where do we stand?"

Jack reached for a plate. "ERT lifted a few viable prints from your car, and they're running them now."

Megan had heard ERT mentioned so many times during Fowler's trial—the FBI's Evidence Recovery Team.

Jack put two slices of bread on his plate. "They're also processing the calendar to see if it has any unusual characteristics. Hopefully they'll figure out where it was purchased. Or recover DNA and prints."

Reid set his sandwich piled high with Swiss cheese and roast beef on the plate and grabbed his soda. "It seemed pretty generic to me."

"It's a long shot for sure." Jack grabbed slices of turkey. "We also found a matchbook from PJ's Sports Bar on the ground ten feet from your vehicle. We'll run the forensics on that too."

"Must be from Fowler," Reid said. "Would be a coincidence if it wasn't, and I don't believe in coincidences."

Jack cut his sandwich in half. "The prints are a better lead. But until we have anything concrete to go on, we've put plans in place in anticipation of Fowler's next move."

Megan looked at Jack. "How in the world can you predict his moves? It's not like he's doing the same thing over and over again."

Lauren grabbed a handful of chips for her plate. "Based on his pattern of contact so far, it makes sense that he'll try to contact you tomorrow when you return for Ella's appointment."

Reid carried his plate and drink to a spot on the end of the island. "You've tapped Megan's phone in case he tries to call though, right?"

Jack nodded and dropped onto a stool in front of his food. "We also have equipment on the way so we can listen in if a call comes in here at the lodge or on her phone. With everything now in place, we wait."

Reid blinked at his friend. "And that's it?"

"You know the drill. What more would you suggest we do?" Jack took a bite of his sandwich.

Reid closed his eyes and took a long breath. He was frustrated but seemed as if he believed everything was being done and he could do nothing else. Oddly that comforted her. If there was anything more to be done, he'd either insist someone do it or he'd do it himself. He was just that kind of man. A man who kept showing he could be counted on.

Reid opened his eyes and faced Jack. "I'm going to make a call to the Veritas Center. See if they might have ideas for forensics we might be missing."

Jack frowned but didn't speak.

"You don't like a private lab butting in," Reid said. "I get it, but I have to do everything I can to make sure we find this guy." Reid drew out his phone and stabbed his thumb at the screen, then tapped the counter. "Trent, good. Glad I caught you. The FBI has taken over the Fowler investigation, and I'm putting you on speaker with two of the FBI agents who are working it. Any news on the fake bomb?"

"We've processed all items for prints and DNA. Device and Megan's vehicle. No viable prints on device. Guy likely wore gloves. Vehicle provided several prints but none that matched to AFIS. We did recover DNA samples from the device, as did Andi inside the vehicle. Those are running. Took longer than normal to isolate the DNA, but last I heard it should complete late tomorrow afternoon. We'll get the results to you then."

That was something at least, but Reid didn't seem relieved at all. "Any hits in ViCAP?"

"None, but we have more. Duct tape was used to strap items to the box."

"I mean no offense, that's not really a big deal, is it?" Reid asked, surprising Megan.

"No offense taken, but why do you say that?" Trent asked, seeming a bit irritated at the comment.

"Forensics techs have been comparing duct tape recovered at a crime scene to rolls recovered from suspects for years, right? Which means we need to find the roll for this to help us. Besides, I thought the process had come under some scrutiny lately and wasn't always holding up in court."

"True, you will have to locate the roll, but thanks to Sierra at our center, the controversy is changing."

"Explain," Reid demanded.

"First a bit about the evaluation process," Trent said. "When a length of duct tape is torn off, it leaves fracture edges. When evaluated and examined we can put the two fracture edges together and demonstrate that they have enough individual characteristics to prove they were once together."

"Yeah, so how has that changed?" Reid asked, sounding like he was losing patience.

"There hasn't been a standardized protocol or industry accepted guidelines for the analysis of duct tape. Now there is. The pilot project Sierra has been working on has shown very low error rates. Get me that roll, and I'll get you court-worthy analysis."

Megan liked the guy's certainty.

"We hope to find it and more," Reid said, sounding equally certain. "What about the box? Anything stand out there?"

"It's handmade like I thought. There are initials, WJS, engraved near the seam inside the box. That ring a bell."

"Not at all." Reid looked at Jack, who shook his head.

"It could be initials for the person who built the box then gave it to your suspect or maybe Fowler didn't leave the bomb."

"Has to be Fowler, even with these initials. He's the only one who has something against Megan. And besides, she saw him outside her daughter's door."

"DNA on the box will help confirm he planted the bomb," Jack said.

"DNA will tell you that Fowler touched the device," Trent said. "But you really need his DNA recovered from the car to put him at the scene."

"True," Jack said.

Megan didn't like that they had so little evidence against the guy.

"What about Fowler's truck?" Reid asked. "Landon find anything?"

"He's working the electronics now, but hasn't reported his findings yet. Not surprising. It takes time to dismantle and thoroughly process a vehicle like he's doing. "

Reid's experience told him that, but it didn't mean he didn't hope for something faster. "Any ideas on forensics we might be missing so far?"

"I can assure you we were thorough with the car and device." Trent's voice rose. "So no."

"Sorry, I didn't mean to imply you weren't," Reid said. "I'm desperate for a lead."

"I understand." Trent's tone once again exuded a sense of calm that even Reid's directness hadn't caused to waver for long. Megan imagined he would do well as an expert on the witness stand. "If you need additional forensics processed, we'll be glad to do it for you, but I'm not familiar enough with the case to suggest what you might be missing. If I think of something, I'll let you know."

That was all they could hope for.

"We appreciate your support," Reid said.

"Landon will phone you with information on the vehicle, and I'll call with the DNA results when it completes or if we find other evidence you need to know about." Trent ended the call.

Reid tucked his phone away and turned to Jack. "Not the answer I wanted, but at least I tried. With you in charge of the operation, I'm content everything will proceed according to plan." Reid took a long drink of his soda and silence descended on the group.

Seemed as if no one had anything else to say. Megan included. So she tucked into her food as did the others.

Though the agents had been upbeat, an ominous vibe throbbed through the air. No matter their planning, no matter their skills, these strong professionals were concerned. Worried even.

Maybe worried that Fowler would best them and get through their defenses.

Megan dropped her sandwich. She couldn't eat another bite. She went to stand in front of the roaring fire that Jack must've built while she was upstairs.

A car pulled into the driveway, and Megan spun to face the windows covered with plantation shutters. Not able to see who'd arrived, her stomach tightened more. Logically she figured the agent bringing the equipment had arrived, but in her heart, she feared Fowler had located her.

Jack and Lauren went to the door, and Reid crossed over to her.

His gaze met hers. "You're tense."

She peered at him. "How can I be anything but?"

He took another step closer but kept an eye on the door. "Now that we know Fowler wants money, we can assume he isn't as likely to hurt you unless you don't cooperate."

His words hit her like ice water. "So what you're saying is

if I follow your advice and don't give him the money, then he's going to hurt me or Ella?"

"No. You're putting words in my mouth. The Bureau won't let it come to that. They'll step in when Fowler contacts you and apprehend him."

"I wish I could give him the money, and then he would leave us alone."

"We've been through this," he said, his tone disturbingly cool. "After he spends the initial payment, he'll keep coming back for more. It'll never end."

"But that could take years."

Reid shook his head. "Not for a man like Fowler. He'll blow through the money in record speed and be asking for more before you can regroup."

She knew he was right, but she couldn't risk Ella's life. If she could buy some time until Ella got well again, Megan could handle another attempt by Fowler. But she didn't want to pay the man if she didn't have to. What should she do?

She rubbed the knot forming in her neck and sighed.

He lifted his hand. "Let me."

She shrank back. "That's not a good idea."

His gaze cooled. "I thought you'd forgiven me. Or was I wrong, and you're going to hold our past against me forever?"

"It's not that."

"Then what?"

How did she answer that? She couldn't tell him she couldn't have him touching her because she'd already come to care about him in a way she shouldn't pursue. She may have forgiven him, but that didn't mean she trusted him with her heart.

A man carrying electronic equipment tromped past her,

and she nodded a greeting to him then turned to Reid. "Now's not the time to talk about this."

His eyes burned into hers. He knew she was running away from him. So be it. Maybe if he thought she didn't want to be around him, he wouldn't question her again.

He gave a sorrowful shake of his head and stepped toward the agents connecting their equipment on the dining table. Reid discussed the equipment with them, but she could see the hurt lingered in the curl of his shoulders.

It hit her then. As much as she wanted him to back off, she hoped he didn't think that meant she didn't want him involved in this mess with Fowler. Because as he conversed with the other men whose eyes were hard and faces all business, she knew beyond any doubt she needed Reid by her side or she would lose the slight hold she had on keeping it together.

19

Nearing dinner time, the recording team finished instructing Jack and Lauren on how to operate the equipment, but Reid let them handle that, and he kept a careful eye on Megan from the end of the sofa. They had a top-notch security team in place, and she seemed less concerned about her physical safety, but she was still worried about Ella. One moment she seemed strong and in control, the next ready to fall apart.

Not an unusual reaction for a parent whose child was suffering. He'd seen the same behavior in parents that he and Jessie visited with Bandit at the hospital. He wanted to take her out of the room, wrap her in his arms, and whisper that she would be fine. That he would make sure she was fine. No way he would do that. Not with the mixed signals she was tossing out. He was better off hanging back and letting her initiate any contact between them.

The tech team headed for the door.

"Hey, thanks," Reid called out.

They nodded and stepped out, letting in a blustery gust of cold air. Jack secured the door behind them and joined Megan and Reid again. Lauren remained seated at the table with the equipment and studied a manual. She was a detail-oriented person, and for that, Reid was thankful. If a call came in, she would be ready to go. No fumbling. Just press the right buttons and record the call.

Megan looked at Jack. "Why do you think Fowler might call me?"

"We really don't think he will, but we want to be prepared," Jack said. "If he does, this equipment lets us listen in on the conversation."

"So when my phone rings you'll know about it, no matter where I am?" she asked.

"Yes. Either Lauren or I will be near the equipment at all times monitoring your phone."

Her expression soured, as if she were imagining the call. Hearing Fowler's voice, raspy and demanding, coming through her phone. His demands urgent and threatening.

Her breathing sped up. "What in the world do I say to him?"

Jack sat in a leather chair across from them. "It all depends on how he starts the conversation, but that's why we're here. We'll have to play it by ear, and we'll be right here to coach you through it."

"What if I'm upstairs when he calls? Or in a car? The doctor's office?" Her tone skated higher with each location.

Reid swiveled to face her. "You can handle it. Just answer the phone and stall until one of us can be with you."

A shiver rippled over her. "I don't know if I can do this."

Hoping to ease her stress, he offered her a smile. "You stabbed him in the bank, remember? If you can do that, you can talk to him on the phone."

She gave a derisive laugh. "It took me time to gather the courage."

"Ah, but that's because he was standing over you in

person. If he calls today, he'll be miles away and can't hurt you."

"And then what? If I'm not allowed to pay him off, how exactly will any of this be resolved?"

Jack rested his elbows on his knees. "If he tries to contact you in person tomorrow at the hospital, we'll have a team in place and make the arrest."

"And if he calls instead?"

"Then we'll schedule a drop for the money, send Lauren in your place, and make the arrest then." Jack gave a smile that Reid had seen hundreds of times and always calmed the person he was talking with.

Not Megan. She studied him intently. She didn't buy their plan, nor did she trust them to carry it out.

"No offense," she finally said. "But I see things like this go wrong in TV shows and movies all the time. How do you know that won't happen here?"

"No offense taken." Jack's flat tone belied his statement. "Movies and TV are nothing like real life. If everything went according to plan on these shows, they wouldn't be interesting or very long. We don't need to make things interesting."

As an agent, Reid had often delivered news like this to terrified parents. He always believed what he said, just as he knew Jack believed his own words. But the calm Reid had possessed on the job wasn't in reach for him right now. Not even close. He was putting on a good show for Megan. At least he hoped he was. He had confidence in Jack and his plan, but something niggled at his brain.

Maybe it was a simple warning to be on alert. To not let anything happen. That Megan—not some stranger—was vulnerable.

Megan was special. The woman who'd come to mean too much to him again to lose her now.

Jack's phone rang grabbing Reid's attention as his buddy answered and listened intently.

Jack tilted his head. "Good. I'll head out there now." Jack tapped his knee with a long index finger. "Text it to me when it comes through, and I'll pay him a visit."

A warrant? Sounded like it to Reid.

Jack shoved his phone into his pocket. "Warrant came in for the video at PJ's."

Reid leaned forward. "I want in on it. Give me fifteen minutes to get Micha and Russ here to take my place on Megan's protection detail, and we'll head out to the bar."

"I need to print the warrant and update Lauren anyway." Jack stepped toward her and the equipment.

Megan nibbled on her lower lip. She didn't like that he was leaving. Reid got that. She might not want to have anything to do with him on a personal level, but she *had* come to depend on his protection.

He worked hard to ignore her additional concern and texted an urgent request for help to Russ and Micha.

As he waited for replies, he turned to her. "You don't need to worry about me leaving. Russ and Micha will provide the protection you need."

"Do you have to go?" She frowned. "Or maybe you want to."

He did and he didn't. Truthfully he missed the action of being an agent. But he didn't like causing her undue concern. "I don't really want to leave you and Ella, but I *do* want to find a lead on Fowler's whereabouts."

"Can't Jack do that?"

Could he? Sure he could, but if they located Fowler, Reid wanted to be in on it. But it was more than that. "I trust Jack to do a thorough job, but with my history with Fowler, the manager might say something that means nothing to Jack but it does to me."

"That makes sense." She twisted her hands together. "I'm just being selfish."

"Not at all." His phone dinged, and he read a text from Micha. "Micha will be here in five minutes."

His phone chimed again. "Russ is on his way too. Same time frame. For once I have to say it's nice to live so close to them."

"I can't imagine having siblings or teammates who come running when I need them."

"It's good."

She tilted her head. "Do you want Jessie to have a sibling someday?"

Did he? Another thing he hadn't considered. Before Diane died, they'd talked about having a second child. But now? "Jess would like that. Me too. If things were normal in our lives. But they aren't, and I'm not sure anymore."

She didn't seem surprised by his answer. "I'm the same when it comes to Ella. She really took to Jessie quickly. She doesn't have a lot of friends. I homeschool her to prevent germ exposure while she's so immunocompromised. She wants to go to school and have that normal life you mentioned."

The sacrifices both of them had made and were making was beyond Reid's emotional comprehension. Sure, he'd given up being an agent due to Diane's death, but that was just a job. He was thriving in Shadow Lake and loved his life with his family and teammates. So in many ways he was thriving, and their life was approaching normal again. If you didn't count the big gaping hole Diane's death left behind.

Jack joined them, ending the personal talk, and he tapped his jacket pocket. "Warrant is printed, and I'm good to serve it."

"You're sure it's okay if I tag along?" Reid asked. "You know protocols and all."

"Yeah." Jack grinned. "I doubt the bar staff will complain about a tagalong to recover a video."

Footfalls pounded up the exterior steps to the porch, and Reid shot to his feet. Hand on weapon, he marched to the door. He confirmed Russ's and Micha's arrival before opening the door for them.

They shed their jackets, and he quickly gave them the lay of the land.

Russ eyed Reid and moved closer to whisper, "I see what Syd was saying about you and Megan."

Megan sat forward. "What's going on?"

Russ waved a hand. "Just family stuff."

She wrinkled her brow at him. Okay, so she didn't buy his evasiveness, but he wouldn't say more. His brothers were gossips when it came to trying to get Reid into the dating game. They figured it was time. He didn't. Or maybe he did now if the woman he dated was Megan.

Jack grabbed his jacket. "Let's get moving."

Reid made strong eye contact with Megan. "Stay inside —away from windows. Listen to Russ and Micha. If you get a call make sure I'm informed when you have a chance."

She nodded, but her focus lingered on him, pulling at him. He took a step in her direction. Paused.

"Come on, man," Jack said. "Time's wasting."

"Go. We'll be fine." Megan shooed him away.

And yet, he struggled to get his feet moving. Jack grabbed his arm and propelled him toward the door.

Outside where snow was falling softly, he stopped. "You've got it bad, man."

Reid couldn't argue. He did have it bad for Megan. Question was, what was he going to do about it?

Jack clicked the key fob for his Bureau-issued SUV. "Go ahead and put the bar's address in GPS while I get out to the road."

Jack cranked the engine, the sound cutting the quiet. Reid took the passenger seat and tapped PJ's address into the GPS program, and the female voice directed them toward the city.

Jack pulled down the driveway, and Reid prepared himself for his buddy to fire off additional questions about Megan that Reid was completely unprepared to answer. Thankfully, text messages coming over the infotainment system kept Jack busy most of the drive.

When he finished, he stared out the window. "Think we'll get much accumulation."

"They're predicting several inches later tonight. Let's hope it hasn't closed down PJ's."

"Nah, sports fans are diehards. A little snow won't keep them home."

Reid chuckled. Snow was a rare occurrence in this part of the state and when it fell, grocery stores emptied out and the cities shut down. Only a few inches of snow could bring the area to a standstill for days.

Reid had no qualms about driving in it. He'd learned as a young guy on the resort to drive utility vehicles and other equipment, then the minute he got his license, he drove pretty much everything he could lay his hands on. He perfected his driving skills in defensive driving courses for work, so a little snow? Nah, that didn't slow him down. A good thing, as Ella had another appointment in the morning, and it was an opportunity for him to show Megan that he was there for them.

At least he hoped he wouldn't let her down again.

～

Reid and Jack got out in PJ's parking lot with vehicles blanketed in fresh snow. Reid had expected the lot to be much emptier, but then, as Jack had said, sports fans were diehards.

"What is it about snow that brings out the kid in you?" Reid asked and took off to slide across the lot.

"Speak for yourself." Jack laughed and balled a handful of snow to throw at Reid.

Reid ducked and bolted for the door. They were laughing when they entered, but it took only a moment for the pair of them to sober to their mission.

Oakley was behind the bar. Tonight she wore a Trail Blazers jersey. She finished drawing a beer from a tap and frowned at them. The bar was emptier tonight so they were able to march right up to her.

"Hang on," she said. "I'll get Guy for you."

Reid slid onto a stool.

Jack took the one next to him, but his gaze trailed Oakley as she delivered the beer to a bearded man at the end of the bar and then picked up the phone. "I take it that's the Oakley you talked to."

"It is."

"You must be losing your charms, buddy boy. She didn't seem so eager to see you." Jack laughed.

Reid didn't think he ever had charms, but he hadn't been unfortunate in the dating department. He'd always found girlfriends by simply being himself. Until he'd gone against everything he believed in and bailed on Megan. Then he deserved to be alone. In hindsight, he had to wonder if that was the reason he married Diane. So he wouldn't be alone. Or so he could forget what he'd done to Megan.

A skinny guy with a goatee hanging down to his chest and long hair in a man bun came out of a door behind the bar. He stopped to talk to Oakley, and she pointed at them.

The man strode in their direction, his goatee swishing. "Manager, Guy Fletcher. Which one of you is Maddox?"

"I am," Reid said. "But not the Maddox you want. The sheriff isn't with me tonight. This is FBI Agent Jack Duger. He has the warrant you require."

Jack fished out his credentials and displayed them, then took out the warrant and slapped it on the bar.

Guy grabbed it and quickly scanned the pages. He reached into his pocket and pulled out a flash drive. "The video you want is on here."

"Were you out here when the man we're interested in was here?" Reid asked.

"Nope."

"Did he ever return for his truck?"

Guy rested tattooed hands on the bar. "I doubt he came looking for it or he would've come in here demanding to know where it was and we haven't seen him."

"Or he could've shown up," Jack said. "Saw the towing sign in the lot and figured out it had been towed."

Guy shrugged halfheartedly. "Now, if that's all, I have a bar to run."

"You have a business card?" Jack asked.

He reached under the bar to retrieve one and slap it on the counter.

Jack took it and studied it. "How long you been the manager here?"

"Going on fifteen years."

"You ever see our guy in here before?"

"Not that I recall." Guy pushed away from the bar. "Now, if you'll excuse me."

Jack flicked his fingers, dismissing the guy.

"Rude much?" Reid asked as they headed for the parking lot.

Jack clicked the key fob, the sounds rising into the night blanketed with snowfall. "I guess he falls into the camp of people who don't have a lot of respect for law enforcement."

"That's the part of the job that I've chosen to forget." Reid's phone rang, and he quickly answered the call from Russ as he carefully stepped through the inch of snow covering the parking lot to the SUV.

"Got the storage unit company for you," Russ said.

"Which one?" Reid asked.

"U-Stor-It-All." He rattled off the address. "It could contain useful information, but I would caution you to leave it alone for now. Give me a chance to get a proper warrant for the motel room and then the storage unit."

Reid understood the value long-term of handling this right, but it didn't matter long-term if they did this the right way if Fowler got to Megan. "I'll give you until morning."

"That's not reasonable, and you know it. With the holiday, more pressing warrant requests will likely keep ours on the back burner. Plus, it's after hours. Gleason won't likely pressure the clerk tonight."

"Do what you can and keep me in the loop," Reid said. "But if you don't come through on a timely basis, I don't promise I won't go get that key and check out the unit."

"You want the guy to go away for maximum years, right? Not be free to do this to Megan again?" Russ let the call fall silent.

"Yeah," Reid said.

"Then do what I say."

"Fine."

"Besides, I've got something else for you. Some good news I heard on the grapevine." Russ took a dramatic pause. "One of the local officers on Fowler's investigation located a woman who saw Fowler at the gas station and heard the whole conversation he had with the attendant."

Reid's pulse kicked up as he slid into the vehicle. "She might've heard something Megan missed."

"Exactly or..."

What was with his brother's cryptic behavior? "Oh, I get it. You think her story might be different than Megan's."

"Could be, and you wouldn't have gotten far at the FBI if you wouldn't have reached the same conclusion in one of your investigations. At least one that didn't involve someone you cared about."

He was right, but Reid wouldn't admit it. "You have a name and address for this witness?"

"I'll text it to you, but you didn't get it from me. Don't want to get on Gleason's bad side."

"From who?" Reid laughed.

Russ chuckled. "I'll get back to you when I have something new to report."

Reid ended the call and shared the conversation with Jack.

"We could head over to talk to the woman now," Jack suggested.

"I was thinking the same thing." Reid stared at his phone screen, waiting for Russ's text with the woman's name and address.

"What's that old saying about a watched pot never boils?" Jack chuckled.

Reid's phone chimed. He read the details and quickly plugged the address into GPS.

"Woman's name is Kim Cole," Reid said and tapped on it to go to the maps program. "Only twenty minutes from here."

"Twenty minutes and we might finally have some actionable information to go on." Jack peered at him from behind the wheel with his cop's interrogating eyes. "So what are your plans with Megan when all of this is over?"

Ah, so Jack hadn't let this drop after all. Just delayed it. "No plans. She returns to her life, and I resume mine."

"Just like that." Jack scoffed. "You both ignore something good going on between you."

"Yep. Just like that."

"You want to throw away what you have with her? I don't have to tell you how hard it is to find someone these days."

Jack wanted to get married. Reid knew that, but even if he had found a likely woman to spend his life with, the job often got in the way. "No matter how I feel about her, I can't possibly handle getting close to a child as sick as Ella. Not after losing Diane."

Jack didn't speak for the longest time. Right. Better prepare for his next comment as Reid knew he wouldn't like what Jack had to say.

He glanced at Reid. "You can't run away from everything in life just so you don't get hurt again."

"Watch me."

Jack shook his head. "You were always too stubborn for your own good."

"Served me well as an agent, though."

"Yeah, you did have one of the highest case closure rates, but at what cost?" Jack stared ahead.

He'd recently ended a long-term relationship that he'd thought might lead to marriage and a family, but she got cold feet over the risks in his profession and totally bailed on him. He was still hurting, and yet, he seemed as if he would consider dating again.

But then his girlfriend wasn't his wife. The mother of his child. She didn't die. That was a whole different thing to face.

The GPS voice broke into Reid's thoughts, announcing a turn ahead and then leading them directly to a small bungalow painted a cheery yellow with black shutters. Reminded Reid of a bee.

Jack parked out front. "Lights are on, so let's hope she's home."

"Home and willing to talk." Reid released his seatbelt.

"I'll take lead and make this an official interview."

"I hoped you'd say that," Reid said as he climbed out. "Most people can't refuse to answer an agent's questions."

Reid missed the implied power that came with the job. Not that he'd abused it, but he liked that people cooperated more often than not when he'd been trying to bring in a bad guy. At least law-abiding people. Criminals were another story.

He rang the doorbell and let Jack take over.

The light flashed on, and the door opened a fraction. A short woman, couldn't be much more than five feet tall, peeked out.

Jack displayed his credentials and introduced them. "Ms. Cole?"

She gave a wary nod, and her short blond hair moved in waves.

"I'm sorry to disturb you so late," Jack said in the calming tone that most always encouraged females to spill their guts for him. "But we need to talk to you about what you witnessed at the gas station."

She opened the door fully but held onto the doorknob with delicate fingers. She wore jeans and a T-shirt, and Reid put her in her early thirties.

"You mean those two guys who were talking to each other?" she asked.

"I do." Reid smiled.

"I've already told the police all I know."

"And we appreciate that." Jack smiled at her. "But we like to hear things right from the witness. Would you mind if we came in for a few minutes?"

"The FBI. I never expected... I mean..." Her words

trailed off as she ran a hand over her hair and tugged on the hem of her T-shirt, then allowed them to pass.

"Excuse the mess." She rushed to the sofa and grabbed a blanket along with a bowl of popcorn and an e-reader. "Have a seat."

She set the e-reader and popcorn on a glass table and dropped onto an overstuffed chair. Reid and Jack took opposite ends of the sofa.

She hugged the blanket against her chest. "What do you want to know about that day?"

Jack leaned into the plump cushion as if this were a simple conversation, not an all-important interview. Reid was too tightly strung to follow suit and admired Jack's ability to play it cool.

"Go ahead and tell us what happened from the time you first saw the two men talking," Jack said.

"I was getting gas, and the attendant had put the nozzle in my car but then didn't start it pumping because this other guy hops out of a trashy white pickup and comes over to talk to him."

Jack held out Fowler's picture on his phone. "Is this the man you saw?"

"Yeah. Yeah. That's him." She shuddered. "I'll never forget that face. So mean looking, and it seemed like the attendant was afraid of him."

"What did they talk about?" Reid asked, starting to lose what little patience he had.

She took a hearty breath. "The visitor was trying to get the attendant to agree to meet him for a drink. I got the feeling that one or both of them were ex-cons."

"How so?" Jack asked.

"The attendant talked about having to stay away from the other guy or go back to prison."

"Did you by any chance catch the attendant's name?" Reid asked, coming to the point.

"I did."

Reid gaped at her before he quickly controlled it as a professional interviewer would do. How had she heard his name and Megan missed it? Or did Megan withhold it for some reason? No, she wouldn't do that, would she?

"And how did that occur?" Jack asked, obviously on the same wavelength as Reid.

"The visitor got kind of mad at the attendant for not quickly agreeing to the drink. So after he said goodbye, he stormed past my car. My window was open, and he muttered, "Stupid Billy Smith. You'll get what's due you if you don't show up.""

"And you're sure he said Billy Smith?" Jack asked.

"Positive. He might've been muttering, but there was an ugly force behind his words and it came through loud and clear."

"How old do you think this gas attendant was?" Jack asked.

"Early fifties, maybe late forties. His beard was graying anyway. His hair too. And he had wrinkles by his eyes."

"Is there anything else that you think we should know about the conversation or these men?" Jack asked.

"Nothing, really. I just got the feeling that the visitor was used to the attendant doing what he asked. That their relationship, whatever it was, wasn't equal."

Reid couldn't wait to track down this Billy Smith, so he stood. "Thank you for your time, Ms. Cole."

Jack stood and fished a business card from his pocket to give to Kim, who was standing too. "Call if you think of anything that you remember that might help."

"What did this guy do?" She shoved the card into her

jeans pocket. "I mean to get the FBI involved it has to be bad, right?"

"You'd be surprised at the boring crimes we investigate." Jack laughed.

Reid appreciated the way his buddy put the woman at ease and still didn't answer her question.

They rushed through the now heavier snow to Jack's SUV. Jack started the vehicle but pulled out his phone and tapped the screen. "Good. Glad I caught you at work. I need you to run particulars on a Billy Smith of Portland, who served time. And before you tell me it's a common name and we'll get a ton of results, I get that. Just do it. Email me with the info for every Bill, Billy, Will, or William Smith who has a record."

Jack ended the call. "Gonna be a long night."

"Even longer. I promised Ella I would watch Christmas specials with her when I get home." He eyed Jack. "Skipping that isn't negotiable."

"Well then," Jack said. "I guess this proves you've changed from the guy I knew so well. Maybe there's hope for you to change in your thoughts on Megan too."

Reid shook his head and turned the radio on. No way he was going to talk about that again. Not while he should be thinking about the guy who could lead them to the man who'd been terrorizing Megan.

20

Megan rolled over on the sofa in the den and stared at the clock. Midnight. The beginning of the day she hoped would be the end of Fowler's reign of terror. Not that the name Billy, Bill, Will, or William Smith had led anywhere yet. Other than to create a list of twenty-three men who had once been incarcerated. Reid and Jack had decided to break the list into smaller pieces and have the team and any agent Jack could spare review it right after they safely escorted Ella to and from her doctor's appointment in the morning.

But they did review the video from the bar right away. She did too. Watching Fowler talk to his friend had turned her stomach. And it didn't reveal anything of use. Sure she confirmed the friend was the guy she'd seen at the gas station, but otherwise there'd been no point in viewing the clip. All it did was stir up her anxiety. Still, Reid had tried to encourage her by saying they often had to exhaust a lot of leads in an investigation before one panned out.

She stood and, using the dim light coming from the hallway, checked on Ella. She'd fallen asleep in the den while watching Christmas programs with Reid. Megan hadn't wanted to disturb her and had left her to sleep in the den.

At least that's what Megan kept telling herself. In reality, it probably had more to do with the fact that she didn't want Reid to offer to carry Ella to bed again. Megan had successfully avoided a personal conversation with him for the rest of the night, but Ella had clung to Reid.

He didn't seem to mind. He'd been patient and kind, warm and caring. The kind of man Megan could see as a stepfather for Ella. The exact kind of thoughts that kept Megan from letting him accompany them upstairs.

She tucked the blanket around her daughter and went to the closest bookshelf. She would go to the family room, where she could turn on a light to read until she got sleepy. She selected a mystery and followed the light down the hallway. She expected to see Jack stationed by the recording equipment as he and Lauren were taking shifts, and Lauren had gone to bed, but she didn't expect Reid. As she entered the room, he jumped from a chair.

His eyes alert, he let his gaze rove over her. "What's wrong?"

"I couldn't sleep."

"But you and Ella are okay?"

She nodded and wished the sudden surge of warmth over his level of caring would go away. "I just couldn't sleep and thought I would read until I get tired."

She headed across the room to a chair near a lamp and quickly opened the book before Reid engaged her in additional conversation. She tried to concentrate on the story, but Reid kept his focus on her, making it impossible. She shifted in the chair, putting as much of her back toward him as possible.

Still didn't work. She couldn't concentrate on the words, much less understand them. Her cell rang. She jerked, dropped the book, and checked caller ID.

"It's not anyone I know." Her gaze flew to Reid's face.

He headed her way, and she met him in the middle of the room.

"Wait." He motioned toward Jack sitting at the table by the listening equipment.

Jack gave a thumbs-up, and she pressed the talk button. She lifted the phone to her ear, and Reid came close to listen.

"Hello," she said, apprehension making her want to throw up.

"Hello, Megan." Fowler's gruff voice came over the phone. "With all those agents around, it looks like you're trying to set me up."

He laughed, reminding her of the way he'd mocked her at the bank robbery. He'd held his hot, evil gaze on her face as he described in detail how he planned to kill her if she didn't cooperate. A visceral pain stabbed her stomach, and she nearly dropped to the floor.

Reid pressed the mute button on the phone. "Easy," he whispered. "I'm right here. Fowler's just trying to get to you. Don't let him do it."

"I don't know if I can talk to him."

"Yes, you can. I've seen how strong you've become over the years." His eyes locked on hers. "Do this for Ella."

His confidence empowered her. She took a deep breath and gave a clipped nod.

Reid unmuted the phone and circled his arm around her back, giving her the courage to talk to the man who'd once threatened and scared her beyond belief.

"What do you want, Fowler?" She forced strength she didn't feel into her voice.

"I want my money and these FBI goons are gonna get in the way. I need you to get rid of them."

"Just tell me where to bring the money."

"And let these goons come instead to haul me in? No way."

"You're the one who got them involved by putting a note in the car, not me. I can't make them leave even if I want to. Which I don't." She let all the anger from his stalking and the robbery flow through her words.

"Hold on there now, little lady. Maybe before you make such a rash decision you should check on your daughter first."

"Ella," she whispered.

"That's right. Your precious Ella might not be as safe as you think at the moment."

Megan pulled away from Reid and charged toward the den.

"Megan, wait!" Reid called after her. "Don't go in there."

Despite his warning she kept going, rounding the corner and flying down the hallway toward the den. Reid's footfalls gained on her. Her heart beat a wild thumping rhythm, nearly exploding from her chest.

Shaking with fear for her daughter, she arrived at the door to the den. A strong arm clamped around her middle and lifted her off the ground. She kicked and tried to break free.

"This could be a trap," Reid said. "Let us take care of this."

Jack pounded down the hall and stopped next to Megan. She quit struggling and fully intended to let them take charge, but her gaze landed on Ella. A red dot glowed from the middle of her daughter's forehead.

A laser. Fowler had a laser weapon trained on Ella.

"Nooo!" Megan screamed and bucked, trying to free herself again.

"Relax," Reid said.

"No!" she yelled. "Ella's forehead."

Reid pivoted, taking Ella out of Megan's view. He stiffened before he muffled something under his breath and settled Megan on her feet.

By the time she turned, he was racing through the den. He snatched up Ella and dove to the floor, protecting her as he fell. He'd safely moved her out of the beam coming through a tiny gap in the drapes.

Megan started for them, but Jack stopped her by getting in her face. "You're safe in the hallway. Don't move out of here until Reid or I give you the all clear."

"But Ella."

"No buts. Reid has her, and she'll be fine. If I can't trust you to stay here, I can't go after Fowler. Will you stay?"

"Yes," she said, despite her motherly instincts screaming to protect her baby.

Jack edged past her and bolted down the hallway. She returned her attention to Reid and Ella. He was whispering to her, and she was smiling at him. She reached up, placed both of her hands on his face, and spoke, but Megan couldn't hear her.

Didn't matter. Megan knew what was going on. She recognized Ella's actions. When Ella wanted to tell Megan she loved her, she would lay her hands on her face and smile. A sweet, angelic smile that melted Megan's heart, and then in a soft voice she would state her love.

Megan hoped that wasn't what was happening in the den, but it seemed likely. Maybe not saying she loved Reid, but that she liked him. Megan couldn't let Ella form a deep connection with Reid. He would only hurt her.

Her cell rang. She jumped. A quick glance at caller ID told her it was Fowler again.

She put the phone to her ear. "What do you want?"

"I want the money delivered without any agents

around." He sounded out of breath. Maybe he'd had to run from Jack.

"I don't have the cash lying around. I have to call my accountant."

"Then you do that, and I'll call you tomorrow with the details for the drop."

She glanced at Ella again. Bile rose in Megan's throat. She swallowed it down.

She was done with this FBI business. No matter their promises, they couldn't protect Ella. It was now her responsibility to meet Fowler's demands and make him back off. She would do anything Fowler asked to keep her sweet little daughter alive.

Anything.

Upstairs, Reid settled Ella in the twin bed, his arms shaking from the threat. When the laser sight had cleared, he'd whisked her out of the den and up the stairs. Megan hot on his heels. Jack and Lauren hadn't returned from their hunt for Fowler, and Reid had to assume the creep was still outside. The safest place for Ella was in a room where she could sleep away from a window and out of Fowler's line of sight. That happened to be Reid's childhood bedroom.

Reid stood over her, his whole body vibrating with anger. Maybe fear. Probably both. Fowler could've killed Ella. Right there in the den. On Reid's watch. He should've been more careful. Checked the windows for the tiniest of cracks in the window coverings.

He let out a breath. It came out in short bursts of tension. He was more shaken than he'd thought. More so than he would like. More than he would expect in this type of situation. Sure, life-or-death situations on the job had always brought a rush of adrenaline, but this was different. He was starting to care for Ella too—and that changed the stakes. He wasn't prepared for the emotions that hit him when Ella put her hands on his face and with a sweet little smile told him she really liked him.

Nor was he prepared for the emotions still churning in his gut.

He had to get out of the room for his own good. He started to back away, but Ella grabbed his hand. Her tiny fingers curled around the edge of his palm.

"That was fun," she said and smiled at him before shifting her attention to her mother. "Did Mr. Reid tell you about the game we played, Mommy?" Her grin widened.

Thank goodness he'd pretended to play a game when he'd snatched her from the sofa so she wouldn't be afraid.

"He did," Megan answered.

Her tone held residual fear, but she put on a brave front for Ella, offering a wobbly smile and sitting on the bed, patting her daughter's knee with a trembling hand.

Ella didn't seem to notice the tension in the room, and her unwavering gaze landed on Reid. "Maybe we can play it again tomorrow."

Her innocence melted Reid's heart, and he settled her hand on the bed. "We'll see about that."

He eased away before Ella could touch him again.

"I'll see you downstairs," he said and gave Megan one last glance.

In the hallway, he sucked in oxygen and leaned against the wall.

"I like Mr. Reid," he heard Ella say. "He's fun. Like Daddy used to be."

"Time for you to get some rest," Megan said.

"Why doesn't Daddy like me?"

"He does, sweetie. He loves you very much." The deceit

in Megan's tone was obvious to Reid, but Ella couldn't understand those nuances at her age.

"Then why doesn't he ever come to see me?"

"He's just not able to be here right now."

Reid tightened his hands into fists. How could any man treat his child that way? The longing and pain in Ella's voice turned Reid's stomach. He wanted to make up for the hurt and show her how a real dad acted.

Whoa. Slow your roll. He didn't want to care about Ella like this, or Megan either, but somehow he was being sucked under and couldn't seem to pull free.

He closed his eyes.

I want to keep helping them, but I don't know if I can. Not without getting hurt again.

A verse in Jeremiah that Reid had clung to when Diane died came to mind. *For I know the plans I have for you, plans to prosper you and not to harm you, plans to give you hope and a future.*

He'd made it through Diane's loss by believing God had a plan for his life. In the midst of his darkness and pain, he'd held on to that hope and made it out the other side. Mostly anyway.

God was still in control, of that Reid was certain. And he was equally certain that God wanted him to help Megan and Ella. But what if something happened to them? Could Reid go through another loss and survive?

Did it matter how he felt? Megan had stepped away from her faith. If something happened to Ella, Megan could sink into a depression too deep to recover from. Reid had to be there for her just as God was urging him to do right now.

Forgive me for doubting You. I still don't want to do this, but I know You'll give me the strength to help them.

The bedroom door latched closed, and he turned. Megan, hand on the knob and forehead pressed against the door, started crying softly. Her shoulders convulsed, and her sobs grew louder.

Reid went to her.

"Don't, Megan," he whispered and placed his hand on her back, rubbing in small circles. "I know that was terrifying, but Ella's okay."

She slowly turned. "For now. But like you said, he'll come back. Or what if she gets sicker again?" She stared at her feet. "I'm so afraid of losing her. I don't know how much longer I can deal with this by myself."

He placed his finger under her chin and lifted her head. "You're not alone. I'm here, and I'm not going anywhere."

A flicker of trust appeared in her eyes. Fear of disappointing her twisted his gut. Only moments ago, he'd wanted to run from her and Ella for his own peace of mind.

How could he now look her in the eye and promise to be here when she needed him?

"Thank you." Her expression softened. She was so vulnerable. He wanted to draw her close, hold her, and never let go, but that was wrong on so many levels.

He let his gaze tangle with hers. His heart opened. Fully. For the first time in years. He should put some distance between them. Now. Go downstairs. Go anywhere other than here.

He couldn't. He gave in and pulled her into his arms. She moved closer and rested her head on his chest, circling her arms around his waist. He stroked her hair and inhaled the fruity fragrance of her shampoo. Holding her felt so good to him. Better than he'd ever imagined when they'd worked on Fowler's case. It was as if after a long absence, he'd come home.

"Reid?" Jack's questioning voice preceded his footfalls up the stairs, and still, Reid didn't want to end contact with Megan.

But she must've heard him approaching and pushed away. "I need to get a tissue." She rushed down the hallway toward the bathroom.

Reid hissed out a breath and turned to face Jack.

"What're you doing?" Jack asked as he planted his feet in a wide stance.

Reid didn't like the accusatory tone. "She was upset. You would've done the same thing."

"No, I wouldn't, and you know it."

"You would see a crying mother and not offer comfort?"

"Of course I would comfort her, but there was more to this. Your face said it all. You've helped plenty of grieving mothers over the years, but I've never seen this kind of reaction from you."

Reid was getting irritated at Jack's interference. "I'm not an agent, and this isn't my job. So it really doesn't matter what happened, now does it?"

"It does if it gets in the way of protecting Megan and Ella."

"Just do your job, Jack. I won't get in your way." Reid charged down the stairs, hoping he could follow through on this promise to his friend and truly not get in the way. But if another threat like this happened to either Megan or Ella, he would risk everything, including his own life, to protect them.

Megan finished washing her face and eyed herself in the mirror. She didn't know she could look so terrified. But she was. Still. With every setback in Ella's health, and Orrin walking out on them, Megan was sure she'd reached the end of her resolve, but she'd rebounded every time.

Tonight was different. Seeing that red dot trained on her

baby's forehead churned up all of Megan's fears of losing her child and they didn't recede. Not one bit.

Megan stared hard at herself. Searched for the strength to go on—to walk out the bathroom door and be brave for Ella. She lifted her still-trembling hands.

She couldn't do this anymore. Not on her own. Like she'd told Reid. She needed someone to help her through it. God? Maybe. Reid? Another maybe. But both of them had abandoned her when she'd needed them most.

Her heart hitched. Had God abandoned her or had she done the running? What? Where had that come from? Out of nowhere. Or maybe out of her talks with Reid. She didn't know anymore. About anything.

She took a few deep breaths and peered into the mirror again.

"You can do this, Megan," she said to her reflection. "Ella needs you. She has no one else. Do this for her like you always do." She forced her voice to grow stronger with each statement and visualized a day when Ella was as healthy as Jessie, and Megan's only worry was typical girlie things like clothes and boys. "For Ella. I *can* do this for Ella."

"For Ella," she said again and lifted her shoulders higher.

She got her phone from her pocket and dialed her accountant, Greg. He answered on the third ring.

She explained her problem. "I need $500,000 in cash as soon as possible."

"You need to get the police involved."

"The FBI is working on the case."

"And they want you to do this?"

"They're coordinating everything," she said, being intentionally vague.

"It'll take me at least a day to ready so much cash."

"Fine. Just do it." She ended the call before she second-guessed her decision to give Fowler the money.

She took one last glance in the mirror to make sure she didn't have a guilty expression on her face from stepping out on her own before marching to the door and down the hallway. At the landing, she paused at the railing. Down below, Reid stood tall and strong, talking with Jack. But it seemed as if they were arguing.

Had something else happened? Fear coiled like a snake in the pit of her stomach, and she ran down the stairs to find out.

Both men turned to face her. Jack's lips were drawn in a tight line, and Reid scowled. But when his eyes landed on her, the scowl changed into a soft smile that eased some of her fear.

"Did something else happen while I was upstairs?" she asked.

"No." Reid stepped closer to her. "We were talking about Fowler and what his next move might be."

She sighed. "I mean no disrespect, but why waste time trying to figure out what you think he'll do? You thought he wouldn't call, but he did. That he wouldn't contact me until tomorrow, yet here he was tonight."

"Being wrong doesn't stop us from trying to get into Fowler's head," Jack said.

"What's to figure out?" she asked. "He wants money, told me he'd let me know where to bring it, and I want to give it to him so he leaves us alone."

Reid stepped closer. "We've talked about this. Fowler will keep coming back for more."

Reid's tone was gentle, but she wouldn't let him sway her. "Well, at least it'll stop him from killing Ella because I didn't follow his directions."

"So he comes back again and again and again and you run out of money. What happens then?"

She raised her chin to minimize the difference in their heights. "I'll tell him I don't have anything left."

"You think he'll believe you?"

"I don't know." Her voice carried the frustration that was mounting inside of her. "I've never done this before."

Jack stepped between them. "Take a deep breath, Megan."

She gulped in air.

Reid moved around Jack and took her hand. "We've negotiated with men like Fowler before, and we know what we're doing." He paused and peered into her eyes, melting her frustration some. "We need you to trust us. Let us help. Don't do anything rash."

She wanted to let them handle things. How she wanted to. It would take a day to get the money together, and for that time, she could let them think she agreed with their plan. If they didn't capture Fowler by the time the money was ready...

She would have to strike out on her own.

21

At the hospital, nearing nine a.m., Reid escorted Megan and Ella from Ella's doctor appointment to his SUV. Reid wanted to drive to be in control, and Jack had actually agreed, preferring to ride shotgun. Lauren and Jack joined him, as did two other agents in other vehicles, but Reid still didn't let his guard down. Despite Jack's warning last night to back off, Reid walked closer to Megan's side than needed. Megan carried Ella, wrapping her arms around her as if they could stop a bullet as they stepped into the hazy morning with light snow drifting to the ground.

"Look, Mommy, it's snowing." Ella squealed and held her hands out, palms up. "Can I play in it?"

"Maybe when we get to the lodge."

"Can you drive fast, Mr. Reid?" Ella asked.

"As fast as I can with it snowing." Reid kept his focus ahead as he didn't want to see if his comment had disappointed the child.

He opened the back door for Megan to put Ella in her booster seat. With Fowler still free, they couldn't allow Ella to play outside, but Megan would be the one to tell her she had to stay inside. Reid didn't envy Megan that task.

After making sure Megan and Ella were settled, Reid climbed into the driver's seat and Jack into the passenger's side. He waited for Lauren to drive off in the lead car and then eased onto the road with a third agency car following them.

Ella chattered about Christmas lights and decorations as they made their way out of town, but Reid focused on the road, where snow started to accumulate fast.

The weather forecast called for three to four inches that morning and more into the afternoon and night. The past few years had been snowier than usual for their part of the state. Still, people around here didn't venture out, leaving traffic light.

Once they were on the highway, Ella drifted off to sleep and Jack communicated with the other drivers, but otherwise silence ensued. The snow seemed to wrap them in a cocoon of protection, but the skies were ominous and overcast, which served to keep Reid on alert.

Nearing their turnoff to the lodge, Reid's phone rang. He glanced at it in the console, and saw that Russ's name appeared.

With the cell phone laws in Oregon, Reid could answer while driving only if he used his hands-free app. No telling what Russ wanted, and Reid didn't want the conversation played on the vehicle's speaker in front of Megan and Jack, so he ignored the call.

Jack glanced at him, a question in his eyes, but Reid let the call go to voicemail and returned his concentration to driving. Seconds later, his phone rang again. Russ again. Call must be urgent.

"That's Russ," Reid said to Jack. "Will you answer and see what he wants?"

Jack grabbed the phone. "It's Jack. Reid's driving." Jack listened. "You're kidding me." His voice rose in an unaccustomed high pitch, stirring Reid's curiosity. "I'll put you on speaker so you can tell Reid."

Jack fumbled with the cell until he located the speaker button.

"Hey, bro," Reid directed his voice toward the phone.

"Looks like you don't need to worry about Fowler anymore." Russ's excited tone rushed through the speaker.

"Really? You have him in custody?" Reid flashed his eyes to the rearview mirror in time to see Megan's surprised expression.

"Not exactly," Russ said. "One of the locals was hiking and found Fowler's body near the ridge. Seems like hypothermia got him last night."

Reid couldn't stop his mouth from falling open for a moment. "And you're sure it's Fowler?"

"He wasn't carrying any ID, but I got a good look at the body. It's him. Still, the medical examiner will confirm his identity with prints. She'll start the autopsy first thing in the morning, and I'll head over there to get preliminary results instead of waiting for the report."

"Let me know what you learn," Reid said.

"Will do."

Reid nodded at Jack to end the call.

"So this is all over, and I can go home?" Megan asked.

"Seems like we'll all get home in time for Christmas." Jack smiled between the seats at her.

Reid checked on Megan in the mirror again. He didn't want to get close to her, but he hated to think that she was eager to be rid of him and go home. He expected to see joy, maybe relief, but she peered straight ahead, her expression one he couldn't decipher. With the snowy roads, he couldn't take time away from his driving to figure it out, so he focused on the road.

At Valley View's driveway, he turned onto gravel already

covered in more than two inches of snow. The wind had picked up, and the light powder blew in swirly circles.

After coming to a stop behind Lauren's vehicle, he looked at Jack. "Wouldn't hurt to clear the place just in case. At least until the ME gets those prints from the body, and we have an official confirmation that Fowler is the guy in the morgue."

"You read my mind." Jack reached for his door handle. "Wait here."

A blast of arctic air peppered with snow swept into the car before Jack closed the door. He strode through the snow, leaving a trail of footprints all the way up to where he joined Lauren on the covered porch. They went inside together.

Reid left the heater running and swiveled to check on Megan and Ella. Ella remained sleeping. Megan, on the other hand, still seemed preoccupied.

"You okay?" he asked.

"I don't know. I want to get excited about this being over, but with the way my life has gone in the past few years, I'm thinking Russ will call again to tell us they made a mistake and it's not Fowler."

"It's about time things turned around for you."

"Says who?" He caught an edge in her voice.

"I know how you feel." He kept his focus on her to gauge her reaction. "I felt the same way when Diane died, and it seemed like I would never come out on the other side. But I did. I could've had a much easier time if I'd relied on God more. And He's also there for you."

"If He is, why don't I feel Him?" Her voice was nothing more than a whisper, as if she didn't mean to speak aloud.

"When Diane died, and I thought He'd turned away from me, my friend reminded me God's never far away. *We* are the ones who let circumstances separate us from Him."

She stared off into the distance as if pondering his

words. Reid wanted to find a better way to help her see his point, but all he could do was put his thoughts out there. The rest was up to her.

"I wish I could take comfort in that," she said at last, "but the more bad things that happen to us, the further away He seems."

"I hear you. Even with my friend trying to help me, I had to reach a point of complete helplessness before I felt God again." He let his gaze connect with hers. "I hope you don't have to do the same."

Her eyes clouded over, and she opened her mouth, but Jack jerked open the door and ended their conversation. As a chill gripped him, Reid wondered what she'd planned to say. With Fowler dead, this could be the last chance Reid had to help Megan work through her faith issues. Issues she needed to resolve to help her deal with Ella's illness.

Please give me another chance with her.

"Everything's clear," Jack said, leaning into the car. "We'll pack our equipment and get out of your way. But I'll be in town a few days to wrap all of this up and maybe we can grab some dinner."

"We—I'd like that." Reid ignored his near slip of including Megan in any future plans.

But Jack didn't. He gave Reid a pointed look before he turned toward the lodge. Jack would definitely not let this drop. For now, yeah, but not for good. But maybe by the time they talked again, Megan would be gone and Reid's life would return to normal.

Normal. Lonely. No Megan.

Gritting his teeth to keep his thoughts on track, Reid killed the ignition and went to get Ella out of her seat. Megan was wearing high heels, and he didn't want her to slip while carrying her daughter.

By the time he opened the back door, Megan had the straps to the booster seat undone.

"I'll carry her." Reid expected Megan to protest, but she gave a quick nod instead.

He lifted Ella, and she settled her head, covered with a bright knit cap, on his shoulder. He motioned for Megan to precede him and, protecting Ella from the snow with a hand shielding her face, followed Megan into the lodge.

She turned to him. "If you'll keep holding her, I'll try to get her jacket off without waking her."

He nodded, and Megan came close, her sweet scent teasing his senses. She reached under Ella for the zipper. Reid shifted to help Megan access it.

Memories of Diane and him working as a team removing Jessie's jacket when she was younger came to mind. He missed sharing the raising of his daughter with a woman. Sharing in the joys and the sorrows. Working together to raise a healthy, happy child.

Megan's face was fixed on her task, and a sudden longing for a relationship with her left him breathless.

Was it Megan in particular, or did the past few days show him how much he'd been missing without Diane?

Megan slipped off the last sleeve. "Can you take her upstairs?"

Reid nodded and headed for the stairs. In the bedroom, he gently settled Ella on the bed and peered down at the little face for longer than was good for him. He shook his head and left the room. At the stairs, he spied Megan in the kitchen. She was reading the box for a brownie mix and humming. He joined her.

The longing returned. Full force. If Megan and Ella didn't go home today, he would have an extremely hard time resisting these feelings. He had no idea yet if he could make a long-term commitment to this woman and her child. Not while Ella was so ill. If push came to shove, he feared he would have no choice but to walk out on her, and he'd never be able to live with being that kind of man.

~

Megan put dinner rolls into the oven and set the timer. They still hadn't gotten a positive ID on Fowler, so Reid asked her to stay put. She'd wanted to leave with Jack and Lauren, but it wasn't a good idea to take Ella out on snow-covered roads where they could slip into a ditch and become stranded. With as fast as the snow was piling up, she didn't mind remaining here for the night. And with Fowler dead, she could enjoy being in this wooded wonderland with snow all around.

An overwhelming feeling of happiness and contentment took hold of her, and she couldn't help but smile. But then it disappeared as fast as it came. She hadn't wished Fowler dead and shouldn't take joy in his passing. But she could be joyful in having their problem eliminated.

A sense of hope was trying to rise to the surface for once. Especially with seeing Ella coloring in a Christmas coloring book at the island and Reid sitting at the dining table with his computer. So homey. So comfortable.

So wrong.

No matter how ideal this setting was, once they went home in the morning when the roads were safe to travel, Reid would be out of their lives for good.

"Can I have a brownie now?" Ella asked.

Happy to have her daughter asking for food of any kind, Megan smiled at her. But she still couldn't give her sweets in place of dinner, which would be ready in a few minutes.

"Sorry, sweetie," Megan said. "You can have one after dinner."

"Aw." Ella hopped down from the counter and crossed the room to Reid. "Mr. Reid, why isn't the tree decorated?"

A warm expression crossed Reid's face. "Jess and I haven't had time to do it."

"Can we do it tonight?"

"Ella," Megan warned. "That's something Mr. Reid likes to do with Jessie, and she's not here."

"I wish she could come over." Ella's lower lip pouted out as if resigned, but then she moved right up to Reid and gazed at him with the angelic face that Megan had a hard time saying no to. "Can Jessie come home?"

Reid narrowed his eyes, and Megan crossed the room to step in. "It's not nice to intrude on their tradition, Ella. Our tree is up and waiting for us. We'll finish it together as soon as we get home."

"I know." Her tone was sullen. "But it hasn't been the same since Daddy left. We're not a family anymore."

"Yes, we are, sweetie. Just a family of two."

"Two isn't fun. I like it better when there're lots of us. Like when Nana and Papa help."

"They'll be here next Christmas."

Ella's lip began to quiver.

Megan offered Reid an apologetic look for putting him in the middle of this. His soft gaze was still on Ella. He was so gentle and patient with her. Far more so than Orrin had ever been. If Reid hadn't chosen his job over her, he would be her child's father.

Oh wow. Talk about coming out of left field. She recoiled. Thinking that way was almost like wishing Ella had never been born, and that was the last thing Megan wished.

Reid took Ella's hands. "Since this is so important to you, I'll call Jess to see if she wants to come home."

"Yippee!" Ella yelled.

"Don't get your hopes up too fast," Reid cautioned. "She might have plans with her grandparents tonight."

"Call her. Call her." Ella danced as Reid took out his cell.

Megan took Ella's hands to calm her before she wore herself out too and was unable to have fun decorating with Reid and Jessie.

Not that Megan was eager for the event. She wanted to see Ella enjoy the tree, but bringing Jessie over here and the four of them decorating would be so much like a family that parting from them would be hard. Not only for her, but for Ella too.

"Her grandpa will drive her over after they finish eating." Reid stowed his phone.

"Then we should have our dinner so we're ready when she gets here." Megan tried to hide her unease over the situation, but it hung in her words, and Reid arched an eyebrow. She ignored him and returned to the oven to remove dinner.

"Go wash up, Ella," she called out.

Ella went down the hall, and Reid joined Megan. "I'm sorry. I didn't ask if you were okay with this."

"I'm fine." She pulled the roasted chicken from the oven and set it on the stovetop.

"No, you're not. Something's bothering you."

"It's nothing." She reached for a large spoon to remove the vegetables from the pan.

He placed his hands on her shoulders and turned her to face him. "What is it?"

She didn't want to tell him.

"I'm not letting you go until you tell me."

"Fine," she said. "I'm worried about how Ella will feel when you and Jessie are no longer part of our lives." She paused to swallow the lump that had formed in her throat. "She's been lonely for her father and wants to be a family.

You're so nice to her, and I think she's wishing you could be there for her all the time."

"I'm pretty sure it's not me in particular."

Megan wasn't so sure. Maybe because she wasn't positive she didn't want Reid around all the time herself, and she wasn't about to share that thought with him.

"You should wash up for dinner too." She pulled away from him and got a bowl from the cupboard.

He didn't move, but she didn't turn to see what he was doing. Instead, she spooned the potatoes, carrots, and onions into the bowl. He finally went to the sink in the island, and the water gurgled into the sink. She took the bowl to the table, and Ella skipped down the hallway. No matter how much Megan was worried about Ella or herself getting hurt, she would make sure this last night with Reid was a special night for her daughter. And that meant no discussions or thoughts about Reid permanently in their lives. That would have to wait for another day—or better yet, never.

Dinner passed with small talk, at times almost stilted, as Megan tried to shut down any real personal exchange between Ella and Reid. Megan received a few strange glances from him for her effort, but she didn't bother to explain. He served the brownies with Christmas sprinkles for dessert, and Jessie and Bandit arrived.

Ella raced to the dog and flung her arms around him for a hug then she hugged Jessie. "We're having brownies. Come have one with us."

Bandit went to curl up by the fireplace and Ella led Jessie to the table. The conversation changed to her grandparents while they finished dessert.

"So," Reid said. "What say I get the lights strung on the tree while the three of you clean up from dinner?"

"I'll do the dishes. Ella and Jessie can help you."

Ella scooted off her chair and grabbed Reid's hand. Jessie cocked an eyebrow at the two of them as if she wasn't sure this was a good thing.

Reid reached out his other hand for her and tugged her close. "Glad to have you home, Bug. I missed you."

"Missed you too." She smiled at him, and the three of them crossed the room to the tree.

Megan gathered the dishes and made a few trips to the kitchen. She tried to ignore the trio, but their festive mood was contagious, and she soon found herself watching them, smiling and forgetting all about the dishes.

"Hurry up, Mommy," Ella called out. "Mr. Reid's almost done, and we can put the ornaments on."

Reid caught her gaze, and the intensity of his expression made her self-conscious. She loaded the last few dishes into the dishwasher before moving into the family room.

Reid finished stringing lights and held out the plug. "So who's going to light it up?"

"Me," Jessie and Ella said at the same time.

They looked at each other and laughed.

"You can do it," Jessie said, her eyes holding no disappointment. "I can plug it in other nights, and you're only here tonight."

"Thanks, Jess." Reid winked at his daughter. "You can hang the first ornament."

"Yeah, thanks," Ella said, eyes twinkling as she went to Reid with more energy than Megan had seen in months. Motherly instincts told Megan to warn Ella to slow down and conserve her energy, but Ella deserved to feel excited, and Megan kept quiet.

Jessie stepped to the table where Reid had spread out boxes of colorful ornaments, and Megan joined her. Jessie, eyes uncertain, her mouth turned down, dug through the boxes as if searching for the perfect one to hang first.

249

"Which one is your favorite?" Megan asked, expecting Jessie to pull out one of the many yearly-themed ornaments in the boxes.

She dug a little longer then withdrew a handmade felt ornament in the shape of a Christmas tree. She held it in her hands as if it were worth millions of dollars.

"This one." She handed it to Megan.

"Why do you like this one best?" Megan studied the ten-inch-tall tree decorated with family pictures cut in circles to mimic balls you might find on a real tree.

"Every year at church we have a decorating party where each family makes an ornament." Her voice got quiet. "This is the last one I made with my mom." Tears glistened in her eyes.

"I can tell you miss her a lot," Megan said softly.

Jessie's head popped up. "How did you know that?"

"I see the same faraway look in your eyes that Ella gets when she thinks about her dad."

"Her dad died too?"

"No, but he left us a few years ago."

"Left you? How come?"

"He had other things he thought were more important," Megan answered honestly.

Jessie's gaze flew to her father. He knelt next to Ella, his arms around her, helping her insert the plug into an extension cord. "My dad would never leave me. He's the best dad ever."

"I know he is," Megan said around the lump in her throat.

Jessie ran to Reid. He pivoted, and she flung herself in his arms. A flash of surprise lit his face.

"Hey." He leaned back. "What's wrong?"

"Nothing, Dad. I love you, that's all."

He ruffled her hair. "I love you too, Jess."

She wrapped her arms around him, while Ella gazed at them, longing in her eyes. Ella had plugged in the tree, lighting it with twinkling lights, but she'd forgotten all about it. She only had eyes for Reid and Jessie. She was so obviously missing her father.

Intent on comforting Ella, Megan headed their way, but Reid drew back and circled his arm around Ella. Megan stopped. Waited. Ella slipped onto his thigh while Jessie snuggled next to him.

"Good job with the lights," he said to Ella.

Her face beamed. Megan's throat constricted. This was exactly what she'd feared. Her daughter forming an attachment to the one man Megan should never pursue, and the same connection burned in her own heart.

22

Reid didn't know what he'd done to get such a frosty look from Megan, but as she sat across the Scrabble board from him, her eyes were cool, if not cold.

Not that this had just happened when he and Jessie sat down with her to play games. She'd scowled at him through most of the tree trimming. Whenever her gaze landed on Jessie or Ella, it disappeared and the warm expression he'd been finding so hard to ignore took over.

Jessie placed the tiles for the word *quit* to grab a triple-word score.

"Nice!" he said, and she glowed under his praise.

She scored the word, and he ran through the day's events. Maybe the change in Megan had to do with his earlier conversation with her. She didn't want Ella to get too close to him and Jessie. He'd planned to keep his distance as they decorated the tree, but when Jessie hugged him and Ella seemed as if she'd lost her best friend, he couldn't stand seeing the adorable little girl so upset. He'd had to reach out and include her.

And if it made any difference, he wasn't too happy about

how Ella had gotten under his skin, either. In fact, it made him downright uneasy.

"Take that." Jessie pumped her fist into the air.

Megan laughed. "You two are pros. I'll have to work harder to win."

An impish smile Reid didn't see often enough claimed Jessie's mouth, but a wide yawn followed. Bedtime was an hour ago, and though he hated to ruin her fun, he needed to send her off to her room.

"It's past your bedtime, Bug." He waited for the groan he knew would come.

"But we haven't finished our game."

"We can finish it in the morning before Ella's appointment."

Jessie opened her mouth to protest.

"It'd be smart to get a good night's sleep," Megan said. "Ella will be awake and pestering you to go out in the snow first thing in the morning."

Jessie's mouth quirked in a crooked smile. "It's fun having her here."

Jessie stood and grabbed Bandit's leash from a hook by the door. She didn't have to call him. He came running at the jingle of the leash, and she clipped it on the dog to take him out for a last break before bedtime.

"She really takes good care of Bandit," Megan said.

Reid nodded. "I thought it might fall on me, but she's doing it all. I think knowing something depends on her helps with her grief."

"I can see that. When Orrin left, focusing on Ella was my saving grace."

"Ditto for me with Jess when I lost Diane."

The door opened, ushering in cold air.

Jessie shivered. "I know. I know. I should've put on a jacket."

253

"You can warm up in bed." Reid held out his arms for their usual bedtime hug.

Jessie hung up the leash then rushed to Megan and gave her an awkward hug instead

Jessie quickly pushed back and turned to him. "Can you come upstairs with me?"

Surprised, he stared at her.

"What?" she said. "Is it a crime to have your dad tuck you in?"

"No crime at all. Just thought you'd outgrown it."

She rolled her eyes. "A girl can change her mind, right, Megan?"

"Absolutely." Megan laughed.

"C'mon, Bandit." Jessie grabbed Reid's hand and tugged him after her. Bandit scampered up the steps ahead of them. In her room, Bandit had settled on the foot of the bed and she sat on the other end. "Did you know Ella's dad left her?"

Reid nodded.

"Megan said he had more important things to do." Jessie's eyes tightened.

Reid sat next to her and took her hand. "And you're worried I'll find something more important than you too."

She nodded, then stared at her feet.

He tipped her head up with his index finger. "Nothing's more important to me than you, Jess. Nothing."

"Honest?"

"Honest."

She nibbled on her lip. "How could he do that, Dad?"

"I really don't know."

"Being so sick and not having a dad isn't fair." She crossed her arms as if defending her friend.

"It may not seem fair, but remember God has a plan for everything. Sometimes we can't understand why things happen the way they do, but He's perfect and so is His plan."

Jessie seemed to ponder his words. They'd had so many conversations about God since Diane died, and Jessie's faith had grown along with his. But she was only eight and still thought life should be fair.

Her brow quirked in question. "It's not wrong to pray for Ella to have a father, is it?"

"Not wrong at all. In fact, why don't we do that now?"

Jessie knelt next to her bed, and Reid joined her, taking her hand in his. Outwardly, he prayed for Ella and Megan in the way Jessie expected. But then he fell silent and offered his own prayer.

Now that this seems to be over, please give me the chance to help Megan find You again.

He didn't add a plea to keep him from growing any closer to her and Ella, but Reid knew God heard his thoughts, and however things between them ended, it would be in his best interest. Too bad that didn't mean it would end without any pain. God often used painful situations to help him grow, but Reid wasn't sure he could handle any more growth right now.

❦

What was taking Reid so long? Without him and Jessie in the room, Megan's jitters got the best of her, and she couldn't sit at the table. She crossed the large room to the window.

Outside, snow drifted lazily to the ground where five or more inches now blanketed the area. She loved snow. Clean and fresh, the white layer covered the dying grass and foliage. She wanted to experience it. Now. Without a window between her and the frosty flakes.

She grabbed her jacket and stepped onto the porch. A sharp chill bit into her, but she zipped her coat and smiled. The snow swirling down in front of her was exactly as she'd expected. Peaceful. Fun. Joyful. But more so, the freedom to come outside without fearing for her life bubbled up in a burst of happiness. Not even eight hours had passed since she'd stood in this very place and climbed in Reid's car with agents flanking her for safety. Now Fowler was gone, and she was free to resume her life.

A sudden need to feel the refreshing snow on her face hit her. She moved carefully down the stairs and into the yard. She lifted her head and held out her hands, spinning with the joy of freedom. The door opened behind her, but she continued to spin, licking the frosty flakes from her lips.

"Our girls will be so mad if they discover we're out here." Reid's teasing tone came from the porch.

She stopped and faced the lake outlined with snow-covered tree branches. "I couldn't help myself. It's beautiful, isn't it?"

"Very," Reid said, his voice seeming so far away.

"It's perfect for catching snowflakes." She could hear him moving on the porch, but instead of looking at him, she lifted her face to the sky and stuck out her tongue.

"It's also perfect for this," he called out.

A thump hit her in the back. She spun, and he pummeled her with snowballs.

"This is war." She laughed and ran behind a tree. She scooped up snow and made a small pile of balls before straightening and firing her first shot where she remembered him standing.

No reaction. She peeked out. He wasn't there.

She cautiously eased around the tree. Her heart pounded from the fun she'd not had in so many years and also from fear over being hit with an icy-cold snowball. She still didn't see him.

"No fair hiding," she called out.

"Fine." His voice came from behind her as wet snow hit her with a thump, then slithered down the back of her shirt.

She groaned and spun. He laughed. She snatched up a snowball and raised it. He grabbed her arm and forced her to drop it. The snow plopped on her shoe, and he laughed harder.

She scooped snow from her jacket and raised it to his exposed neck.

"Oh, no, you don't." He clutched her arm midair and peered at her with a sweet smile.

Their gazes collided, and she forgot about the snow to concentrate on his eyes. The sharp blue had warmed and held fire. He loosened his grip on her arms and wrapped them around his neck. He bent forward, his lips seeking hers.

The warmth of his lips sent all cold fleeing. She rose on her tiptoes and kissed him with all the emotions she'd kept bottled up this week. He pulled her closer, and she reveled in finally letting go of emotions she'd had to keep pent up.

She'd fallen for this man again. Big time. And at this exact moment, held tightly in his arms, she didn't care about all the problems that would or could bring to her life. Like the fact that he'd once betrayed her. Or that he didn't live in the same town.

All that mattered was she cared for him, and he cared for her.

The front door creaked open, but she didn't want to break contact to see who'd stepped out.

"Dad!" Jessie yelled. "Dad, are you and Megan out there?"

Reid lifted his head, and cold immediately took the place of his mouth.

"Busted," he whispered and turned toward the door.

Megan moved out of his arms, her face starting to flush

at being caught kissing by his daughter. At least a huge tree hid them from view.

"What do you need, Jess?" Reid smiled down at Megan and plucked snow out of her hair.

"It's Ella. She says she doesn't feel good, and she's calling for Megan."

Ella! Megan whipped around the tree and jogged toward the house. She knew better than to let her guard down and have some fun. Every time she did, something happened to snap her back to reality.

She raced for the house, passing Jessie. She heard Reid following at a slower pace. Inside, she stomped the snow from her shoes and charged up the stairs to burst into Ella's room.

She sought out her daughter's face. She grimaced in pain and clutched her stomach.

"What's wrong, Ella?"

"I have a stomachache."

Megan sat on the bed and rested her hand on Ella's forehead. She was burning up. She turned to Reid, who'd come to the door with Jessie. "Do you have a thermometer?"

"I'll get it." Jessie raced away.

Megan stroked Ella's back. "Tell me about your tummy."

"It hurts really bad when I breathe." She wrapped her arms tighter around her middle. Wheezing came from her chest as Ella struggled to take breaths.

Jessie returned with an electronic thermometer. Megan turned it on and inserted it in Ella's mouth. The silence in the room, save the intermittent beep of the thermometer, was nearly palpable. Megan kept stroking Ella's back until the thermometer beeped the final time.

She lifted it and read 102.6. She looked at Reid. "I need to call Dr. Browne. Will you stay with Ella?"

"Of course."

"I'll be right back, sweetie." Megan got up.

At the door, Reid stopped Megan. "How high is it?" he whispered.

"It's 102.6."

He gave a grave nod, and Megan rushed out of the room. Reid knew as well as she did that this temperature, which might not be dangerous for a healthy child, was too high for Ella.

Megan dug her phone from her purse and dialed Dr. Browne's answering service. Megan left a message and knew the doctor would return the call in a few minutes. Megan desperately wanted to be with her daughter while she waited. Of course she did. But it was better to be able to talk freely with the doctor without Ella overhearing the conversation.

Megan glanced around the hallway. Her jacket lay on the floor where she'd tossed it as she'd run toward Ella. She hung it on the newel post next to Reid's, taking a smidgen of comfort from her jacket touching his. She really wished he was next to her, holding her and telling her Ella would be all right.

Her phone chimed, and she jumped, almost fumbling the phone before answering. "Thank you for calling me so fast." Megan relayed Ella's fever and stomach pain.

"With her recent infection, I think it's best if you bring her in as a precaution." Her tone was calm, as usual. A tone she used even when delivering the worst of news.

Megan could never tell what the woman was thinking because of that. "What do you think it is?"

"I won't know until I examine her. I'll meet you at the hospital."

"We're in Shadow Lake, so it'll take us an hour or so to get there."

"I'll be waiting."

Megan shoved her phone into her pocket and ran up the stairs. Reid was holding Ella, who'd curled up in his lap. Jessie looked at them both with terror-stricken eyes.

Megan took a breath to calmly walk into the room. "Dr. Browne wants me to get Ella to the hospital."

"I'll call Russ. His vehicle has chains, and he'll be our fastest transport."

"Thank you." Megan sat on the bed.

Reid transferred Ella to her lap. Ella moaned, her eyes glazed.

"Hang on, sweetie," Megan said. "We'll take you to see Dr. Browne, and she'll make this all better again."

Reid pulled his phone from his pocket and stepped into the hallway.

Jessie sat next to Megan and looked as if she might cry. Megan barely had enough presence of mind to deal with Ella, but Jessie needed reassurance too.

"I know you're worried, Jessie." Megan managed a weak smile. "But Ella will be okay."

Megan could see Jessie didn't believe her. Probably because Megan's words were hollow and weak. It was hard to convince another person that her child was going to be fine when she wasn't convinced of her own words.

Reid waited in the hospital lounge outside intensive care for word on Ella's condition. The doctor's initial diagnosis was pneumonia. The very thing that had shortened Diane's life. But this was different. Diane had a cold that gradually developed into pneumonia. Ella had very few symptoms, and it came on fast.

When they'd arrived, Megan lamented letting Ella do so much tonight, but Dr. Browne said it could happen fast no matter what Ella had been doing. Still, Megan didn't hide the fact that she was blaming herself.

Jessie slipped under his arm. "Is Ella going to be okay, Dad?"

From the moment they'd seen Ella pale and sweating, then heard the diagnosis, Reid knew Jessie would ask about her new friend. He'd been thinking about what to say to her. If he painted a rosy picture and Ella didn't make it, then Jessie wouldn't be able to trust him again. His only option was to be honest.

He pulled her closer. "I don't know, Bug."

Her chin trembled. "So she might die, like Mom did."

"Maybe." The single word came out in a croak, surprising him at the intensity of pain he was experiencing over the possibility of losing Ella.

A tear trickled down Jessie's cheek, and she swiped it away. "Can we pray for her?"

"Of course." He took Jessie's hand and bowed his head.

"I'll start," Jessie said. "God, I need Your help. My new friend Ella is really sick, and I'm afraid she might not make it. I know it's all up to You, but don't let her die like a lot of the kids around here."

Jessie's voice cracked, piercing Reid's heart. He took over. "Please direct the doctors to the right treatment and cure Ella's pneumonia. Amen." He squeezed Jessie's hand.

"This is so hard." Her eyes glistened with tears. "I really like Megan and Ella, and I don't want anything bad to happen to them."

Reid had brought Megan and Ella into their lives, and now he opened Jessie to more pain. The anguish in her eyes again cut him to the core. He wanted to do something to ease her pain, but there was nothing he could do. Nothing. So he quietly stood there, holding her by his side.

Russ and Sydney came into the room, and Jessie spun

out of his hold. Sydney had driven Reid's car to leave so he could stay with Megan, and Sydney and Russ would take Jessie home in the squad car.

Sydney came over to Jessie and wrapped an arm around her. "So it's you and me again, huh?"

"Yeah," Jessie answered, her tone gloomy.

"How's Ella doing?" Russ asked.

"They think she has pneumonia." Reid could hardly get the words out over a throat that was closing.

"Really?" Russ's eyes narrowed. "She was fine yesterday."

Reid figured Russ was comparing Ella's situation with Diane's.

Reid swallowed. "I'm surprised too, but the doctor says it can come on suddenly."

"And her prognosis?" Russ asked.

Reid gave a quick shake of his head to stop the conversation before they had to talk about it in front of Jessie.

"It's okay," Jessie said. "I know how bad it is, but maybe God will heal her."

"Hey," Sydney said. "Not maybe. Let's believe God *will* heal her."

Sydney was right. They should all believe in Ella's healing. God had chosen to take Diane and so many others to be with Him, but that didn't mean He would take Ella too.

Reid opened his mouth to say that very thing to Jessie. He tried, he really did, but the words wouldn't come out. He'd thought he'd made it through losing Diane with his faith intact. But had he? Maybe when it came to life-and-death matters, he still didn't trust God. And if he didn't trust God with Ella's life, was there any way he could be there for Megan as he'd promised?

23

Megan went into the hallway to catch a breath. They'd been at the PICU for more than eight hours, and Ella's condition had worsened. Dr. Browne visited Ella's room often and was preparing Megan for the possibility that Ella may not make it. Her tears had fallen for so long that they'd dried up, and she could only sob inside.

"Megan." Reid came to stand behind her. He placed a hand on her shoulder, and she turned into his arms.

"How is she?" he asked.

"No change." Megan laid her head on Reid's chest, listening to his heartbeat, his strong arms holding her.

This man had disappointed her once, but here he was, helping her through the toughest night in her life. She was beyond thankful.

She tried not to seem helpless but she had to let him know how she felt. "I'm so afraid."

"I know how hard this is for you." He stroked her cheek. "Syd and Russ took Jessie home, and they're adding Ella to the prayer chain at church."

"Do you really think that'll help?" She was surprised at the hope in her voice.

"Of course it will." He'd answered the way she expected, but something in his tone made her search his eyes. Did he really think Ella wouldn't make it? Did he doubt the power of God?

He looked away and dropped his hands. "When Diane was here, it helped to get out of the room every now and then. I took a walk. Maybe you should try that."

"I don't want to leave Ella alone for that long."

"She doesn't have to be alone. I'll sit with her."

Megan drew back. "Are you sure?"

His gaze wrapped around her, warm and comforting. Their past pain and anguish disappeared like a wisp of smoke. He was here. Solid and true. By her side. He hadn't run. Hadn't bolted.

When the going was the toughest ever, he stayed. For her. For Ella. She could now fully trust this man. Her heart swelled with a burst of joy, but her body sagged from fatigue.

He was right. A quick walk outside in the brisk cold would help, and she would be better equipped to face whatever was coming.

She squeezed his hand. "I *will* take that walk. I won't be gone long."

She retrieved her jacket and rested her hand on Ella's cheek for a moment. "I'll be right back, sweetie. Mr. Reid is here with you." She loved the sound of that and gave him one last lingering look before hurrying from the building.

A blast of cold hit her hard, waking and invigorating her. She took the sidewalk surrounding the hospital. One quick trip around should do it.

The snow had stopped, and the sidewalk had been shoveled. Still, she walked carefully through slippery patches left behind. She glanced at the sky, clear and bright, the sun hinting at morning and revealing the end of the storm.

But not the end of the storm in her life.

She shivered and picked up her pace. She couldn't believe only four days had passed since she'd come here with Ella and first run into Reid again. Four days to reconnect and see how much he still meant to her. To change her mind about his strength and commitment now.

Fowler had threatened in so many ways, but Reid had kept her strong. What Ella faced was a different kind of threat. Something Reid could do nothing about.

No. That isn't true. He could stand by her side like he was doing now. To be with her and help her get through this. Maybe teach her how to trust God again and actually pray for Ella.

She would cling to that—and to him.

Hope swelling in her heart, she rushed toward the building. With Reid by her side, everything would be okay. It just had to be.

Reid stood by the door to Ella's intensive care room. She was so pale and fragile-looking under the oxygen mask. Wires and tubes ran from her body to various machines, and memories of Diane flowed like raging, ugly river rapids rushing over him.

He swallowed once. Twice. Wanted to flee.

You can do this. You promised Megan.

He crossed over to Ella and took her little hand. She didn't wake, didn't move at all. He sat in the chair and watched this little urchin who'd snuck into his heart when he wasn't looking. Seeing her so ill gutted him.

What if she didn't make it? How could he handle that? How would Jessie handle it?

What have You done by bringing them into our lives?

He didn't wait for God to answer. He really didn't want an answer. It just didn't seem fair that more pain entered his life.

Listen to him. How could he be so selfish? Thinking about his and Jessie's pain? What about Megan? He'd seen the anguish on her face before she went outside. Heard it in her voice. Remembered it so well from his time with Diane.

Oh, Father. Why?

His heart was crumbling into pieces.

What should he do? Could he stay and support Megan?

Panic near the level he'd experienced with Diane robbed him of breath. He promised Megan that he'd stay with Ella. He couldn't. He had to get some air or the medical staff would be picking him off the floor.

He laid Ella's hand on the bed and kissed her forehead. "Get well, little one."

He raced out of the room and to the elevator. The doors opened, and Megan stepped out.

"What's wrong? What happened to Ella?" Panic took hold of her voice.

"Nothing." He grabbed her hands and squeezed as if it could make her understand. "I'm sorry, Megan. I thought I could do this, but I can't. I have to go."

"You're leaving me?"

"You're better off without me." He stepped onto the elevator.

She stared at him as the doors closed. Her anguish changing to anger. Hot and living in her eyes.

The car jolted into action, and he slammed a fist into the wall. He'd done exactly what he said he'd never do to her again. Leave her alone. This time she would never forgive him, and if she did consider forgiving him, he didn't deserve it. Not at all.

He jogged to his SUV and headed out of town, letting

the miles flow under his vehicle. The sun was barely peeking over the horizon, and Reid hoped for a sunny day to brighten everyone's moods. Not that mere sunshine would brighten Megan's day. He pictured her sitting beside Ella and holding her hand as he'd done. Terror gripping her heart, with maybe a little room left for hurt from his betrayal.

What kind of man was he to leave her like that? He'd been so judgmental of Ella's father for bailing on her. Now here he was, doing the same thing. Disgust for his behavior settled like a lump in the pit of his stomach.

He pulled into a gas station and laid his head on the steering wheel.

I don't want to run. I don't want to be that kind of man. I want to be there for Megan, for Ella, but I can't do it alone. I need Your strength to do this.

He sat there, time ticking by until God's presence surrounded him.

If only Reid knew if Ella was going to live, but God didn't work that way, revealing the future. He prepared people to handle everything they would face, however.

Reid needed to use his grief and pain from losing Diane to help Megan survive this situation. Whether Ella lived or not, Megan needed him. God needed him. To be with Megan.

My purpose is clear now. Thank You. Now give me the strength to do Your will and let Megan accept my help.

He lifted his head, feeling as if he could do anything. Eager to get back to Megan, he shifted into drive and pointed his vehicle toward the road for the return trip.

His phone rang. He glanced at caller ID. Russ.

"What's up, bro?" Reid asked.

"Fowler's been dead for three days and he didn't die from hypothermia. Was strangled."

"What?" Reid blinked rapidly as he processed the news. "Three days? Strangled? Impossible. He's been communicating with Megan during that time."

"Or someone else was pretending to be Fowler."

"Someone else." Reid thought about it. "Then Megan could still be in danger."

"That's why I called."

"Megan's alone at the hospital, and I'm thirty minutes out. Can you get someone there sooner?" The panic in his own voice nearly had him losing his breath again.

"I'll do my best with the chief, but with the snow, there's bound to be countless accidents in town tying up officers. I wouldn't count on it."

"Then what? What do I do?" Reid could hardly keep it together.

"What about Jack?"

"I'll give him a call." Reid ended the call and dialed his friend. "Fowler's been dead three days. Couldn't be the one stalking Megan. She's alone at the hospital, and I'm thirty minutes out. Can you get there sooner?"

"I'm on my way, but I'm on the other side of town."

"Just hurry." Reid whipped out of the lot and onto the street. He cut off a car, their brakes screeching to a stop, the car nearly taking Reid out. He needed to calm down. He wouldn't do Megan any good if he was hurt in a car accident.

At a stoplight, he thumbed through his cell to Megan's number. It rang.

"C'mon, Megan. Pick up." Voicemail. He left a message warning her about another man impersonating Fowler, then dialed hospital security.

"Security. Ingerman speaking."

"This is Reid Maddox," Reid said. "Ella Cash is in the PICU. We think someone may attempt to hurt or abduct her or her mother. I need you to get up there right now. Call me the minute you locate them."

The light turned green, and Reid floored his gas pedal. The tires slipped on the wet street, and he eased off. He maneuvered through traffic nearly at a crawl.

Why had he left Megan? And why now, in rush-hour traffic when snow clogged the limited traffic and brought it to a near standstill?

He honked his horn at a slow-moving car and swerved into the next lane. The driver gave him a dirty look, but he didn't care. He whipped in front of him and floored it again. But soon thick traffic completely blocked his way.

His heart constricted. He'd left the woman and her daughter who'd found their way into his heart, opening it and giving him a chance to live fully again. He would always love Diane, but it was time to move on. *If* Megan didn't come to any harm.

Please let me get there on time. And keep Megan and Ella safe. I can't lose them.

He should trust God and leave the situation in His hands. But overwhelming fear threatened to swallow him whole. If he didn't hear from Ingerman soon, Reid might lose his mind.

Megan sat in the chair by Ella's bed and took her sweet little daughter's hand. So small and fragile. From the day they'd diagnosed Ella with a tumor, Megan feared a day like this could come. She'd known it intellectually but never allowed herself to feel the terror to the fullest in her heart.

And after Orrin had walked out, she'd known if the horrific day ever happened, she would be alone. When Dr. Browne announced Ella had pneumonia, Megan had called

Orrin, but he was out of the country on an assignment, and he couldn't come home. Maybe didn't want to come here.

And Reid? Well, he'd shown his true colors.

A chill took hold of Megan. Not the cold she'd found outdoors, but the freezing realization that Reid abandoned her again. This time, the pain nearly doubled her in half.

She laid her head on the side of the bed and thought only of Ella. Her baby clinging to life. Megan couldn't control her tears any longer, and she sobbed into the sheet until she could cry no more.

She stared at the textured ceiling.

"God, what did I do to deserve this? Please don't punish Ella for something I may have done. Punish me in some other way, but don't take my Ella."

Exhausted, Megan laid her head on the bed. A door opened behind her and footfalls came close. She was almost too tired to lift her head and see who it was. She hoped it might be Reid coming to his senses, but she knew he was gone for good.

"Megan," Dr. Browne's soft whisper drifted over Megan.

Not more bad news. Please, not more bad news.

Megan didn't open her eyes right away. She wanted to pretend she was asleep. If she did, she wouldn't have to hear more bad news, but she had to know.

She raised her head and peered at the doctor, whose face told of her sleepless night.

She smiled. "Ella's stats have improved a bit."

Megan shot up. "She'll be okay, then?"

Dr. Browne held up her hand. "Let's not jump ahead of ourselves. I'm hoping this means that by getting her here so quickly, we've caught the pneumonia in time."

Thanks to Reid calling Russ and his speedy transport. "But she's not out of the woods?"

Dr. Browne shook her head. "It'll take some time for the

drugs to really take hold, but this may be a positive indicator that they could be working."

"You really don't know, right?"

"Right." She squeezed Megan's arm. "I'll be back to check on her soon."

Megan nodded and the doctor left. Megan appreciated the visit, but she couldn't let even a fraction of hope take hold only to be let down again, but she could at least cling to the positive test result.

The nurse came in carrying IV bags and went straight to the stand. "We've got coffee and pastries in the lounge, Ms. Cash. This early in the morning, there won't be many people around. You could have a few minutes to yourself before your day gets started. Why don't you go grab something while I take care of this?"

Megan didn't want to leave Ella, but she had to eat something. With the nurse in the room, it would be a perfect time to do so.

"Thank you." Megan left with a backward glance at Ella.

The small lounge set up for families of patients in the PICU was nearly empty, as the nurse predicted. Megan pumped coffee into a paper cup, stirred in a generous helping of cream, and listened to the sounds of the hospital coming to life for the new day. Breakfast trays clanging, people chatting, and wheels churning down the hallways. Life was going on, no matter what happened in her world.

She sipped the coffee and walked to the window. The sun grew in the sky as a glorious ball of light. It sparkled on the freshly fallen snow and seemed as if it would be a beautiful day. Megan would embrace that along with Ella showing a bit of improvement. That was a start. She would think positively and leave behind all her doubts.

"You thought you were smarter than me, didn't you?" A deep male voice came from behind.

Megan spun. A man, eyes narrowed and angry, stood in the corner of the room. She'd seen him when she'd entered the lounge, but she'd figured he was here visiting a patient and hadn't paid him much attention.

"Did you say something to me?" Megan asked.

"You gonna pretend you didn't hear me."

"Do I know you?" She studied the bearded man who bore a brief resemblance to Fowler, but he was dead so it couldn't be him.

"You know my work."

"Excuse me?"

"You should've given me the money like I asked." He pulled a gun from behind him and pointed the barrel at her.

She gasped. "Who are you?"

"Billy Smith at your service. Norman Fowler and I go way back. He told me everything I needed to know to get a nice payoff from you." A slow, mean smile crept across his lips.

"Fowler was the one demanding the money, not you."

"Are you certain?"

"Yes," she said, but she was beginning to doubt herself.

He jerked a Rainiers baseball cap from his back pocket and put it on. "This look familiar?"

She gasped again. Had they made a mistake? Had this man, not Fowler, terrorized them of late?

"Fowler didn't have the brains to pull this off," he said. "Sure, he scared you that day outside Ella's door, but then I made sure he didn't get in my way again. It was me who planted the bomb. Me in the Santa suit. Me with the rifle trained on your kid."

"I don't believe you," she said, but she was starting to. "Fowler could've told you about all of these things."

"It doesn't matter if you believe me. I killed Fowler coupla days ago, and I'm holding the gun."

She still wasn't convinced this man had done all of those things, but as he said, it didn't matter.

He jerked his gun toward the door. "Now, let's get out of here and get that money you owe me."

"I don't owe you a thing," she said bravely, even as a pang of fear tugged at her.

"You do if you want your little missy to live." He fixed his hot, ugly eyes on her. "I have a friend in the lobby. If you and I don't walk out of here in a few minutes, he'll pay a visit to your kid."

"She's in intensive care. The nurses will never let him in," she said, but in the back of her mind, she knew. She knew he could get to Ella if he wanted to. Nothing Megan did would stop him.

He laughed. "You underestimate us. Now move."

Megan didn't know what to do. She couldn't go with this guy, but she couldn't let him hurt Ella, either.

She tried to take a deep breath, but her lungs refused to expand. She searched the room for a way out, but she didn't see anything to help her. He came her way, and she shot out her hand, flinging the scalding coffee at him.

He jumped back, and the liquid splashed onto the tile. His eyes grew meaner, and he jerked out his cell phone. "You want me to make the call that ends your kid's life?"

She shook her head.

"I said move." He dropped his coat over the gun and jabbed it into her ribs.

She had no choice but to comply. She headed toward the door. All she could hear was the thundering in her chest.

If this man was to be believed, he'd killed recently. Proof positive that he wouldn't hesitate to strike again—and if she didn't do as he asked, he would kill her precious daughter.

Of that she had no doubt.

24

Reid raced through town, time ticking like an alarm clock in his head. Loud. Sharp. His hands sweated on the wheel, and his heart raced. His phone finally rang with a call from the hospital. Ingerman. Good.

Reid punched the answer button on his steering wheel. "You better have good news."

"The kid's in her room, but the mom is AWOL," Ingerman said.

Reid's heart took a dip. "What do you mean AWOL?"

"Nurse says the mom went to the lounge for coffee and never came back. No sign of her in the lounge."

No. Oh no. Reid's mind raced, searching for a logical answer. Found none. "You have a camera in that area?"

"Not the lounge, but the hallways."

"I'm a few minutes out. I want to see the footage of that area and all exits when I get there." Reid ended the call and careened around a slower vehicle. He called Megan again and waited for her to answer.

Please, let her answer.

Voicemail.

I'm begging You. Please let Megan and Ella be okay.

Reid moved as quickly as he could, but ten minutes passed before he reached the main entrance. He jumped from his SUV and ran to the security office, hurdling a snowbank and being careful not to slip on snowy patches.

A man he assumed was Ingerman sat at a computer.

"What'd you find on the feed?" Reid asked breathlessly.

He frowned. "She left with some man."

Reid's heart nearly stopped. "Cue it up for me."

Ingerman played the feed with a time stamp of less than twenty minutes ago. A man walked next to Megan. His back was to the camera so Reid couldn't get a good look at his face, but he wore a baseball cap. Rainiers cap? Reid couldn't be sure. Together, they exited the south side of the building. It appeared as if the man had a gun concealed under his jacket. Made sense or Megan wouldn't have walked off with him. Unless he was a friend, but still, she would never voluntarily leave Ella at a time like this.

"What about parking lot footage?" Reid asked, desperation settling in.

"Haven't gotten to that yet."

"Do it now. Start with the lot this exit dumps into. Cue it up to the same time as this one."

Ingerman clicked through computer screens until he retrieved the correct parking lot. He rewound the feed to the same time stamp as the exit camera.

"There." Reid pointed at the screen where Megan and the man walked into the lot. Reid squinted, hoping to see the vehicle they climbed into, but they walked out of camera view.

He slammed a hand on the monitor. "He knows the camera angles and parked out of view."

Where could this man have taken Megan? Did she leave some sort of clue for him upstairs?

Not likely. Why would she? She thought he bailed on

her. But maybe he left a lead for the police or security? He had to find out. "I'm heading to the PICU. Call the local PD and give a description of this man and Ms. Cash. Report that she is under duress and likely being held at gunpoint."

Reid flew out of the room and to the same stairs he'd climbed after chasing Fowler a few days ago. When he exited the stairwell, he punched Jack's number on his speed dial.

"He's got Megan," Reid explained.

"I'm still a few minutes out."

"Stop at the gas station where Megan saw Fowler. See if we can get Billy Smith's address. If we go with William Smith, the WJS could be his initials in the bomb box, and he could be the one behind this. And put in a request to triangulate her cell. She's not answering, but that doesn't mean she doesn't have it with her."

"You got it."

Reid made his way down the hallway Megan had walked with the intruder. He searched for anything that might lead him to her. He reached the nurses' station with nothing to go on.

"Excuse me," he said to the two nurses staffing the desk. "Megan Cash is missing, and I'm trying to find her. Did you see her leave?"

"Not me," the guy said.

The woman, whose name tag identified her as Dora, looked at him. "I saw her in Ella's room. I had to hang some fluids so I told her I would stay with Ella if she wanted to go to the lounge for coffee."

"Did anything seem odd when you saw her?" Reid asked.

"No. She was upset and tired like most mothers whose children are in the PICU. But nothing else seemed odd. But then she didn't come back, and I had an urgent call for another patient and had to leave Ella."

"Did either of you see a man wearing a Rainiers cap in the hallway?"

They both shook their heads.

"See any man go into that lounge?"

More head shakes.

Dora's eyes narrowed. "Is she in some kind of trouble?"

"That's what we're trying to find out." Reid didn't want to worry the nurses, so he kept his answer vague. "Can you tell me how to get to the lounge?"

"It's easier if I show you." Dora came out from behind the desk.

He followed her down the hallway, his eyes alert. Near the end of the hall, she stepped into a door on the right. He surveyed the route Megan would have taken from Ella's room. They'd passed only five rooms, and the foot traffic would've been light. Especially this early in the morning. It would be a miracle if anyone had seen her.

Reid entered the lounge. An empty paper cup lay on the tiles, and coffee pooled on the floor. Maybe a struggle. Maybe she tossed her coffee at the guy. Maybe it had nothing to do with Megan.

"Did you actually see Ms. Cash come in here?" he asked.

"No. All I saw was her leaving Ella's room."

"And you're sure you didn't see a man who didn't belong in this area?"

"If I had, I would've called security." She twisted her hands together. "I'll get housekeeping to clean up this mess."

"No!" Reid shot out a hand. "There may be some evidence in this room that could help us find Megan. Call security and have the room sealed off until the police arrive."

"You're scaring me."

"Nothing to be afraid of. The police are on the way and this man is long gone." Reid smiled, but he knew it came out tight and flat and did nothing to ease her concern. "Go ahead and make that call to security. I'll be in Ella's room if you think of anything that might help."

He left the room and made his way down the hall, checking the area with every step. He arrived at Ella's room without locating a stitch of evidence. Ella slept with Boo-Boo tucked under her arm. Her skin had lost some of the gray pallor and pinked up. A good sign? Hopefully.

Megan's jacket and purse remained in the room. If he hadn't seen her on camera, this would tell him she hadn't planned to leave the building. She wouldn't have gone out into the cold without the jacket or leave the building without her purse.

He sat in the chair by Ella's bed, drew out his phone, and dialed Megan again. He heard the ringtone not only from his cell, but also from Megan's jacket. He dug into the pocket and located her phone. No wonder she wasn't answering. He clicked through the recent calls. Only one call had been made in the past few hours. One to her ex-husband. Reid would follow up on this, but he doubted it had anything to do with Megan's disappearance.

He held the cell in his hand and stared at the black screen. They couldn't use it to locate her. His best hope in finding Megan was now gone. How could he find her before this man who had taken her did her irreparable harm?

He wanted to be here for Ella but he also had to find her mother. At this point finding Megan had to take precedence. He dialed Russ, and he agreed to take Jessie to stay with their parents and return with Sydney to watch over Ella.

Reid ended the call, his mind searching for how to locate Megan. But where? Where?

Ella stirred. He bent over the child and gazed into her eyes.

"Hi, sweetheart," Reid said softly.

Ella blinked rapidly. "Where's Mommy?"

"She had to go out for a few minutes." He took her hand and swallowed down the lump that had lodged in his throat.

"When will she be back?" Her sweet little face peered at him with trust and, if he was right, affection.

He didn't know what to do. What to say. How did he answer an impossible question?

"I'm not quite sure, sweetheart, but she'll be here as soon as she can."

Ella clutched his hand. "But you're here."

"Yes, I'm here."

Her eyes drifted closed, and her hand fell away. He laid it softly on the bed and stepped into the hallway to pace.

His phone rang. Was it helpful information? Bad news?

He could barely get his shaking hands to comply and dig it from his pocket to answer. No caller ID. Who? What?

Panic threatened to swamp him.

"Reid Maddox," he got out through a closing throat and resumed pacing.

"Trent Ingram here."

"Good. Trent." Reid's spirits lifted. "Tell me you have something for me."

"I do. DNA has completed on both the device and vehicle, and we have a match."

"Who?" Reid demanded.

"A William Smith. Goes by Billy."

Billy Smith? The gas station friend? "So that's proof positive that Fowler didn't place the device."

"Correct. We did recover Fowler's DNA from the baseball cap and business card found at Megan's house. The

279

business card Santa delivered at the hospital had both Fowler's and Smith's DNA."

"So maybe Fowler started this and then Smith killed him and took over to demand money."

"You'll want to be careful with this guy. He's a piece of work. Record a mile long. Did time for manslaughter so could be dangerous."

And he has Megan.

"Can you get a last known address for him?" Reid asked as Jack and Lauren strode down the hall toward him.

"Wish I could," Trent said. "But that'll be up to law enforcement. I *am* sending you a printout of GPS locations Fowler visited in the past month. Perhaps Smith's address is on it."

"Thanks, man," Reid said and hung up. He explained the latest news to Jack and Lauren.

"No worries about the address," Jack said. "Lauren played on the manager's sympathies and he caved."

Lauren rattled off an address not far from the hospital.

"I doubt he took Megan to his place," Jack said. "But we'll scope it out to see if we can find a lead."

No way Reid wouldn't be in on that visit. "Lauren, can you stay here with Ella until Russ and Sydney get here?"

"I can," she said, but shuffled her feet.

He got it. She wanted in on the bust, but she was putting her needs aside to help him.

"Thanks. I owe you big time." Reid turned to Jack. "Let's move."

They charged out of the hospital.

"The manager also told me Smith hasn't shown up for work since his encounter with Fowler at the station," Jack said

The news fired off a red-hot alert in Reid's brain. So the

guy hadn't returned to work. Gave him plenty of time to take care of Fowler and stalk Megan.

Meant he had nothing to lose, and if he had Megan—she had everything to lose.

⁓

Megan's heart pounded wildly. Her mind flooded with terrible possibilities. And her heart broke for Ella, her baby waking up to find her mommy gone.

All because of this lunatic named Billy Smith seated next to her in his ratty pickup truck. The interior was as gross as he was. Vinyl seats had split open, and the cracks were filled with trash, as was the floor. They'd been traveling for ten minutes in this mess, heading deeper into the city. She kept her gaze trained out the window, searching for help. A police car, fire truck, anything—anyone not too busy trying to get to work in the snow to stop and notice her. Plus, it helped her know exactly where she was at all times, in case she had a chance to escape.

Escape how? He held a gun trained on her, and she knew she couldn't get the door open and run away faster than a bullet could pierce her body.

"Here we are." Smith pulled the vehicle into a grocery store parking lot.

Odd. Why would he be taking her to a store?

He eased into a space next to a small blue sedan near the outskirts of the lot. He turned off the engine and took out his phone, resting it on his knee.

"I just need to type a little text." He jabbed the gun into her ribs. "Try anything and you're dead. Then your little brat will get the same treatment."

She bit back the pain from the gun and desperately glanced around. The lot was nearly empty save snow plows mounding up the fresh snowfall in the distance. She was alone. A crazed man sat with a gun in her side and no one cared. He tapped on his phone, but she barely heard it above the pounding of her heart.

"There." He held the phone out to her. "Read."

Kill the kid now.

Her blood turned to ice. Four little words, but so deadly.

He retracted his arm. "You so much as try to run, and I'll press send. The text will go straight to my buddy, and he'll snuff out Ella on the spot." He lifted the gun and rubbed the cold hard muzzle against her cheek. "Got it?"

She closed her eyes and swallowed, but she couldn't form the words.

The gun barrel ground into her cheekbone.

"I got it," she said through clenched teeth.

He tucked the gun into his belt then held his thumb over the send button. "Stay here." He climbed out and ran around the truck to her door. "Get out and get into the car."

Keeping her eye on his cell in case he got distracted and she could grab it, she did as told. Once in the new vehicle, he fired it up and took off, merging into traffic. So all he wanted to do was ditch the truck to confuse the police. Her hopes of anyone finding her plummeted.

If anyone was even looking for her. The hospital staff might wonder where she was, but there was no one else on this earth who would miss her right now.

Ella's and her lives were in her hands. Hers alone. But what could she do when only the tap of a thumb could end Ella's life? Nothing, right? Nothing.

No. No. Fight off this desperate thinking. Clear your mind.

She focused on the streets, memorizing their route until Smith pulled into a gas station.

"Time to call your accountant. I want you to tell him to deliver the money to the Starbucks on the corner, where you'll be waiting inside for him." He pointed across the street. "Make sure he comes alone."

Megan let her focus stay on Starbucks. Once Smith had the money, he would kill her and maybe have Ella killed. She had to delay. "I don't have my phone."

"That's why we stopped. To use the phone." He jerked his head at the pay phone mounted on the building. "Let's go."

"But I don't have the number."

"Ever heard of directory assistance?" He snarled and held out his cell, thumb above the send button. "Now get out."

She climbed out and trudged carefully through the snow toward the building. Without her jacket, the cold bit into her, but she relished the chill as it helped clear her head. He came up behind her and nudged her forward at a faster pace.

She reached the phone and stared at him. "Payphone. No money."

"Enough stalling." He dug into his pocket, leaving his cell exposed. She shot her hand out to grab it.

He moved his hand out of reach and laughed. "Knew you'd try that." He produced a few coins and offered them to her. "Hold out the phone so I can hear the conversation."

His thumb returned to the perch above the send button.

She snatched the coins and got Greg's number from information then dialed. He answered on the third ring, and she held the receiver between them, hating that Smith moved close enough for her to smell his disgusting breath.

"It's Megan," she said, letting her distress flow through her words, hoping he would notice it. "Do you have the money ready?"

"Yes."

"I need you to bring it to Starbucks." She gave him the

location and waited for him to ask why she was on the opposite side of town.

"Why there?"

She wanted to tell him but Smith held out his phone reminding her of the threat to Ella's life.

"That's where the FBI agent asked for me to meet you," she lied.

"I don't know, Megan. This seems weird. Why wouldn't he have me bring it to your house?"

Smith elbowed her in the ribs and mocked pressing his thumb on his phone.

She stifled a groan and glared at him. "We're not staying at home right now because of the threats. Look, Greg, this is hard enough without you arguing with me. Can you please meet me at Starbucks?"

"Sure," Greg said. "I'll get there as soon as I can."

"Thanks." She hung up.

"There," Smith said. "That wasn't so hard, was it? Now let's get over to Starbucks."

Megan headed for the coffee shop. She hated that Smith had bested her, but she had to admit his plan of using his cell instead of a gun to keep her in line was a good one. They could move around in public, and no one would suspect anything. He would get what he wanted, the money.

And what about her? What would happen to her?

She glanced at him, his eyes glazed with greed and rage. Once he had the cash in his hot hands, she was certain she would die. The only questions left.

How would he kill her and would he kill Ella too?

∾

Reid and Jack charged down the dark, dank hallway toward Smith's apartment. Reid only hoped that the last known address was good for him.

They reached the door and both of them drew their guns, though neither of them really expected him to be home. It would be highly unlikely to bring Megan here where she could be readily found.

"A quick reminder," Jack said. "This is official business, and you shouldn't be here. I'm in the driver's seat. Stay in the background and let me do my thing."

Reid gave a quick nod, and Jack pounded on the door. "FBI."

No answer.

Jack pounded again. They waited in silence. Time ticked by. Second after precious second when they could be rescuing Megan.

"Are you going to break it down or what?" Reid asked.

Jack rolled his eyes. "What about staying in the background?"

"Don't worry. I'll stay behind you as you kick it in."

Jack turned the knob first, and the door swung open.

"So much for brute force." He cocked a brow at Reid and lifted his gun to enter the apartment.

"FBI!" Jack yelled.

No response.

He motioned that he would go to the right and directed Reid to the left. Reid checked a closet, the kitchen, and behind a sofa for Smith, while Jack went to a bedroom.

"Clear," Reid shouted and glanced around at the sparse furnishings.

A sofa and small television on a warped TV stand filled the cramped living room. The place had the look and feel of a cheap furnished apartment where ex-cons like Smith often ended up.

"Clear," Jack called out from the other room.

So Smith wasn't here. Not surprising. But that didn't mean there wasn't some piece of evidence here that could lead them to Megan. At least he prayed they would find something.

He went toward a rickety card table where mail sat unopened and a large bulletin board was propped against the dingy wall. Pictures of Megan and Ella filled the board. He moved closer, disgust twisting his stomach as he walked.

Photos of Megan at the grocery store, at Ella's school, drugstore, in the park, and at the hospital overlapped each other. Smith or Fowler had been there watching in the shadows while Megan went about her life unaware and unprotected.

Reid wanted to rip the pictures off the board and tear them into shreds. Instead, he sat on a chair to take them down one at a time and flip them over to search for any clues.

"Bedroom's a bust." Jack came up behind Reid and gave a low whistle. "Smith's definitely our guy. I'll check the kitchen while you finish going through those."

Picture after picture, Reid studied them. Rage built. Higher and higher. Reid tried to swallow down the anger. Failed.

"Nothing in the kitchen either." Jack clapped Reid on the back. "We won't let him get away with this." Jack moved to the stack of mail and started sifting through it.

Reid wanted to believe Jack, but unless they found something here, they had no other lead to go on.

"Nothing," Reid said, tossing down the last picture. "We must be missing something."

"Sorry," Jack said. "There's nothing here. I'll call the office to see if they've retrieved Megan's banking info yet."

Reid had hoped they would find something here that

would take them directly to Megan, but it wasn't going to be that easy. Their next step was to find out if Megan had withdrawn money, and if so, where. Then maybe surveillance footage would provide another lead.

Unfortunately, if she'd already withdrawn the money, Smith had most likely killed her by now.

A desperate fear climbed from deep inside and tried to swamp him with despair. What should he do? Megan had depended on him, and he'd let her down in the worst way by turning his back on her—again. Now she could die, all because of him and his crazy fear of losing her.

The irony hit him hard, and he didn't know where to turn. He lifted his head in prayer.

Please help us here. Don't let Smith hurt Megan. Give me another chance with her to tell her how much she means to me.

"You're not going to believe this," Jack said and clicked his phone off. "Megan's accountant just called the office. Yesterday, she'd instructed him to get the demand money together, and he delivered it to her about thirty minutes ago."

"Where?"

"At a nearby Starbucks. The accountant said she was alone, but he could tell she was under duress."

"Smith was probably there too." Reid slammed his fist into the table and cringed from the pain. "So he has the money, and we have no way of finding them."

"But we do, my friend, we do." Jack grinned.

"What? How?"

"When Megan asked to have the money delivered to a Starbucks, the accountant figured the FBI wasn't involved anymore. So he put an Apple Air Tag in the bottom of the bag. We're tracking her as we speak."

Reid jumped to his feet. "So we'll be able to find her."

Jack nodded, but his pained expression immediately burst Reid's bubble.

The Air Tag would soon give them Megan's location, but with the money delivered to Smith, he no longer had a reason to keep Megan alive.

25

Megan's blood froze. Smith was driving toward Mill Creek Falls, just northeast of the city. He had his money, and he was taking her out there to kill her and dispose of her body in one of the many secluded areas.

Their route had taken over an hour, passing Lost Creek Lake with the Rogue River running alongside them. All of it was so beautiful in the pristine snow, and yet she didn't enjoy the scenery. Instead, she pondered her fate. The falls. She'd never been there but could easily imagine a quick shove, and she'd drop into icy cold water, plunging to her death to boulders below.

He pulled into the parking area for the steep falls she suspected she would soon be splashing down with a fierce intensity, and her breath caught in her throat.

This was it. Her death was imminent.

"Okay." He held out his cell, his thumb ready to tap send without hesitation. "Let's do this."

"And what exactly is *this*?" Her voice trembled.

He laughed and exited the car without answering.

As she waited for him to open her door, she looked at the single car in the lot. The beautiful tourist area was nearly deserted in this weather. People were home sledding. Making snowmen. Playing in the snow and then heading inside for a cup of hot cocoa. Not visiting a nearly frozen falls with giant icicles dangling alongside.

She climbed out, and the howling wind hit her hard. She wrapped her arms around her body and wished for a coat. Maybe someone would see her and wonder why she wasn't wearing one. Maybe stop and talk to them.

"Go. Follow the path." He shoved her forward.

She trudged ahead, dragging her feet through the snow in the parking lot toward a wide, flat path. He prodded her as if she were a lumbering cow up the path that gently wound higher.

They crested the hill. The waterfall roared in all its majesty on the other side of the river but a cavernous ravine opened in front of her. So he couldn't push her into the falls, but he could push her to a certain death. She stopped but Smith shoved her ahead.

How many times as a child had her mother warned her on trails like this one to hug the hillside? She'd always tempted fate and crept toward the edge to peer down, only to be jerked back by her mother and scolded. How she wished her mother was here today to protect her, but only a miracle could keep her alive now.

A miracle from a God who she was certain had turned away from her.

Reid didn't seem to think God had left her. But then, Reid had also bailed on her. How could she trust his judgment?

She looked around.

The scenery was breathtaking. Vivid green foliage peeking through the snow, crystal-clear water running free. God's country, her mom liked to say. She claimed it was proof that a God big enough to create such a wondrous display was plenty big enough to have a plan for their lives as well, and it was pure foolishness to try to do things on our own.

As Reid had said, no matter God's way or His method, He was here watching over her with a plan.

Tears pricked her eyes, and she bowed her head.

Forgive me for turning from You. Forgive me for questioning Your every move. And I know whatever You have planned for me is what needs to happen. Help me to trust You, and help me to do the right thing now to save my precious child.

"Keep moving," Smith sniped from behind and gave her a shove.

She stumbled and fell to her knees, the cold snow biting through her clothing. No matter. This was the opportunity she needed. She grabbed an ankle and rocked back and forth, pretending injury. He couldn't expect her to climb the path with an injured leg.

"Get up."

"I'm hurt," she said, hoping to slow him down.

"It won't matter in a few minutes."

His sardonic grin unsettled her stomach. "But I can't stand."

"You haven't even tried."

She glanced ahead and hoped to spot another person, but the trail was deserted. "I can't move."

He came over to her and bent, putting his snarling face in hers. "One push of my finger and that little brat will die."

She glared at him.

"Suit yourself." He stood. "I have my money. It's no skin off my back if she dies." He lowered his thumb.

"Wait." She got up. "I can make it."

He laughed. She wished for a weapon to end his life as callously as he wanted to end Ella's.

"Move." He jabbed her in the back.

She gave him one last glare then slowly started off. Her heart sank and despair threatened.

No. Think positively. God was here with her. She was now certain of that. But what she wasn't certain of was His plan for her.

With one small shove, Smith would send her toppling to her death, and if she wanted to save her baby girl's life, she would be powerless to stop him.

~

Reid bolted from the car and ran along the path, following the pair of footprints in the snow. One large. One smaller. Megan and Smith for sure.

"Slow down," Jack called from behind. "I know we're dealing with Megan here, but you need to keep your head or you won't do her any good."

Reid heard Jack's warning, and as much as he wanted to keep pounding along that path, he knew his friend was right. Reid needed to slow down and take a more cautious approach. Smith and Megan could be around any one of the turns ahead, and Reid didn't want to spook the creep into pushing her over the edge.

Jack caught up. "I'll take point."

Reid didn't want to relinquish control, but if there was a man Reid could trust with his life or the lives of people he loved, it was Jack.

And he loved Megan. Beyond any doubt, he loved her. This situation stripped everything else away. He could see it so clearly now and couldn't let anything happen to her. So he slowed and let Jack move past him on the narrow path.

They continued to climb in silence until Jack held up a hand and pointed. Reid came forward. His heart plummeted.

Smith had backed Megan to the edge of a cliff.

Reid's breath left him, and he struggled to gain another one. Jack motioned to retreat, and they did in unison.

"He's not holding her with a gun, so there must be some other reason she's cooperating." Jack jerked his head behind him. "I'll climb into position to get a clean shot at Smith."

"Are you sure that's a good idea?" Reid asked. "He could take Megan down with him."

"You have a better one?"

Reid frantically searched for something, anything. "Maybe we can talk him down."

"Not likely."

"Why not give me a chance at it first?"

Jack's eyebrow rose. "You think you can keep it together?"

"Yes," Reid answered, hoping once he saw Megan again that he'd be able to come through.

"It's worth a try. If you can't talk him down, I'll take him out. Let me get into position before you move."

Reid nodded and waited as Jack picked his way through the snowy, thick brush to reach a vantage point. Reid figured the odds of his plan working were slim. But they had to do something, or Megan would surely die.

Please give me the words to say that will keep Megan alive.

Jack reached a high perch and maneuvered into a prone position. He propped his arm on a stump and sighted his gun. He gave Reid a wave to indicate it was time to move.

"Please, please. Keep her safe," he whispered as he took off.

"Smith," Reid called out without drawing his weapon when everything in him urged him to do so. But Jack had his gun pinned on Smith and Reid trusted Jack to take him out if needed.

Smith spun, his back now to Megan. His eyes flashed in surprise, and his gaze traveled around the area.

Taking advantage of his confusion, Reid signaled to Megan to run, but she gave a slight shake of her head. Smith was controlling her, but how?

"This is over, Smith," Reid called out. "Let Megan go and come peacefully."

"Not a chance. I'd rather die than go back to prison. Take one more step this way, and she goes over the edge." He jerked his thumb at Megan.

"Hold on now," Reid said, making sure his voice sounded calm when his insides were quaking in fear.

No matter what they said, Smith would try to push Megan to her death. His best bet was to distract him so Jack could get a clean shot.

Reid stepped closer. "We can work something out."

Smith held out his cell phone. "I mean it. One more step and I push this button."

"Listen to him, Reid," Megan cried, clearly in distress. "If he sends that text, Ella will die."

So he was controlling her with his phone, and it had to do with Ella.

"How can a text kill Ella?" He shuffled a few more inches.

"Stop, Reid, please!" Megan screamed, breaking his heart. "He has a man in the hospital lobby. The text instructs him to kill Ella."

Reid had to admire Smith's method of controlling Megan. It was likely a scam. Russ had texted to confirm that Sydney was sitting with Ella, and he was stationed outside the PICU, protecting her. But Reid couldn't take a chance without confirming everything at the hospital was okay.

For that, he had to buy time with Smith. "Tell you what,

Smith. Let me make a call. See if we can work out a deal for you."

Smith wetted his lips. "What kind of deal?"

"To keep you out of prison."

"You can do that?" He bounced on his toes.

Reid nearly laughed. Of course he couldn't do that, but if Smith thought it was possible, it would buy them some time.

Reid dredged up as much enthusiasm as he could put into his tone. "Yeah, man. Let me try. Okay?"

"Make it quick."

Reid pulled out his cell and pressed his speed dial for Russ.

"You with Ella?" Reid asked, keeping his voice low.

"Yeah."

"She okay?"

"Yeah. Doc Browne was just here and said she's come through the worst."

A flash of joy lit him, but it died off instantly. "Smith might have a man at the hospital prepared to kill her. Keep an eye out."

"No worries, bro. No one is getting through us."

Knowing his brother spoke the truth, Reid disconnected. "It's looking good," he yelled to Smith. "One more call and we should be good to go."

As Smith started appearing antsy, Reid dialed Jack. "You still have a clear shot?"

"Affirmative."

"When I nod, take him out."

"Roger that."

Reid stowed his phone and eyed Smith. "No deal yet, but if you surrender and come with me, we can probably work something out."

"No way, man, You're playing me." He held up the phone. "I want out of here or I kill the kid."

"I can't let you leave."

"Then the kid dies."

"No!" Megan screamed and charged Smith's hand.

He held tight to the phone and took threatening steps toward Megan. "I'm so tired of your interference. One way or another. This ends now."

Reid couldn't let Smith get his hands on Megan. He locked gazes with her. "Do you trust me?"

Her eyes held a moment of unease, but then they cleared, and he knew she trusted him with her life and her child's life. He smiled at her then held his breath and nodded for Jack.

A crack sounded. The bullet pierced Smith's chest and lifted him off the ground. He plummeted backward over the cliff.

"Nooooo!" Megan screamed and dove for the cell phone.

"Megan, stop!" Reid shouted and raced forward. "Russ is with Ella. She's fine."

Megan swiveled to look at Reid as she tumbled toward the cliff. He dove to grab her leg. He hit the ground hard. Missed her ankle. She teetered then rolled off the cliff before his eyes.

"Megan!" He shouted, his voice holding all of his agony.

He pushed to his feet and went to the edge. He heard Jack crashing down the hill behind him.

Megan lay in a crumbled heap on a jagged ledge.

"Megan!" he shouted again.

She didn't respond. He searched the hillside for a way down to her.

"Call for help," he told Jack. "I'm going down there."

Jack grabbed Reid's arm. "Don't even think about it. There's no safe way down, and the snow is covering everything. You won't be able to see what you're stepping on, making it even more treacherous."

"I don't care. I'm going."

"What about Jessie? What'll happen to her if you break your neck?"

Reid was pulled in two. "I can't just leave Megan alone."

"Accidents like this happen on trails all the time. A rescue team will be here in no time."

"Then call them." Reid searched again for something, anything, he could do.

He spotted a fallen tree. If he could maneuver it into place, he could prop it between two trees and shimmy down to Megan. He ran to the tree and started it rolling toward the cliff.

"Help me with this," he said to Jack the second he hung up. "If we perch it on the ledge, I can use it to climb down."

Reid expected Jack to argue, but his friend came up the path and helped him turn the tree perpendicular to the cliff. They both held tight and eased it through the base of two sturdy pines and out over the edge. The massive log quivered, and the muscles in Reid's arms and thighs screamed from the exertion of directing the large tree to the right spot.

They began to lower the massive tree, and it swung wildly.

Please don't let this hit Megan.

"Now!" Reid shouted, and they dropped it onto the ledge.

The tree landed with a thump and bounced a few inches toward Megan's head.

Reid held his breath until it settled. "I'll need you to brace it at the top so it doesn't roll."

Jack dropped to his knees and lay on his stomach, holding the log with outstretched arms. "Good luck, man."

Jack's hours in the gym would keep the log stationary,

and Reid didn't waste a second climbing on. Hand over hand, he descended. Already taxed, his muscles begged for relief, but Reid powered through until his feet hit the ground.

He gave Jack a thumbs-up and moved to Megan. She lay with one leg twisted under her body. He dropped next to her and ran the ABCs of an emergency through his brain.

Airway, clear. Breathing? He stared at her chest. Waited for it to rise. Good. She was breathing. Circulation. He felt for a pulse. Strong, but rapid.

Thank You for keeping her alive.

He would watch all three until the medics arrived. He took off his jacket and laid it over her body then searched for external injuries. A large knot pulled the skin tight at her temple. Could be the reason for her unconscious state. He'd taken enough first aid classes to know this could be a very serious head injury.

He moved farther down to her leg. A jagged edge of her tibia protruded through her jeans. Bleeding was minimal, but he still ripped off his shirt and applied pressure. It was probably a good thing she was unconscious, or she'd be in a tremendous amount of pain.

"She okay?" Jack yelled.

"Compound fracture. Unconscious with a large knot at her temple." Reid glanced at his friend. "How long before rescue arrives?"

"Anytime now."

The authorities in this area were prepared for such an emergency, and she would be in good hands and rushed to the nearest hospital. Once they arrived. Which could take more time if they were already deployed due to the snow.

Megan stirred and moaned. He shifted closer to her head.

She opened her eyes and blinked at him, confusion

dulling the otherwise striking color. She glanced around, wincing with pain as she moved. "What happened?"

"You fell off the cliff. Looks like you broke your leg, but otherwise you're safe."

"Smith?"

"He's dead. He won't hurt you again."

She seemed to ponder his words, then tried to shoot up. "Ella. I have to get to Ella."

"Ella's fine." He restrained her and helped her lie back.

"I have to see her." She struggled against his hands.

"We're stuck here for a little while. How about I call her?"

"Please." Her weak and pitiful voice scared him.

He settled her body gently on the ground then made a video call to Russ. "Smith's dead, and Megan's injured. She needs to talk to Ella to see that she's okay."

"Hang on, I'll go in there."

"Russ is getting her." Reid gently moved a strand of hair from Megan's face. "Dr. Browne says she's come through the worst."

She smiled, soft and sweet and breaking his heart. "You came back."

"I'm so sorry I left," he said, filling his voice with the urgency driving him. "There's no excuse for what I did, but when I saw how sick Ella was, I freaked out. After losing Diane the same way, I didn't think I could survive if Ella didn't make it." He cupped the side of Megan's face. "I didn't get far before I knew I'd made a huge mistake. You needed me by your side, so I turned around."

"God sent you back to me."

"God, huh? Sounds like you patched things up with Him. When did that happen?"

"Let's just say a man holding his gun to your head has a way of making things clear."

"I'm so sorry about that, Megan." He gently stroked the side of her face. "That would never have happened if I hadn't taken off."

"You don't know that. Besides, if Smith hadn't taken me, I might not have discovered God really was with me." She held his hand. "Just like you said. I let my circumstances separate me from Him. But when I reached the end of everything I could do for myself, my only choice was to admit He didn't exist or decide He was with me regardless of what happened in my life. Now, thanks to Smith, no matter what I face in the future, I'll know God is by my side."

"I'd like to be by your side too. I love you, and if you give me another chance, I'll never leave you again. Never."

"Here she is, bro," Russ said over the phone, interrupting any response Megan might have to his admission of love.

He handed the phone to Megan. "Ella," she said, then stared at the screen.

He couldn't see what Ella was doing, but Megan smiled, and the world opened up as if a ray of sunshine had broken through the tree canopy and illuminated them.

He sucked in a breath at this woman's beauty. He'd been such a fool to leave her. He loved her so much. But his feelings didn't matter right now, did they? Not after bailing on her.

He gazed at her, fear filling the void in his chest and replacing the optimism of a future together. No matter how much he loved her, would she ever be able to forgive him for abandoning her a second time?

~

Ella's excited voice bolstered Megan, as did her smile, but it came from an illness-ravaged face. Still, it didn't lessen

Megan's joy. It even covered the excruciating pain radiating through her leg.

Her precious child was out of the woods and getting better, and Megan had survived Smith's attack. Only one way that had happened. God had heard her prayers or prayers offered on her behalf by others.

How could she doubt that He was close after that? Sure, skeptics would say if He was watching out for her that she would never have been held hostage by Smith as that was a terrible experience. She would counter with the fact that no one could know God's reasoning. She could only believe God's promise in the Bible that He would work this and everything for her good.

Ella chattered away, telling Megan how her new friend Sydney had been reading to her. Ella looked tired, but she was on the mend again, and people who cared for her well-being surrounded her. No, not just people, but the Maddox clan—a family who seemed to be reaching out and drawing her and Ella into their midst.

Ella described the latest Christmas book, and Megan peered at the one Maddox who mattered the most to her. Their gazes met. Desperation lingered there.

I love you...

His words spun through her head. She wanted to reach out for them. Grab hold. Believe in them. Let them convince her to accept something better than she'd ever known. But how?

"Mommy, did you hear me?" Ella demanded.

"Sorry, sweetie, what did you say?"

"I asked if we could spend Christmas at the lodge with Jessie and all of her family."

Another glance at Reid. "We haven't been invited."

"Yes, we have," Ella said. "Sydney told me Jessie asked if we could come."

"I don't know, Ella. You may still be in the hospital, and I doubt Jessie asked her dad if we could come."

"Come where?" Reid asked.

Megan held her hand over the phone. "Jessie asked us to come to the lodge for Christmas."

He smiled a sweet, crooked little grin. "Consider it an official invitation."

Megan returned her attention to the call. "We can talk about this when I get there. Okay, Ella?"

"'K. But how long before you do?"

"I'll be there as soon as I can, sweetie. I love you." Megan disconnected and handed the phone to Reid.

His lips were pressed tight, and the intense desire to gently swipe away whatever was bothering him surprised her. She wanted to be angry with him for leaving. Or at least wary of him, but he took her hand and bent close, his gaze heating up as he drew near, and she lost the resolve.

"I really want to be mad at you for walking out on us," she said firmly.

"But?"

"For the first time in a long time, I'm seeing clearly. Maybe my renewed faith is helping me take risks I might not have taken before. It hurt so much when you left me the first time and even more when you took off from the hospital. But it wouldn't hurt so much if I didn't love you." The warmth of his hand cut through the cold, and she knew everything between them would work out. "If I learned anything in the past few days, it's that risking it all for love is so much better than living in fear of rejection."

"Does this mean you'll give me a chance to prove I'll never leave you again?" His intense gaze left her breathless.

She watched him carefully. "How do you propose to do that?"

He sat up taller. "By standing by your side from this day

forward, no matter what happens, until you know I'm in this for the long haul."

His commitment lifted her spirits even more, but could she buy into it? "That could take a long time."

"I don't care how long it takes. I'll be there if you let me." He caressed the side of her face, and his warm gaze further thawed her resolve.

"My heart tells me to trust you," she admitted.

"But?"

"But my head says I can't."

"Then think with your heart. That's what I'm doing." He paused as if trying to compose his words. "I knew the minute I kissed you last night that I was in love with you and wanted you in my life forever. But I let seeing Ella so sick scare me. It took Smith kidnapping you for me to realize I want nothing more than the chance to be with you. No matter the risks. I love you and want to be with you forever." He bent forward and settled his lips over hers before she could speak at all, much less protest.

But she didn't want to. She drew his head closer and lost herself in the kiss. His lips were warm, strong, and tender all at the same time. She didn't want him to let her go. She'd always loved this man and had never stopped. This kiss proved it. ~

"The medics are here," Jack called from above.

Reid groaned and pulled back. "He needs to stop interrupting us."

Happiness flooded her heart, and it escaped in a grin. "We'll have plenty of time without him around."

Reid blinked rapidly and stared at her. "Are you saying what I think you're saying?"

"Yes. I love you too, and want to give us a chance away from all of this mess to see if we work in the real world."

He softly stroked her hair. "Oh, we'll work all right. Better than you could ever imagine."

She smiled at him and knew he spoke the truth. She never imagined a future with him and two sweet girls like Ella and Jessie. Her life with Reid had started out when she witnessed something terrible, but now that Fowler and Smith were out of their lives, she could imagine the four of them together forever, starting this week with their very first perfect Christmas at the lodge.

EPILOGUE

Christmas Eve one year later.

Megan fussed with the lace on her wedding dress, trying to get it to lie perfectly flat, but the fabric refused to obey. She needed to get a steamer and work on it, but she doubted anyone kept a steamer here at the lodge. She'd chosen a simple dress for the semiformal event shared only with family and a few very close friends, but she still wanted everything to be perfect.

"Stop fidgeting," Sydney said and stepped back. "The lace is fine."

"I don't know." Megan stared in the full-length mirror. "Everything has to be perfect."

Mia laughed, and Megan turned to look at her soon-to-be sister-in-law.

"You and Reid are perfect together, and that's all that matters." Mia came forward and put her hands on Megan's shoulders. "You're madly in love with him, and your face shows it. Just look in the mirror. What difference does a little piece of lace make?"

Megan peered at the taller woman's reflection behind her. In the past year, Megan had grown close to both Mia and Sydney and didn't know what she would do without her two new friends. They'd become the sisters she'd never had, and she admired the strength in both women.

Megan turned to smile at Mia. "When did you get so wise?"

"I don't know about being wise, but I can see in your eyes the same feelings I have for Ryan and Syd has for Russ."

"She's right." Sydney ran her hands over her belly, swollen with an expectant child. "Our lives aren't perfect, but I've never known such happiness, and Mia here—when she's not dead tired from getting up with the second baby—would say the same thing."

"Hey, I don't look that tired," Mia said to Sydney. "You'll find out real fast the joys of waking up multiple times per night. Am I right, Megan?"

Megan nodded. "It's been a while since Ella was a baby, but it does take time to adjust to being a parent."

Sydney's beautiful eyes turned wary. "If you're trying to scare me, you're doing a great job."

Mia winked at Megan. "It's the trip to the hospital that should be scaring you."

Sydney blanched.

"Cut it out, Mia." Megan patted Sydney's shoulder. "It's not that bad. I mean, Ella is seven now, and I've almost forgotten how hard it was."

Mia and Megan laughed. An impish grin lit Sydney's face. "Let's hope I don't go into labor during the ceremony."

Megan groaned. "Great. Something else for me to worry about."

A knock sounded on the door, and Mia went to answer it.

Ella, Jessie, and Megan's mom came into the room and

Bandit scampered in behind them, a bright blue bowtie around his neck.

"Hold up, Bandit," Sydney's teenage sister Nikki called out. "You are not getting away from me again."

She grabbed the dog up and snapped on his leash.

"Sorry," Jessie said. "He's a little excited over all of the commotion."

"No worries." Megan smiled. "He has every right to be as excited as we all are."

"I know I am." Her mom rushed across the room and hugged Megan. "You look beautiful, sweetheart. I'm so happy for you."

Megan took in her mom's powder-blue mother-of-the-bride dress that fit her to perfection. "You look really nice too, Mom."

"What about me?" Ella twirled in her flower girl dress. The white organza swirled, and her eyes twinkled. Her hair had grown in after chemo ended, and now she had a pixie cut highlighted today with pearl bows.

Megan drew Ella into a hug, laid her chin on Ella's hair, and smiled at her family. Everyone returned her smile except Jessie, who toed her shoe into the carpet and looked ill at ease.

"Come here, Jessie, so I can see your dress too," Megan encouraged.

Her eyes lit up, and she wobbled across the room in her first pair of heeled shoes.

Megan shifted Ella to one side and drew Jessie to the other. "You two are the prettiest of us all."

She pivoted so they could see their reflections in the mirror. The sight of the three of them brought tears to Megan's eyes. She couldn't be any happier. Everything had worked out in the past year. Megan had moved to Shadow Lake to be closer to Reid and Jessie, and the four of them had fallen into sync, their lives perfectly entwining as if they were meant to be together.

Now this. Her wedding day. Perfection.

She closed her eyes.

Thank You. For the good times, the hardships, for everything. But most of all, thank You for bringing me back to You and into this family I am about to become a part of.

"It's time to get started." Reid's mother, Barbara or Barbie, as she preferred to be called, poked her head into the open doorway.

Jessie and Ella rushed out the door, followed by Nikki with Bandit then Mia and Sydney. Megan moved slower, butterflies swirling in her stomach. Not from fear but in anticipation of seeing the man she loved.

She stopped to hug Barbie, who wore a free-flowing flowered dress and had pinned her usually free-flowing long hair into a fancy hairdo. Megan had been so surprised to see such a throwback hippie kind of woman as Reid's mother, but his more straight-laced father standing off to the side in a formal black suit seemed more natural as one of Reid's parents.

"I'll make sure the girls get to their marks," her mom said and gave her a quick hug.

Barbie linked arms with Megan and led her toward the stairway. Near the top of the stairs, yet out of view for guests below, she stepped back and smiled, revealing Reid's physical resemblance to this strong woman who'd made Megan and Ella so comfortable in the Maddox family. "Welcome to the family, Megan."

Tears pricked Megan's eyes, but she fought them off. "Thank you for everything, and especially for welcoming Ella as if she were your own grandchild."

"When you marry Reid, she is my granddaughter in every way." Tears glistened in Barbie's eyes, and she cleared her throat. "Now let's make that happen, shall we?" She cupped Megan's elbow and directed her toward her father, who stood at the top of the stairs.

Megan's dad came close and circled her shoulders with a strong arm, then gave a firm squeeze.

Megan looked over the balcony. Reid stood tall next to his brothers, Ryan and Russ. All three of the men were beyond good-looking, and with their black suits setting off the startling blue of their eyes, she didn't want to take her focus off them. Correction, off Reid. But Ella started skipping down the aisle lined with rental chairs, and her daughter glowed with happiness.

Sydney and Mia followed, and Jessie looked up at her, waiting for the signal that, as Megan's maid of honor, she could proceed. Megan nodded. Jessie nervously held her flowers out and started the slow walk.

"Looks like we're up," her dad said. "You ready, princess?"

"Absolutely."

She slipped her hand into the crook of his arm and started her descent down the stairs with pine boughs, red bows, and twinkling lights circling the banister. The smell of fresh pine greeted her, but her gaze met Reid's, and her attention returned fully to him. She blushed from the intensity of his emotions shining in her direction.

She didn't look away, but kept her eyes firmly connected to his. Not that she thought he'd be going anywhere, as he'd proved his willingness to stay by her side. Even when Ella had another health scare this past year, he'd remained true and tough, standing strong with her. Megan simply wanted to see the man who'd watched her go from a scared witness to a woman about to become a bride on Christmas Eve.

They reached Reid, and her father slipped her hand into Reid's. Her father took his seat by her mother, and she stepped toward their pastor, but Reid tugged her toward him. He slipped his other arm around her waist and pulled her close. His lips descended on hers, and the love she'd seen as she walked down the aisle filled his kiss.

She forgot about their family and friends and deepened the kiss to let him know how much she loved him. A sudden outburst of applause brought her back to reality, and she gently pushed against his solid chest. She gazed at the man she was to marry, and he smiled, a sweet little smile just for her that sent her pulse racing.

Then he turned to their audience and said, "Sorry about that. I couldn't wait for the I dos."

Their friends and family broke into laughter, the booming tone of Reid's team members rising above the others. This wasn't exactly what she had planned, but that this man loved her so much he couldn't wait to kiss her spoke volumes about their future together.

She and Reid made their way to the pastor hand-in-hand. Megan glanced at the tall Christmas tree, twinkling with bright lights that the four of them had decorated during the week. Bright white lights reminding her of God's light in a dark world and how He'd watched over them last year when Fowler and Smith came after her. This was just the first Christmas of so many to come with this special man and two very precious girls, and with God on their side, nothing could stand in their way.

~

Thank you so much for reading *Shadow of Truth*. If you've enjoyed the book, I would be grateful if you would post a review on the bookseller's site. Just a few words is all it takes or even leave a rating.

You'll be happy to hear that there will be more books in this series. Read on for details.

SHADOW LAKE SURVIVAL SERIES
When survival takes a dangerous turn and lives are on the line.

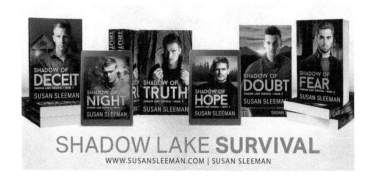

The men of Shadow Lake Survival impart survival skills and keep those in danger safe from harm. Even if it means risking their lives.

Book 1 – Shadow of Deceit
Book 2 – Shadow of Night
Book 3 – Shadow of Truth
Book 4 – Shadow of Hope – March 2, 2024
Book 5 – Shadow of Doubt – June 2, 2024
Book 6 – Shadow of Fear – October 2, 2024

For More Details Visit -

https://www.susansleeman.com/shadow-lake-survival-series/

STEELE GUARDIAN SERIES
Intrigue. Suspense. Family.

A kidnapped baby. A jewelry heist. Amnesia. Abduction. Smuggled antiquities. And in every book, God's amazing power and love.

Book 1 – Tough as Steele
Book 2 – Nerves of Steele
Book 3 – Forged in Steele
Book 4 – Made of Steele
Book 5 – Solid as Steele
Book 6 – Edge of Steele

For More Details Visit -
www.susansleeman.com/books/steele-guardians

NIGHTHAWK SECURITY SERIES
Protecting others when unspeakable danger lurks.

A woman being stalked. A mother and child being hunted. And more. All in danger. Needing protection from the men of Nighthawk Security.

Book 1 – Night Fall
Book 2 – Night Vision
Book 3 – Night Hawk
Book 4 – Night Moves
Book 5 – Night Watch
Book 6 – Night Prey

For More Details Visit -
www.susansleeman.com/books/nighthawk-security/

THE TRUTH SEEKERS

People are rarely who they seem

A twin who didn't know she had a sister. A mother whose child isn't her own. A woman whose parents lied to her. All needing help from The Truth Seekers forensic team.

Book 1 - Dead Ringer
Book 2 - Dead Silence
Book 3 - Dead End
Book 4 - Dead Heat
Book 5 - Dead Center
Book 6 - Dead Even

For More Details Visit -
www.susansleeman.com/books/truth-seekers/

The COLD HARBOR SERIES

Meet Blackwell Tactical- former military and law enforcement heroes who will give everything to protect innocents... even their own lives.

Book 1 - Cold Terror
Book 2 - Cold Truth
Book 3 - Cold Fury
Book 4 - Cold Case
Book 5 - Cold Fear
Book 6 - Cold Pursuit
Book 7 - Cold Dawn

For More Details Visit -
www.susansleeman.com/books/cold-harbor/

ABOUT SUSAN

SUSAN SLEEMAN is a bestselling and award-winning author of more than 50 inspirational/Christian and clean read romantic suspense books. In addition to writing, Susan also hosts the website, TheSuspenseZone.com.

Susan currently lives in Oregon, but has had the pleasure of living in nine states. Her husband is a retired church music director and they have two beautiful daughters, two very special sons-in-law, and three amazing grandsons.

For more information visit:
www.susansleeman.com